Early Praise for *Dad:*

"Heartfelt and uplifting, *Dad* is Steven Manchester at his best. An absorbing story of reconciliation, love, and the ripple effects of the past."
— Carla Neggers, *New York Times* bestselling author, *Cold River*

"Steven Manchester's *Dad* is a poignant portrait of fatherhood and the triumphs and tragedies of being a husband, a father, and a son. A must read for men of all ages."
— Robert Dugoni, *New York Times* bestselling author, *The Extraordinary Life of Sam Hell*

"Steven Manchester is a master at understanding the psyches of ordinary American men, and a poet at writing about them. You will reach the end of this book smiling through your tears."
— Judith Arnold, *USA Today* bestselling author, *The Daddy School* and *Full Bloom*

"From a perspective too seldom explored, Steven Manchester offers a sensitive and sympathetic recounting of the significant challenges and rewards of fatherhood through the eyes of three men experiencing its different stages."
— Donald Hubin, PhD, Chair of *National Parents Organization*

"*Dad: A Novel* demonstrates the psychological power and importance of fatherhood and a father's love. This is a welcome addition to the culture's growing interest in and appreciation for fathers' emotional engagement with their family."
— Raymond A. Levy, PsyD, Founder and Director, *The Fatherhood Project at MGH*

"Steven Manchester writes with heart. Raw, probing, and honest—keep the hankies close."
— Tanya Anne Crosby, *New York Times* bestselling author, *The King's Favorite*

"Few fathers know how important they are to their kids and Steven Manchester's *Dad: A Novel* has the potential to show them. Mothers may appreciate it even more."
— Greg Bishop, Founder, *Daddy Boot Camp*

T0018411

"*Dad: A Novel* is a beautifully written and brilliantly executed tale that spans three generations in elegant fashion. Steven Manchester's expertly wrought family saga takes us on an emotional roller coaster, in which the dips and rises become the perfect metaphor for the varied challenges that come with youth, maturity, and aging. A stunning literary tome, as ambitious as it is effective."
— Jon Land, *USA Today* bestselling author, *Murder, She Wrote*

"Steven Manchester once again proves he doesn't just tell a good story so much as he paints a vivid, multilayered portrait. Enthralling from its frantic start, and written with all the confidence of a seasoned literary veteran, *Dad* is both a poignant and inspiring read."
— Vincent Zandri, New York Times Bestselling Thriller Author, *The Girl Who Wasn't There* and *The Remains*

"Prolific author Steven Manchester writes from the heart and leaves nothing on the table in his latest inspirational novel, *Dad*. Three generations of Earle family members are in crisis, struggling to find common ground. Love, communication, and true-grit allows them to change course and heal old wounds with new life lessons. *Dad* is a must read in these troubled times and, like many of Manchester's novels, be sure to have a full box of Kleenex tissues close at hand."
— John Lansing, national bestselling author, *The Fourth Gunman*

"Men are too often portrayed as being shallow, unemotional, and stoic in modern fiction, which is why *Dad: A Novel* is a refreshing change of pace. Focused on the dilemma of the modern man and his relationship with other men in his life, Manchester also offers a thoughtful exploration of the often-difficult father-son relationship."
— Dave Taylor, single father and blogger, *GoFatherhood.com*

"In Steven Manchester's newest work, *Dad*, every character is fully realized—having the same human foibles we can recognize in ourselves. With many wonderful twists and turns along the way, the reader will feel very much included in this story."
— Donna Foley Mabry, *Wall Street Journal* bestselling author, *Maude* and *The Right Society*

"Steven Manchester clearly understands the complexity of intergenerational relationships and how critical the role is that fathers play in their children's lives. His portrayal of these relationships in *Dad: A Novel* shows how they can truly shape a family's future."
— Michael Ramos, National Fatherhood Engagement Trainer and Consultant

"Few topics are as timely and critical as the role of men in the family and generational fatherhood. Hearts lie in the balance. *Dad: A Novel* hits home, literally, at an incredibly critical time in America."
— John Smithbaker, author and Founder, *Fathers in the Field*

"Steven Manchester's latest novel, *Dad*, is a heartfelt tale. Expecting the unexpected, prayer and never losing hope is how Oliver Earle learns how to mend the broken hearts around him—while showing us how to cry, laugh, and find hope in others."
— Charley Valera, award-winning author, *My Father's War*

"Steve Manchester's latest work tackles the balancing act of fatherhood across generations by holding in perspective the inescapable mistakes and quiet moments of learning that link us in our humanity."
— Ken Goldstein, bestselling author, *This Is Rage* and *From Nothing*

"There is a profound simplicity and depth of heart in Steven Manchester's writing. In *Dad: A Novel*, be prepared to laugh, cry, and admire a great story from an amazing storyteller."
— Dr. Keith Carreiro, author, *The Penitent* series

"No matter what stage of the parenting journey you are at, *Dad: A Novel* will connect with you. One of the many relatable thoughts from this novel is that 'Constant worry is the price of fatherhood.' Steven Manchester perfectly encapsulates the essence of fatherhood and the journey we take as life throws us all kinds of curveballs."
— Richard Sayers, *One Hull of a Dad*

"*Dad: A Novel* is a heartfelt examination of love, loss, and life across three generations of fatherhood. It'll have you nodding, reflecting and, most importantly, wanting to right wrongs while you can."
— Daniel Lewis, co-founder and editor, *thedadwebsite.com*

"Steven Manchester does a fantastic job of telling a multilevel story with heart and hope. Fatherhood isn't simple. It isn't supposed to be. *Dad: A Novel* is an emotional journey into the complicated nature of fatherhood, family, and the ever-changing world of masculinity. I highly recommend the read."
— Joel Gratcyk, blogger, *Daddy's Grounded*

"Every dad has a story but the differences that divide us leave some men unwilling to read about the success and failure, joy and fear, love and loss, and intense pride and guilt that fill each of our chapters. In cracking open *Dad: A Novel*, we discover a reason and a method for reconciling the past and appreciating how each unique fatherhood journey shapes us and those we hold dear."
— Jeff Bogle, blogger, *Out with the Kids*

dad

A Novel

Steven
Manchester

THE
STORY
PLANT

The Story Plant
1270 Caroline Street
Suite D120-381
Atlanta, GA 30307

Story Plant Hardcover ISBN-13 978-1-61188-308-4
Fiction Studio Books e-book ISBN-13: 978-1-945839-53-5
Story Plant Paperback ISBN-13: 978-1-61188-334-3

Visit our website at www.TheStoryPlant.com

First Story Plant Hardcover Printing: June 2021
First Story Plant Paperback Printing: October 2023
Printed in The United States of America

For all the men who were blessed with fatherhood,
but then went on to earn the title, *Dad*

Lo, there do I see my father. Lo, there do I see my mother.
And my sister and my brother.
Lo, there do I see the line of my people, back to the beginning...

CHAPTER 1

*H*ow *in the hell did I ever end up here?* Oliver wondered for the umpteenth time. Recently, it had become his pathetic mantra.

Jonah's young face suddenly popped into Oliver's head like a frightened Jack-in-the Box. *Oh shit, Ginny asked me to pick him up from school today.* He checked his watch. *Three minutes ago.* Panic struck his heart. *And his school's ten minutes away.* He took off at a sprint for his car, feeling for his cell phone on the way. Racing toward the school, he managed to place a call. *No answer.* With his heart rate now at a dangerous pace, his breathing turned quick and shallow. A bead of sweat formed across his forehead. *This one's on me,* he realized, *I screwed up big this time.* He considered calling Ginny, who was a few miles closer. *Nah.* Although it was a brutal decision, in the end he decided that he couldn't take her relentless ridicule, or glares from her disappointed—even convicting—eyes. He stepped on the pedal, risking himself and everyone else in his path. He'd made an honest mistake that now felt like sheer abandonment.

Suddenly, young Jonah's face became twisted and contorted in his mind—as one horrific scenario after the next played out in vivid and morbid detail: The white van pulling up and snatching his kid. Oliver's throat began to constrict, threatening to close. He then pictured Jonah wandering off in search of his neglectful father. Oliver stopped breathing for a moment when he screeched up to the back bumper of a car that was stopped. He beeped his horn, pushing down on the center of the steering wheel much longer than needed. The guy's head snapped up, his snake-like eyes now in his rearview mirror. He gestured toward the red light before he flipped Oliver the bird. *Maybe I should have called Ginny?* Oliver questioned, squealing around the angry driver. His heart racing faster than the car, he tried calling the school again. This time, someone picked up.

"I'm sorry, who did you say this is?" the woman asked.

"Oliver, Jonah's dad. I'm on my way to pick him up. I..." He stopped, suddenly aware that an honest confession might turn into a case of neglect. "I'm...I'm almost there."

"Jonah Earle, you say?" There was a lethal pause. "I haven't seen him. Let me check for you."

As the line went silent, Oliver stopped breathing again. *Oh God, please!* he silently begged, as more scenes of abduction and grisly torture flooded his buzzing mind. He pushed back the sensation to dry heave. *Come on...come on...* Even with every unintentional attempt to hit everything in his path, the brick-faced school was now in sight. He hung up the phone, screeched to a stop and began sprinting toward the building—a final prayer to God on his lips. *Please Lord, please let Jonah be okay. I swear I'll never...* His mind froze. Jonah was not outside, waiting.

Oliver threw open the front door, screaming, "Jonah! Jonah!"

An elderly woman stepped into the yellow-tiled hallway. "Can I help you, sir?"

"My son, Jonah, I was supposed to..."

"He's in here, Mr. Earle," she said. "Students who miss the bus or their ride..." She paused, as if in condemnation, "are required to wait in the library."

"Oh, thank God."

She checked her watch and grinned. "Although you're not that late, Mr. Earle," she said. "There are parents who won't be here for another twenty minutes or so." She rolled her eyes. "Trust me, it's a daily routine with some folks."

Oliver stepped into the desolate library to see Jonah sitting quietly in a chair, reading a book.

The boy looked up. "Oh, hey Dad."

Rushing to him, Oliver wrapped his arms around the confused boy.

"What's going on, Dad?" the kid asked, now worried. "Did something happen to Mom, or...?"

"No, son, I'm just really happy to see you, that's all."

On the way home, Jonah asked, "Dad, were you all freaked out because you were a few minutes late?"

Oliver looked in the rearview mirror and offered a partial shrug.

The little guy chuckled. "You worry too much."

"I'm your dad. That's my job," Oliver told him, thinking, *And you have no idea just how much.* He looked back at his son again and grinned. *But you will someday.*

They drove—slowly—for a mile or two when Jonah added, "And don't worry about Mom. I won't tell her you were late coming to get me."

"I appreciate that, son," Oliver said, smiling, "but we don't keep anything from your mother, remember?"

"I know, Dad," the kid said, smiling back, "but I still won't tell her."

The boy's learning, Oliver thought.

◊◊◊

Oliver sprang straight up in bed, panting like a dog. Ripping the CPAP mask off his face, he frantically searched the darkness. *Jonah...* While his heart raced out of his chest, he did all he could to calm his breathing and collect his thoughts.

"What is it, Oliver?" Ginny asked, half-awake beside him.

"Noth...nothing," he whispered in a stutter. "Go back to sleep. It was only a bad dream."

"Again?" With a yawn, she did as instructed—a light snore quickly following her head hitting the pillow.

Although forgetting Jonah at school was only a bad dream, it was one that repeated a couple times a year—every year since the actual incident occurred.

Constant worry is the price of fatherhood, he thought. After taking a few deep breaths, he slowly lay his head back down. *I'll gladly pay it.*

Oliver set the alarm on his cell phone. *I have my weekly therapy session at eight o'clock, and I don't want to be late for that.* He smiled. *And God forbid if I'm late for work.* He wore his sarcastic grin right up until he began snoring like an asthmatic bear.

◊◊◊

Oliver had hit the snooze button like he was keeping beat to a dreadfully slow song, while the morning arrived as unwelcome as any of them over the past few years. He tried to focus on his therapist sitting across from him.

"So, how's the job going?" Dr. Borden-Brown asked, her leather notepad and pen at the ready. "Any better?"

Startled from his thoughts, Oliver shook his head. "Same," he said, adding a half-shrug. "Just working to feed my kids, you know?"

"Is there anything you want to discuss on that this week?"

"Not really. Nothing worth wasting our time over." He shook his head. "Just the same old grind." As Oliver spilled his guts each week—regardless of the topic—he felt like his life was circling the bowl.

She nodded. "And how are your children?"

"Same," he repeated. "They're fine. Layla's off saving the world, and Jonah..." He stopped.

She jotted down a note, causing Oliver to lean forward in curiosity.

"And your marriage?" the doctor asked.

He looked up at her. *Neither you or I have enough time to figure that one out*, he thought, *and I don't have the energy right now to even try to explain it*.

Dr. Elizabeth Borden-Brown was a cognitive behavioralist. With kind eyes and a knowing smile, she reminded Oliver a lot of his late mother, so he'd trusted the woman right away—which even he knew was key to making any type of progress in therapy.

When he'd first met her, she said, "My name's Elizabeth Borden, but I prefer my middle name, Stephanie. My parents clearly had a sick sense of humor."

"The whole ax thing?" Oliver asked.

She shrugged. "I try to stay away from them," she joked, "just in case."

Oliver laughed. *She's a good egg*, he thought.

"So, Ginny still doesn't want to join us?" Dr. Borden-Brown further prodded, dragging him back into the present.

Now there's an understatement, he thought. "She doesn't."

"And you've asked her?"

"Weekly," he said.

"This week?"

"Every week," Oliver said, sucking in a deep breath. He'd sensed long ago that he would end up in therapy at some point in his life; what he didn't predict was that he'd feel this lost in so many areas of his life—*marriage, work, the future*. He was hoping that this compassionate woman would help him rediscover the ground beneath his feet.

Dr. Borden-Brown nodded. "Okay then." She jotted down a note into her leather-bound notepad. "What do you want to work on then?"

He smiled. "Whatever," he said. "You know I'm only here to help manage my stereotypical mid-life crisis."

In some respects, this was true. Oliver was no longer climbing in his life, nor did he feel like he was on the back end just yet. He was supposed to be sitting at the top. Instead, life felt like a treacherous seesaw. *I'm not young anymore, and I'm not an old man yet.* He had a good number of years ahead of him, with not nearly as many dreams or aspirations to fill them. It was such a strange time in his life, a rut that he couldn't seem to get past. *The passion, the drive—each of these are a real task now, and both used to come so easy for me.* Life had become a frustrating struggle. Occasionally, the battle was a valiant one. Most days, however, sheer exhaustion—of body, mind, and spirit—took the clear win. *It's a good thing I stopped keeping score a long time ago,* he thought.

"Well?" Dr. Borden-Brown prodded.

"I need to work on everything," Oliver half-joked, "but for now, I'd like to talk about my fear of public speaking."

Although the middle-aged, strawberry-blonde therapist tried to conceal it, her squinted eyes betrayed surprise. "Really?"

Oliver knew there were much bigger fish to fry than his lifelong battle with public speaking. *But at least this will keep the conversation going,* he decided, *and buy me some more time before I have to wade into deeper waters without a life jacket.*

"Fear of public speaking is very common," Dr. Borden-Brown said, kicking off another squandered session, "and believe it or not, it ranks just behind the fear of death."

Oliver nodded, aware of the statistic. "Although I can do it, and do more public speaking than I care to," he explained, "I'm absolutely tortured every second that leads up to it. From the time I'm asked to deliver a speech or even a few words in front of an audience, my stomach starts to flop and a rush of anxiety rushes through my body."

Dr. Borden-Brown opened her notebook again, clicking her pen into action. "Take me through the symptoms you feel," she said.

Oliver's mind drifted off to the more pressing issue in his life. *I wonder what Ginny's doing right now?* he thought. Not long ago, he considered his wife to be the best thing in his life. *But something definitely changed,* he realized, *and it wasn't good.* Although he and Ginny still slept together, they did not share a marital bed. *There's a big difference,* he thought. The lack of affection in their marriage was difficult for him to reconcile.

"Are you still with me, Oliver?" he heard the doctor ask.

"Yeah, yeah...sorry," he said, taking a moment to reset and return his attention back to the distraction at hand. "It's...it's not like this anxiety begins with self-defeating thoughts leading up to the speaking engagement. It always starts with a wave of bad feelings, followed by my need to analyze them."

She placed her notebook into her lap. "What are you afraid of, Oliver?" she asked.

Although his eyes remained locked on hers, he was already drifting off again. *I wonder if Ginny's alone right now.* She had recently started to work out regularly. "If I don't take care of my body," she'd claimed, "then nobody else will." Oliver remembered choking on a laugh, thinking, *That's one way to put it.* As of late, the more he considered her statement the less he felt like laughing. *I wonder if she's...*

"It looks like you left our session again," Dr. Borden-Brown said. "Maybe we should talk about what's really going on with—"

"No matter how bad my anxiety gets," Oliver blurted, quickly cutting her off, "I refuse to back down from this internal fight." He nodded twice, making sure she knew he was no coward.

"Okay," she said, working her pen again, "good."

"But I always suffer terribly," he said.

"As a cognitive behavioralist, my primary objective is to help you challenge those fears," she said.

"Okay."

"You see, when you're afraid of something," she explained, "it's easy to overestimate the likelihood of something bad happening to you."

"Okay," he repeated, struggling to focus on the conversation.

"So it's important that we document—or list—your specific worries. From there, we can directly challenge them by identifying probable and alternative outcomes, as well as any evidence that may support your fears or the likelihood that they'll come true."

"Whatever we need to do to make public speaking more bearable," he confirmed.

She nodded. "Very good," she said, before looking up and locking her eyes onto Oliver's. "It's hard to see where you're heading when you don't remember where you've been."

"Oh, I know where I've been," he told her, grinning at the thought of it. "Trust me, I remember."

"Most fears are deep-rooted and originate in childhood," Dr. Borden-Brown said. "In many cases, the past holds the answer to the root cause of present fears."

"I think my entire childhood was rooted in fear," Oliver joked.

"That's true for most people," she countered, without cracking so much as a grin. She leaned in toward him. "I think it makes good sense for us to revisit your past. You may be surprised at how those early fears rising to the surface begin to explain what you're experiencing today."

"I doubt I'll be too surprised," he said, smiling.

She nodded. "I need you to do some homework, Oliver."

"Homework?"

She nodded. "I need you to start putting your thoughts and feelings down on paper."

"I can do that."

"Good, and I need you to start as far back as you can remember."

"How's that?" Oliver asked, unsure of where this was going.

"I'd like you to start keeping a journal. Go back as far as you can. You'll be surprised of the things you can remember and how one of those things are more than likely the basis of your distress."

"Ummm, okay but..." he said, "I'm so busy at work and with the kids—"

"A half hour a day," she interrupted. "That's all it takes." Her smile suddenly appeared. "A half hour a day and you may not need to see me for too much longer." Her eyes softened. "Not a bad trade off, right?"

"Okay, I'll do it."

"Wonderful," she said. "Again, start as far back as you can recall and work your way forward. Same time next week?"

"Same time."

"And maybe next week, you can start telling me what's really bothering you?"

"Maybe."

"Please ask your wife to join us," she concluded.

He shot her his best fake smile. "Every week," he confirmed.

On the way out, Oliver caught his reflection in the doctor's etched glass door. Although clean shaven, he had his father's facial structure and brown hair—now peppered with gray—as well as the old man's height. He'd always wished he had his father's piercing blue eyes. Instead, he got brown—which his dad never let him forget. "You're full of shit, kid," his old man would say, smiling. "I can see it in your eyes."

Oliver peered harder at his own face. *Age difference aside, Dad and I could easily be mistaken for brothers,* he thought, taking a step closer to the glass. *Maybe not twins, but close.* Adjusting his new eyeglasses, he scanned his once fit physique. *Somebody's been snacking between meals,* he chastised himself, studying the start of a second chin. He was chubby now, bordering on obese, the extra weight earning him a CPAP machine to help him sleep and medication to control his high blood pressure. Even with the extra weight, much of him had dissipated over time—*at least all the important stuff.* As he recalled, he was a skilled hunter in his prime. Over the years, he'd been reduced to becoming more of a gatherer—his prowess best displayed when picking fresh produce at the local supermarket.

He glanced at his cell phone for a time check. *I need to get to work,* he thought, *before the new regime finds some passive-aggressive way to punish me.*

◊◊◊

The only real benefit of early morning therapy was missing the brutal commute alongside his fellow robots. The highway had become dangerous, with most drivers texting behind the wheel. When Oliver thought about it, although he didn't text and drive—pleading with his kids to never do the same—he drove on autopilot, more and more of his life being controlled by his subconscious. He'd tried the commuter train a few years back, but that was even worst. *Until then, I never realized that hygiene was optional for a lot of folks.*

Oliver pulled into the long line at the coffee shop. *A few more minutes late isn't going to kill anyone,* he thought, crawling along. When he reached the window to pay for his medium regular and toasted bagel, he glanced into his rearview mirror. A woman and her two kids—a boy and a girl—were arguing. He smiled. "I want to pay for the car behind me," he told the pretty girl standing in the drive-through window.

She looked at her computer screen. "They've ordered quite a bit," she warned.

The smile never left Oliver's face. "Of course, they did," he said, "she's feeding growing children." He handed over his debit card. "I'll pay for their order too."

Grabbing his coffee and bagel, he pulled away. *At least I get to do one good thing today*, he thought. *It's not like I'll ever get that opportunity at work.* He was just pulling onto the road when the lady behind him beeped her horn. He looked in the rearview again to see her and the kids waving at him. "You're welcome," he said, waving back. "Happy to do it."

◊◊◊

As an indentured servant of Corporate America, Oliver worked as a Disaster Recovery Manager. Essentially, if the company's technology failed and the business was disrupted as a result, it was his job to coordinate the IT teams toward successfully failing over the bad server—or even the entire data center—from production to their secondary data center. Most of his time, however, was spent in planning and testing, with the goal of being able to resume business operations during an actual outage. He also worked with the business continuity teams to help coordinate alternate site recovery plans—whereas, if a building went down and was inaccessible for one reason or another—the staff would be relocated to a vendor-hosted site. From this alternate site, they could resume normal operations—having imaged desktops and working telephones—within a single day.

Oliver was a skilled planner and project manager, a master facilitator who worked as a translator between technology and the business. It had taken him many years to gain the knowledge and experience needed to be consistently successful within his role—*which are the only reasons this company still retains me at my current salary.*

For years, his flimsy, partitioned cubicle took up four square feet of prime real estate—less territory than the two urinals located down the hall—consumed by his neat and organized desk. Only one framed photo was allowed per desk; his family's picture—him, Ginny, Layla, and Jonah—had been replaced by a photo of his now-grown children.

"Nice of you to join us today," Oliver's new boss, Sadie, commented.

He turned to find a woman—fifteen years his junior—smirking at him. "I'm super excited to be here," he countered, jumping right into their usual banter.

"Taylor needs help on the training modules," she said, cutting to the chase.

"Of course he does," Oliver commented.

"Is that going to be a problem?"

Oliver shook his head. "I'm on it, boss," he said, nearly chewing his tongue off.

Within this progressive new culture, the millennials were quickly taking over—squeezing out the "old-timers"—or "the boomers," as they called them. *It's difficult to complain, though,* Oliver reminded himself. Long ago, he'd made a very conscious and intentional decision not to move up to management—*which would have changed my life, selling my soul to a soulless organization that's in the business of making more money for stakeholders who already have more than they could ever spend.* In his current position, Oliver had hit the ceiling, watching helplessly as others with less talent, experience, and intelligence sprinted past him. Although this wasn't easy, he continually reminded himself, *It's the sacrifice I've made to spend time with my family.* Otherwise, the price would have been too much—*memories lost with my kids. Time I could never get back,* he thought. *And for what, more money?* He snickered. *I don't think so.*

Even though he'd been very careful to stay under the radar, Oliver still found himself lingering in the danger zone, making too much salary for a job that two millennials could do for less money.

"I appreciate it," Sadie said, "and I need something on my desk by the end of next week."

"Next week?" Oliver repeated. "Hasn't Taylor been on this project for two months?"

"He has."

"And how far did he get?"

"Not far enough," she admitted.

"So I need to land another plane for him, huh?"

She half-shrugged.

Great, Oliver thought. *And I think you need to go back to Management 101,* he thought. *A true leader pulls from the front. She doesn't push from the rear.*

"I don't want to get into it with you again," Sadie said. "The work needs to get done and I'm assigning it to you—period."

"Fine, Sadie," he said in surrender. "I'll do Taylor's work."

"Good to hear," she said. "And remember, you have the AVP presentation on Friday, so make sure you're prepared. All the big wigs are scheduled to be there."

"Looking forward to it," Oliver fibbed, thinking, *Seeing Dr. Borden-Brown once a week might not be enough.*

Don, one of Oliver's disgruntled coworkers, stopped at his desk. "Sadie reminds me a lot of my wife," he whispered.

"Sorry to hear that," Oliver replied.

"I used to think I had a trophy wife," Don added, smirking. "Now she feels more like a participation ribbon."

Oliver shook his head. *And the day just started.*

◊◊◊

Oliver returned home to the same game of emotional roulette that awaited him daily. As usual, Jonah was out of the house, doing his own thing. Oliver had just gotten off the phone with a potential landscaper when Ginny complained, "Why are we wasting the money, Oliver, when you can be out there cutting the lawn yourself?"

Committed to not cussing, he took a seat across from her in the living room. "For the same reason you sit on this couch and watch the housekeeper clean." Not long ago, they'd hired a cleaning lady, who went through the house once every two weeks. *Money well spent,* he'd always thought.

"This house is a lot bigger than that yard," she contended.

"True, but I'm the one who..." He stopped, knowing this conversation was going nowhere constructive.

Somewhere along the way, he and Ginny had fallen into stereotypical roles. While she took care of the inside of the house, he took care of the outside. In time, this evolved into Oliver helping indoors as well—washing dishes, making the bed, doing laundry. *And Ginny's never once lifted a finger outside our front door.*

"The sink's still leaking," she said, happy to continue the bickering. "Do you think you might find the time to fix that broken faucet at some point?"

Oliver was the opposite of handy around the house, for which his wife pointed out any chance she could. "I guess I must have gone to the same plumbing school you did, Ginny?" he said. "As the man in this relationship, I should know how to fix everything, right?"

"I'll just call your father and have him come over to fix it," she said.

He opened his mouth, but rage caught his words and wouldn't let them go. *For someone who's the furthest thing from a great cook or refuses to work a toilet brush...* Happy that his true thoughts became trapped, he decided to take a few deep breaths and ignore the satisfied smirk leaking from his wife's face. *At least the therapy's paying off.*

He wasn't sure when it had happened, but two different set of rules had been established in their relationship—*one for me and the other for her.* He shook his head. *And I've just about had it with that!*

"Stop being so sensitive," she mumbled.

He ignored the comment, thinking, *Love can cast some long, cold shadows when you think back on the way it used to be.* "Where's Jonah?" he asked, almost by default.

"Who knows," she said, never looking up from her magazine. "Your guess is as good as mine."

"Have you heard from Layla?"

"I haven't," his wife said, adding a half-shrug. "She's in Montenegro, Oliver. I don't think we'll be hearing from her every day." Her eyes remained on her magazine article.

Oliver's mind flashed back to the moment their family dynamics had changed.

◊◊◊

"Mom, Dad," Layla said, "I have something I need to tell you."

"Okay," Oliver said, his hackles raised. "What's wrong?"

She smiled. "Why does there have to be something wrong?"

"What is it, sweetheart?" Ginny asked.

Layla took a seat on the edge of the couch before handing over a folder of important-looking documents. "I've applied for a Fulbright Scholarship to study abroad."

"Abroad?" Oliver echoed, his heart rate picking up.

"Montenegro," she said. "It's near Bosnia and Serbia."

What? Oliver swallowed hard. "What do you have to do to apply?" he asked.

Layla took a deep breath, exhaling slowly. "That's the thing...I already have." She slid down to the couch cushion. "I have a 3.9 GPA, and I also got the professor recommendations that I needed."

"Ummm...okay," Ginny said, her face filling with worry.

"I submitted a five-prong essay about becoming a student of the world in order to become a teacher worth learning from."

Clever approach, Oliver thought.

"It's all about the story," Layla added. "The *why*."

"That's right," Oliver said, his mind sprinting like a racehorse.

"Well, it looks like all that time and effort paid off," she happily announced.

"What does that mean, Layla?" Ginny asked, her voice going up a full octave.

"The Fulbright Board met in New York and recommended me among five other candidates for the scholarship." Her tiny grin began making its way toward a massive smile. "Montenegro then selected me and one male counterpart for a grant period of two semesters."

Two semesters? Oliver lost his breath. He'd never been so proud and terrified at the same time.

"So, what does all this mean?" Ginny asked; she was on the verge of tears.

"This is a good thing, Mom," Layla reminded her. "It means that I'll be an English Teaching Assistant for ten months in the country of Montenegro."

Ten months? Oliver thought, his heart now thumping hard in his ears.

"Ten months?" Ginny gasped. "Are you sure this is what you want?"

"Are you kidding, Mom? This is a dream come true!" She smirked. "Of course, I'll miss you and Dad fighting all the time, but this is exactly what I want," she half-joked.

Oliver maintained his best fake smile, while he struggled not to dry heave.

Layla grabbed her mother's hand, and then looked Oliver straight in the eye. "You guys raised me to be independent, to go out into the world and make a real difference. This is exactly what I'm doing." Her eyes glossed over with sincere emotion. "I'm so thankful to both of you."

"When do you leave?" Oliver asked.

"In two weeks," she said.

Ginny's face bleached white.

"I was waiting to tell you, until I knew for sure," Layla said, still smiling. "And here we are."

"Will we be able to communicate with you when—" Oliver began to ask.

"From what I'm told," Layla interrupted, "cell phone service is available for calls and texts." She grinned. "Though I don't know how much time I'll have to—"

Ginny pulled her daughter in for a strong embrace, silencing the room.

"Congratulations, baby girl," Oliver said.

After a round of hugs and best wishes, Layla grabbed her thick folder and headed off to her bedroom. Oliver searched his wife's eyes. Ginny was as scared as he'd ever seen her. "Layla will be fine," he said, trying to make them both feel better. "That Fulbright Program's been established for many years. I'm sure there are lots of safety precautions in place."

"I know that," Ginny said.

Oliver continued to watch her face. *Maybe it's not Layla who she's afraid for?*

◊◊◊

As Oliver's mind returned to the living room, he took the opportunity to study his wife's face again. *Ginny's still a beauty,* he thought, *even now as an older woman.* Ample bosom, with the rest of the good stuff locked away in her trunk. Her eyes were the color of the Mediterranean Sea— *much too easy to get lost in.* Dirty blonde hair with some natural curl. *She's cute and sexy at the same time.* He shook his head. *But she's no longer mine— at least not in the ways that count.*

"So how was your therapy session today?" she nonchalantly asked, surprising him.

"Fine."

"What did you talk about?"

"Do you really care?" The question felt involuntary to him, driven more on emotion than thought.

She glared at him from her perch on the couch.

"Listen, I don't want to fight again over this, Ginny, but I really would like you to come with me. I think it could help us."

"Help us?" She shuffled to the edge of her seat. "I'm not going to therapy, Oliver. You know that!"

"But why?" he asked, with as much empathy as he could muster. "I just don't get it."

"I have my reasons," she huffed.

"Sure, you do."

"Don't be a jerk, Oliver."

"A jerk?" he fired back. "I'm not a jerk, Ginny. I'm alone, that's what I am." He could feel that the end was getting closer and wondered if the light at the end of the tunnel was an oncoming train.

"Alone?" she asked, as though it came as a surprise.

"If there's ever a hug or a kiss shared between us," he said, "it's because I initiated it."

"That's just not true," she countered, laying the magazine in her lap for a moment.

"Really? Name the last time you came to me with a hug or a kiss?" She went silent.

It is true, he confirmed in his aching head. *Whether it's in the morning or at night, it's always the same cold story.* Ginny always reciprocated the affection, but never initiated it. *And her words never accurately reflect her actions*, he decided. *Her "I love yous" are shallow now—empty.* He shook his head.

Months earlier, being incredibly frustrated, Oliver had decided to start giving his wife only what he received from her; offering Ginny the same affection that she gave him. *And that's when it all shut down*, he realized. *There was nothing between us anymore—no hugs, no kisses, nothing.* In some ways, it also felt like the point of no return.

"Can you even remember the last time we've said good night to each other...or greeted each other in the morning?" he asked.

She continued to stare at him. "And that's my fault?"

He shook his head. "No, Ginny, it's our fault—yours and mine."

My test failed miserably, Oliver decided, making him feel conflicted. *Because of me, there's no more warmth at all between us.* But he also knew, *It was only because of me that any expression of love existed to begin with.*

"I don't know what you want from me anymore, Oliver," she said. "I honestly don't." She stood. "It seems like all you want to do now is fight."

A plume of bile lifted into his throat, where it began to bubble. "That's not true!" he roared, immediately sorry for the sudden increase in volume. "I'm the only one who even cares enough to talk about it. You never have anything to say about this marriage, and how bad things have gotten between us."

"I don't want to fight, Oliver," she said; "that's what I know."

"And neither do I," he said, returning to a calmer and even tone. "But we need to communicate, Ginny. I don't know about you, but I know I don't want to keep living like this."

"Like what?"

"Like I'm married to some cold zombie, who would rather—"

"Nice, Oliver," she yelled, glaring at him with pain in her eyes. She grabbed for her pocketbook. "I'm going out," she announced."I have an appointment."

"You have a lot of appointments lately," he snapped, allowing his anger and frustration to get the better of him. "Forgive me, Ginny," he said, being sarcastic. "I'm sorry I bothered you with something as menial as our marriage."

Without another word, she stormed out of the house, leaving him to fend for his own dinner.

After the front door slammed shut, Oliver sat still for a good hour to process their dreadful situation. He was still in shock over how far he and Ginny had fallen together. *How did we get here, to a place where our marriage could go either way?* Although he didn't want it to end, he also understood, *Ginny and I are hanging on by a bare thread.*

For most of their marriage, the kids were the perfect all-consuming distraction. Between school and extracurricular activities—karate and basketball, dance and theatre—there was little time for much else. *But that seems like a lifetime ago.* For all those weeks and months, Oliver couldn't wait until Layla and Jonah got their own driver's licenses. *But once they did, life completely changed,* he thought, *and not for the better.* Those licenses led to part-time jobs.

Although Jonah's hanging on to his childhood for dear life, Layla's in the wind. It made him sad. Several years before Layla had ever gotten her driver's license, Oliver no longer played the role of hero in her eyes. He'd been reduced to her taxi driver and then mobile ATM, handing over twenty-dollar bills like they were Monopoly money.

Even though I constantly complained about it, he thought, *I really miss it now. Maybe that's why I'm letting Jonah get away with murder?* he wondered, still holding on to the last remnants of a phase that was quickly fading away.

Searching for a cold beer, he noticed that the refrigerator was packed so tight that it looked like a Jenga puzzle. *One wrong pull and it's all coming down,* he decided, studying it for a moment. *The tub of butter seems to be holding everything together.*

Closing the fridge's stainless-steel door with beer in hand, he studied all the souvenir magnets—each one of them telling a story of where their family had traveled together. *We were so happy back then,* he thought, taking a long swig of beer. *How in the hell did we ever end up here?*

He turned his back to the fridge and surveyed everything before him, considering all he'd worked for—*for all these years.* Ginny had furnished the house piece-by-piece, like bringing twigs back to a perpetually un-finished nest. *She did a great job,* he thought, *making this house our home.*

Downing the rest of the beer, he grabbed another Corona and head-ed back to the deserted living room. Collapsing into his leather recliner, he grabbed the TV's remote control and clicked through a few channels before landing on some ominous documentary on shark attacks. *It's bet-ter than the silence, I suppose.*

CHAPTER 2

I woke up one morning and realized, I'm 72 years old, Robert thought. *Now how in the hell did that happen? Although I'm retired, I—*

"Are you still with me, Dad?" Ginny asked, yanking him from his daydream.

He shook off the cobwebs and laughed. Taking a break from the sink repair to catch his breath, he caught his reflection in the kitchen window where he lingered. Not quite six feet tall, Robert had blue eyes with crow's feet in the corners. His hair—once chestnut brown—was now long, white, and ungroomed. Although he always enjoyed a muscular physique, time and diminishing levels of testosterone had methodically melted it away. Retaining two full rows of teeth, he had big hands and a nose to match. *You old bastard*, he told his reflection, grinning.

"So, are you enjoying your retirement?" his daughter-in-law asked, pulling him out of the window. Before he could answer, she added, "It looks like you've lost some weight, Dad." She opened the pantry door, grabbed a granola bar, and handed it to him.

"I guess I can afford the extra calories," he told Sophie, the tiny dog playing under his feet.

"Sophie, come see Mommy," Ginny called to the teacup poodle. "Grandpa's trying to work."

Sophie never left Robert's side; she was clearly in love with him, as all dogs were. She stood on her hind legs, resting her front paws on his shin.

Robert looked down at the dog and laughed. "You're pretty aggressive for a stuffed animal that pees, aren't you?"

"Are you enjoying retirement?" Ginny repeated, a hint of annoyance in her tone.

He grinned. "I am, my dear! I love being retired." He thought about it. *If it wasn't for feeling so exhausted all the time.*

She waited for details.

"Life's a funny thing, Ginny," he told her. "For a while there, I thought I was still climbing, never realizing that I was already sliding down the back half of my life." He nodded. "Don't wait for anything, my girl," he said, surprising himself to be jumping into the deep end of the pool with his son's wife. "If you need to do something, then do it. Don't wait. If you need to say something, make sure you say it. Got me?"

With a single nod, she smiled.

"Before you know it," he added, "the sun won't be rising on your life; it'll be setting."

The smile evaporated from her face.

Robert lifted his greasy wrench, returning to the job before him. "I think I work harder now since I've retired," he joked, trying to catch his breath.

"Well, we appreciate the help, Dad," she said, her voice seemingly rattled. "We always do."

Looking up from the newly-installed faucet, Robert feigned a smile. "So, where's my lazy son, anyway?" he asked, playfully.

"Who knows," she shot back. "Oliver doesn't tell me anything anymore." Her own fake grin disappeared.

Robert studied her face. *I like Ginny well enough. She's been a great mother.* But if he'd been able to pick his son's partner for life, the woman would have been a bit more easygoing. "Can you let Ollie know I was here, asking about him?"

"I will."

"And how are my grandbabies?"

"They're hardly babies, Dad."

He grinned. "They'll always be babies to me." He kept his eyes locked on hers, awaiting an answer.

"Jonah's at the college library, studying."

One of his unruly eyebrows rose to attention.

She chuckled. "At least that's what he told me." She half-shrugged. "Layla called a few nights ago. She says she's enjoying Montenegro; that the food is different, but that the people have been very warm to her."

"Glad to hear it." He nodded. "I'm proud of that girl. She's really going to make something of herself."

Ginny nodded in agreement. "Thanks again for the help today."

"My pleasure," Robert said, preparing to step out of the house.

"You're a good man," she commented, stopping him dead in his tracks.

Oh, I'm not so sure about that, he thought.

As though she were reading his thoughts, she went on. "Everyone who meets you, loves you, Dad. And you've always been the perfect example of kindness and true friendship for your grandchildren."

"All right, then," he said. At a loss for words, he nodded his appreciation and made a beeline for the door. *I need some fresh air*, he thought, hobbling off to feel some type of breeze on his sweaty back.

Luna, the old man's well-behaved mutt, was waiting patiently in his faded red convertible. "Thanks for being so patient, girl," he told her, opening the driver's side door. "I would have let you in, but you might have accidentally eaten Sophie."

The old mutt looked at him blankly.

He raked his wrinkled fingers through her neck's thick fur. "I'll give you a few licks of my ice cream later." He thought about it. "Somerset Creamery's still open 'til late, I think."

As he eased into the Chrysler Sebring's duct-taped seat—the car had been beat to hell and back but refused to call it quits—he felt a pang of gratitude.

The second-hand ragtop was a far stretch from the junk station wagon Robert had driven most of his life; all those years he'd spent taking care of his wife and only son, Oliver. He'd been a blue-collar stiff, a hard-working man, and his work was his religion—as though being able to provide for his small family was a sacred covenant with God.

Once Oliver was raised and proved self-reliant, Robert grew out his hair and lived life by his own rules—the days of being a conformist gone forever.

As he fired up the beater, Andrew Souza—one of the town's mailmen and friends—passed the front of the car, knocking on the hood. "I think it might be time to trade in this thing for something a little newer," he suggested with a mischievous grin.

Robert man snickered. "Something newer? Why the hell do I need something newer, Andrew?" He looked over at Luna. "This sled's plenty reliable. Besides, me and my girl just putt around town, is all. Right, Luna?"

The mutt's tail and tongue began wagging.

Laughing at the sight of the odd couple, Andrew kept right on marching to finish his day's route.

Chuckling, Robert shot a sideways glance at his partner in crime. "Ready to roll? We could swing by the beach if you want to?"

The tail and tongue kept right on wagging.

In their retirement years, Robert and Luna spent many quiet hours down at Howland Beach. They loved to ride the back roads of Westport together, the old man's unruly white hair and the dog's Swedish fish tongue flapping around in the wind. *There's nothing better than experiencing that feeling of freedom without the danger of riding a motorcycle,* Robert thought; he especially loved the warm summer nights. Given the speed Luna's tail swung from side-to-side, he knew she felt the same.

"Well, all right then." He turned on the radio to listen to their favorite country music station, *Cat Country 98.1.* "Top down, radio up," he said, sucking in a few lost breaths before slowly pulling out onto the road.

◊◊◊

After feeding and watering Luna for the second time that day, Robert filled both bird feeders. Still feeling exhausted, he swapped out his T-shirt and headed for the quiet of his backyard. He loved sitting alone in the old wooden rocking chair situated under an even older oak tree.

He scanned the yard, aware of how blessed he was to have been raised in New England, and then to have stayed and raised his own family. When he thought about it, the four seasons weighed heavily on his decision to stay. He loved the start of spring when the black, exhaust-stained snowbanks began to disappear. By many measures, the previous winter had been a mild one for New England. *I do love spring, though,* he thought, with the rich smell of the earth giving new life to a recently hibernated world. The birds reappeared to offer their song in the morning; small animals scurried about to forage for the day's nutrition. Everyone seemed to be smiling again, happy for the milder temperatures and the opportunity to spend some time outdoors—to feel the sun on their faces once again. In one minute, new plants were sprouting and, in the next, those mild days were heating up, requiring less clothes. The summer also created a natural decrease in appetite. *Maybe that's what's going on with me?* he considered. The summer days were long, though—

sometimes too long. *I like the heat, but the humidity was a beast this year.* For him, it caused random headaches. Open screened windows were closed to support humming, bulky air conditioners, with most people returning to hibernation—*no different from winter.* But when he considered the cookouts, the ice cream runs, and the Boston Red Sox baseball playing every night at seven o'clock on the tube—*I'll take it over a New England winter any time, even if I do have to shower a couple times a day.*

As Robert settled into the stillness, his mind began filling with unwelcome thoughts—one after the next—each one passing through the landscape of his brain. *I hope Layla's keeping her wits about her over there. I hope she's safe. It seems like Ginny and Oliver aren't doing well. And Jonah, man, that boy needs a good swift kick in the ass.*

He recognized each thought—negative or positive—and gave them a nod before letting them pass through. He didn't latch onto any one thought or become fixated, as he had his entire life—dissecting and analyzing, trying to make sense of it all before placing each one into the compartment he believed it belonged. A few years back, he'd realized that this lifelong process did nothing but fill his heart and mind with more worry than hope. *And I'm all done with that,* he decided. *Worrying is a lot like sitting in this rocking chair. It's one way to pass the time, but it doesn't actually get you anywhere.* He vowed to never give another negative thought the kind of attention he once did. *They'll never hold control or power over me again.*

Another thought arrived. *I wonder how bad Ginny and Ollie are fighting?* Although he recognized it, he merely allowed it to pass by. It was the first time in Robert's life that he understood peace. *At this point in the game, there's not a whole lot left for me to do.* His only job was to be still—to feel the sun on his face; to feel the breeze on his neck; to recognize his surroundings without being a part of them. The only work he had left was to breathe—in and out, in and out. *Although even that's become a chore lately.*

He squinted at the sun filtering through the colorful leaves above him. *I wish I'd known this secret earlier in my life,* he thought. *I might have been able to live worry-free—no fears, no regret, no shame.* He shook his head. *I might have even been able to avoid all the bad decisions and mistakes I made.* For a moment, he considered this, realizing, *That's only a pipedream. I had a wife and son counting on me. There's no way I could've just sat still like I can now,* he thought. *I needed to worry and make my mistakes. I needed to play all the different roles I played.* But that work was done now. *Now I can finally be still.*

As the thought passed through his mind, Luna—licking the last crumbs of dinner from her chops—sauntered over to him, where she flopped down at his feet. For a while, they sat in silence together, watching the chaos ensue at the bird feeders.

At one point, Robert took note of the two faded tattoos on his forearms—both of which had also shrunk over the years. His right forearm hosted a little devil holding a pitchfork; on his left, a pair of angel's wings, with the initials *GG*, branded into his flesh for life.

Georgey Gouveia, he thought, smiling, *it's been too many years, my old friend.*

It felt rewarding to reminisce. After having lived a full life—experiencing all its joys and pains—it seemed almost criminal not to recall them. *Maybe travelling down memory lane is the only good reason to experience life in the first place?*

◊◊◊

Robert had served in the U.S. Navy during the Vietnam War, an experience that he took as much pride in as avoided remembering. His best friend, George Gouveia, was the only exception to that rule.

From 1965 through 1966, he and Georgey had served side-by-side on the Destroyer USS Ingersoll. Sailing out of San Diego, they headed for the coast of South Vietnam. Although her primary mission was to conduct 'market time patrols' to intercept Viet Cong men and supplies, she was also called upon for 24 gunfire missions against 116 targets along the Vietnamese coast, as well as three perilous missions up the Saigon River. She also operated with two aircraft carriers—the USS Independence and USS Midway—for plane guard and screen duties.

Robert could still picture that final weekend pass as vividly as when he and Georgey had taken it.

Georgey was a prankster, reputed to be the "craziest bastard" on the ship. They were in a local bar, a hole-in-the-wall that served brief escapes from reality through some murky drinks disguised as legitimate cocktails. One of their shipmates, Paul Faria, staggered off to the head when Georgey waited a few minutes before following him in. Robert also joined them, knowing he was in for some type of spectacle. Georgey's unsuspecting prey was sitting in the bathroom's closed stall when Georgey threw open the door to find Paul sitting on the dirty toilet, his pants gathered down around his ankles.

Robert laughed. "Oh, here we go."

With one grunt, Georgey tore the door clean off its hinges, handing it right to Paul where he sat.

Paul was fit to be tied. When he walked back into the bar holding the shithouse door, everyone held their sides in laughter—Robert the loudest.

"We'd better get out of here," Robert told Georgey, "before you end up getting us killed."

"But I haven't finished my hooch yet."

"Oh, you've finished it, all right." Grabbing his friend by the arm, they staggered out of the bar, laughing all the way back to the ship.

As the destroyer came into view, Georgey slurred, "I love ya, man... you know that, right?"

I love you too, brother, Robert thought. Instead, he replied, "I bet you say that to all the sailors."

Georgey laughed. "So...so, what are you gonna do when we get home?"

"Forget about this place," Robert answered, assisting his friend in staying upright.

"No...no, I'm being serious."

"And so am I."

Georgey stopped. "Are...are you crazy, man? This is the adventure of our lives and we...we get to share it together. Now how lucky is that?"

Robert nodded. *I'm not sure that good luck plays into any of this,* he thought, *but you're right, at least we have each other.*

Unfortunately, their adventure together was two weeks away from coming to a bloody end—at least for Lucky Georgey.

◊◊◊

Robert hurried back from memory lane to recognize that, at his advanced age, his memory had become selective and kind. Earlier in his life—even a few years back—he would have never been able to recall Vietnam with any sense of fondness.

After the war, he'd committed himself to helping as many people as he could, as though it would purge his soul from all the darkness he'd witnessed. *But the one thing I failed to take into account was my own family,* he realized. While he was always off helping one stranger after the next, he didn't spare all that much time for his son—and he knew it. *Guilt has made me pay dearly for it, though.*

He could still see his son's face. *I wonder how Ollie will remember me in the end.* He pictured his young son sitting up on his shoulders and giggling; he recalled teaching the boy to overcome fear, and to stand up and fight when somebody brought it to him. In Robert's mind, there was little evidence of all those father-son arguments or the long periods of silence that followed and made everyone's guts churn. *The memory certainly is kind*, he confirmed, *no anger or disappointment to be found.*

◊◊◊

Robert's flip phone rang. He picked it up, squinting at the tiny screen to see who it was. "Oh shit, it's Peggy," he told Luna before sending it to voicemail. "Peggy's a good woman, but she's also a pain in the ass." He looked back down at the mutt. "I just want to be friends with her, nothing more. But she doesn't seem to be getting the message."

Luna moved in closer until she was leaning up against his shin.

"That's right," he said, smiling, "*you're* my girlfriend."

Twenty minutes later, a tornado of dust whirled into the air, as Peggy's car came barreling down the dirt driveway. Robert looked down at Luna. "What did I tell you?" he asked. "She's a pain in the ass."

"What are you doing?" Peggy asked as she approached, her car still sputtering. With frizzy blonde hair and green eyes that were as sharp as her mind, the rest of her appeared wrinkled and weathered.

"Just sitting," Robert reported, shifting his weight in the hard chair.

"That's it?"

"Taking stock, I suppose."

"Oh yeah, taking stock of what?" she asked.

He shook his head. "My life, and how I might have squandered the greatest gift I was ever given."

She took a seat on the faded red Igloo cooler beside him. "I'm listening."

He just kept shaking his head. He couldn't help it. "My son, Ollie, was no more than ten when he was doing his daily chores without complaint." He stopped to look at Peggy. "Though I imagine his mother slipped him a little extra in his allowance every week."

"I hope she did," the older woman commented, laughing, "because we both know you're as cheap as hell."

Robert ignored the comment. "The boy kept asking, 'How am I doing, Dad?' His big brown eyes pleaded for acceptance, so I nodded my approval—careful not to give away anything too easily."

Peggy shook her head. "Men," she mumbled.

"'A solid work ethic and a strong back is all you'll ever need in this world, Ollie,' I told him. 'Being dependent on someone other than yourself is like being placed into a cage. You can never control your own destiny.'"

Peggy nodded in agreement.

"'Now go back to work, you lazy bum,' I teased him, and the boy did as he was told, never cracking a smile." Robert's grin faded, as he began to labor for oxygen. "Later that afternoon, once his work was complete, he asked me, 'Dad, can we go fishing? I finished all my chores and I'd really—' 'Fine, we'll go fishing in the morning,' I told him, my skin already starting to crawl at the suggestion."

"Skin crawl," Peggy repeated. "Why's that?"

He peered into her deep emerald eyes. "I served in the Navy during Vietnam," he told her, his throat starting to constrict. "I haven't felt comfortable around the water since."

Peggy placed her veiny hand on his forearm and left it there as a show of support.

"It was just past dawn, and unusually warm for an early morning," Robert recalled aloud. "I can still picture that long flowered field we had to walk through before reaching the wood line, a blue body of water shimmering just behind it." He shook his head. "That damned pond."

Peggy gave his arm a reassuring squeeze. It felt good.

"'I bet I catch more fish than you do, Dad,' Ollie told me, more excited than I'd ever seen him. 'I hope you do, son,'" Robert added, a lump wedging itself halfway down his throat. "'I love fishing,' he told me. 'But how do you know?' I asked him. 'You've never been.' 'I just know, Dad,' he said, and he meant it." He paused to take in some air. "I remember wiping that cold sweat from my brow with a trembling hand, making sure my boy never saw it. Up until that point, I'd been careful to steer clear of the water since returning home from Nam. I'd never talked about it, so there was no way Ollie would have ever known about my pain." He looked at Peggy again. "And I was going to do my damnedest to make sure it stayed that way."

Peggy's eyes filled with empathetic tears; her hand now clutched onto his tanned arm.

"We reached the water's edge where I decided that my best strategy was to concentrate on the tasks at hand; baiting hooks, teaching the boy how to cast on his own, untangling fishing line and unhooking the fish."

"Good plan," Peggy whispered.

"From the moment that first red and white bobber hit the water, I focused on my breathing. *Slow and steady*, I kept reminding myself, *slow and steady*." He gulped in a few lost breaths. "As I expected, Ollie felt bad for the worms, happy that I was willing to replace each bare hook."

The old woman smiled.

"Suddenly, the bobber went under the water. I grabbed the pole and gave it a jerk sideways, helping to set the hook. And then I handed the pole back to Ollie, watching as my happy boy reeled in his first fish. Ollie's eyes went wide when he saw the small blue gill convulsing wildly from the end of the bloody hook. And then he looked away. *You love fishing, all right*, I thought, sliding the fish off the hook, and placing it into a bucket half-filled with pond water, so Ollie could admire his prize for a few minutes. 'He's a little one,' I told him, 'so we should probably throw him back at some point to be with his mother.'" Robert's eyes wet with tears, he chuckled. "Don't you know, he just picked up the bucket and dumped it out—fish and all—back into the pond."

He turned to Peggy. "I can still hear that giant splash," he whispered, extending both his tattooed forearms to show her the goosebumps that now covered him. "I still hate being anywhere near the damned water," he confessed.

Peggy stacked her right hand on top of her left.

"We stayed an hour longer," Robert added, "an eternity for me...so we could kill a dozen more night crawlers and release half that many small fish. 'Okay, Ollie,' I finally told him, 'I don't know about you, but I've about had my fill of fishing for the day.' He was not happy. 'But Dad—,' he started to complain. 'We're leaving!' I snapped back, sorry for my sharp tone." He paused to breathe again. "But I couldn't help it. My heart hadn't stopped racing from the moment we'd stepped up to the water."

Robert stopped to scratch Luna's thick neck. He was buying time. "As we packed up to leave, the boy was clearly disappointed," he went on, "but by the time we reached the station wagon, a giant smile returned to Ollie's innocent face. 'Maybe we can try fishing from a boat sometime?' he suggested." Robert shook his head hard, but still couldn't stop the tears. "Although I meant nothing by it, I screamed at him, 'Get that idea out of your head, boy! I'll never step foot on another boat for as long as I live.' His face dropped again, staying that way all the way home."

Peggy stood to give Robert a long hug. "I'm so sorry," she said. "I'm sorry you had to suffer that."

"Even though Ollie claimed to love fishing, that was the first and last time I ever took him," Robert muttered into her bony shoulder—his old, stinging tears staining her blouse. "I should have told him why we never went again rather than let him believe that I didn't want to spend the time with him. So stupid..."

Peggy leaned back to meet his gaze. "Why don't you just talk to him about it?"

Robert shook his head. "Because he'll think me a fool. He's probably forgotten all about it."

Chuckling, she grabbed his large hand and kissed it. "You boys are something else," she said. "You can get all cozy and comfortable with violence if you have to, but God forbid you need to share your feelings." She stood. "Are you okay?"

"Better now, thanks."

"Good," she said, letting his hand go. "It looks like you haven't eaten in a while?"

He shrugged. "I eat."

"Let me go fix you something," she said, kissing his cheek before heading for his front door. "You have eggs?"

"Always," he said.

"Omelets it is, then."

As she walked away, the old man looked down at Luna. "Don't give me that look. I've got to eat, right?"

She wagged her tail slowly.

"I already told you," he whispered, scratching under her ears, "you're my girl."

While Robert continued to rock in his weather-beaten throne, he looked down at the mutt. "The time has flown by too fast, Luna," he told her, feeling the first twinge of panic he'd experienced in years. "And then I got busy helping other folks."

The dog inched in closer to keep the massage going.

"How in the hell could I have put other people before my own son?" He took a few deep breaths to ground himself. "I'll just have to find a way to make up for all that lost time," he added. *But is there enough runway left?*

◊◊◊

Although he was beyond exhausted, Robert tossed and turned in his bed that night, struggling to take in easy consistent breaths. He finally fell asleep only to awaken an hour later in pain. His upper abdomen felt like it was being squeezed in some invisible car crusher, sharp pains that wouldn't subside. *At least there's no pain radiating down my arm,* he reasoned, *so it's probably not a heart attack.*

Propping himself up with another pillow—until he was nearly sitting straight up—he tried to breathe past the pain so he could fall back asleep.

Luna nudged closer to him, laying along the length of his left side like a living body pillow.

Ugh, I have to pee, Robert realized, laboring to deepen his shallow breathing. Looking over at the alarm clock, he did the math. *Maybe I can hold it until morning?*

CHAPTER 3

*H*ow *in the hell am I supposed to know where to go from here,* Jonah wondered, *if I have no idea where I am?*

It was his first year in college and he was still undecided on a major—as well as anything else in his life. *I feel so lost,* he admitted to himself.

For the immediate future, he had a big decision to make. *Do I play Call of Duty or Madden Football?* Jonah grew up addicted to video games. He spent a great deal of his time playing them. Even when his parents yelled, "You need to find a job instead of staring at a screen all day," he continued to master his craft. *I hear them,* he thought, *but I can't help myself.* All he wanted to do was play games. *Madden, it is,* he decided, grabbing for his trusty controller.

From the moment he turned on the magical machine, he felt excited, confident, and in control; he was completely in his element. *Too bad Quinn's not here to play duos with me.* Smiling, he shook his head. *He'd just slow me down anyway.*

As Jonah played—his thumbs moving in rapid sync—he fantasized about making it to the big leagues of video gaming. *If I keep playing in competitive game mode, I could qualify and get invited to the Madden Championship. I can already see it...Jonah Earle sitting at the top of the 32-player bracket, competing for the $100,000 prize.* As he threw a long pass to score his second touchdown, his smile grew wider. *I can definitely see it!*

It was nearly noon, when Jonah made his way out of the dark cellar to the kitchen to eat. *Not bad for a Saturday,* he thought, checking the wall clock. He took one step in to find his parents waiting for him at the kitchen table.

"What's the problem, Jonah?" his dad asked, holding up an unfolded letter. "The college has informed us that you haven't been attending two of your classes?" He shook his head. "Can you explain to me why the hell we're paying for them?"

Great, he thought, *an intervention.*

Jonah's mom, seated by her husband's side, nodded in agreement.

Well, that's rare these days, Jonah thought.

"College is not really an option today," his father continued. "Without it, you won't be able to compete in today's job market...or even be able to survive in this world."

"I know that, Dad. I do. But..."

"But what?"

"No one wants to succeed more than I do, believe me, but what I'm doing right now, some of the classes I'm taking—it just feels like a total waste of time."

"A waste of time?" his mother asked him.

Jonah nodded, wishing he had the right words to explain. "The whole college thing is criminal," he complained, "making freshmen pay for classes to learn things they'll never apply in their entire lives."

"How do you know the information they're teaching you won't benefit you later on, Jonah?" his mother asked.

"I have a science class as part of my core curriculum, Mom," he explained. "What's that about? I have absolutely no interest in any career field related to science."

"So what field are you interested in?"

"I don't know," he said, shrugging, "not yet anyway."

Both of his parents stared at him until it became more than uncomfortable.

"If only I could figure out a way of making money playing video games," he muttered under his breath.

"Video games?" his mom echoed, her voice rising a complete octave.

"And therein lies the problem," his dad said, adding a snicker. "He thinks he can play video games for a living."

"There's a boatload of money to be made in gaming, Dad," Jonah snapped back, defensively. "People have very successful careers in the field."

"Really?" his dad fired back.

"Yes, really! Bugha won the Fortnite World Cup last year and took in three million bucks over a couple of days."

"Bugha?" his mom repeated, confused.

"Then beat *Bugha* and maybe you can start skipping classes," his father said.

Although the comment was infuriating, Jonah still tried to share his frustrations. "I wish I could explain it to you. I really do. I'm not trying to be lazy or stupid. I just need to figure out what..." He stopped, inhaling deeply. "I want to do something big with my life, I promise." The teenager went silent, considering his own words. *Sorry, not sorry.*

His mom opened her mouth a few times before the words came. "So, what's the plan, Jonah, play video games in that basement for the rest of your life?"

"Well, we all know that's not going to happen," his dad said, interrupting. "Are you interested in joining the military?"

What? he thought. *Are they even listening to me?* "No, Dad," he quickly replied.

"The military?" Ginny repeated under her breath, glaring at her husband.

His father ignored the bad look. "Are you interested in learning a trade?" he asked.

Jonah shook his head. "I'm not very good with my hands, you know that."

"Great, then it's settled," the scowling man said, shocking everyone; "college, it is!"

Jonah sighed heavily. "And I'm fine with that. I just wish I had a clearer direction on which way I should move forward."

"Just move forward, Jonah!" his father said. "Attend the classes you're signed up for and apply yourself." He looked at his wife. "Mom and I couldn't ask for anything more than that."

Jonah nodded in surrender. *Got it, Dad. Just waste my time and your money until I figure out how to get to where I need to go. Makes sense.* Although he tried to contain it, he could feel a smirk twitching at the corner of his mouth. "I wish I had things figured out the way Layla always has."

"No need for comparisons, Jonah. We don't do that in this family, you know that," his father said. "We each find our own way and create our own shadows. I never wanted to live in my father's shadow, the same way I never wanted you to spend a single minute in mine." His dad grabbed his forearm. "You were raised to be your own man, son, so just be that—nothing more, nothing less."

That's a lot, the teenager thought, *it really is.* He nodded. "Okay, Dad. I'll attend the classes and complete the prerequisites for other classes I probably won't need."

His father sneered at the sarcastic comeback.

"Fine," Jonah surrendered, "I'll go to class." He turned, prepared to leave the kitchen—hungry and uninspired.

"Nothing more, nothing less," his dad repeated to his backside. "There's no secret to success, Jonah." His voice grew louder. "Dreams don't work unless you do. It's as easy as that."

Yeah, yeah, yeah... Jonah thought, offering another dismissive nod—though he never bothered to turn back. *I can't count how many times I've heard these same words before.* Although he didn't question their validity, a sense of terrible inertia was prohibiting him from putting his father's theories into practice.

"It's all about putting the sweat equity in..." His dad's voice began trailing off.

Sure, Dad, he thought, as he began descending the cellar stairs, *but I also need to eat.*

Jonah returned to his dungeon to daydream about becoming the next e-sports champion—*the modern-day rock star.* As he grabbed for his video controller, deep down he realized, *If only I were good enough.* The reality of it made his stomach flop. *But if not video gaming, then what?* Every other profession seemed like a dreadful consolation prize, making him feel even more frozen in place.

He looked up to find his mother standing on the bottom step. "Come for a ride with me," she told him.

"To where?" he asked.

"I need your help," she said. "Let's go."

Ugh, he thought, abandoning his video game, *you're really cutting into my training time, Ma.*

◊◊◊

They were in his mom's car and backing out of the driveway—with Jonah buckling in—before she admitted, "I'm going grocery shopping and I need your help."

"Ma!" he complained. *You've got to be kidding me?*

"Listen, the only time I can get you to talk to me is when I trap you in a car." She smiled. "And I'm guessing that your eyes can use a break from those video games." She shook her head. "You're too young to lose your eyesight."

He took a deep breath and exhaled heavily, surrendering to the imprisonment. "What's up with Dad lately?" he asked.

"What do you mean?"

"He seems so sad or upset all the time."

She sighed. "Your dad's been going through a tough time for a while now. He hates his job and—."

"He does?" Jonah was shocked by this. *And they want to condemn me to the same future in middle management—punching a clock and paying bills?*

She nodded.

"Then why doesn't he just quit?" Jonah asked.

She gave him the side eye. "Because he has a family to support, that's why. People don't just quit when things get tough, Jonah."

He watched her face, wondering whether they were still talking about his dad's work. "I get it."

"Your father's a good man, Jonah. He's a great dad and husband, and—"

"If you think he's so great, then why do you two fight all the time?"

She sighed again. "We need to work on that," she admitted. "Marriage can be difficult sometimes, two different people needing to be in the same place...in synch all the time." She shrugged. "Sometimes, it's..." She stopped.

Jonah waited.

"Sometimes, it's important to remember why you got together in the first place."

"Okay," he said, already missing his video games.

"Listen, all I'm saying is, give your dad a break...and try your best to do what he asks of you, okay?

"Okay," Jonah repeated, hoping this was the end of it.

As they pulled into the supermarket's giant lot, she found a spot up front before parking and turning off the ignition. "Are you coming in with me?"

Grabbing for his cell phone, he shook his head. "I'll help you load and unload the groceries," he said. "That's my job."

"Fair enough." She stepped out of the driver's seat. "Is there anything specific you want me to pick up for you?"

He nodded. "Can you please get me some more Pop Tarts," he said, "the strawberry ones."

"You can't survive on Pop Tarts, Jonah," she told him.

He smiled, thinking, *I have so far.*

◊◊◊

Marissa DeSousa, Jonah's girlfriend, was a Portuguese beauty with dark hair and matching eyes. Her skin was olive toned, even a light caramel, giving her the appearance of having a perpetual tan. From the moment Jonah saw her walking out of the school cafeteria, he was infatuated. From the moment they spoke—weeks later, after he'd finally drummed up the courage—he was in love. That feeling only grew with each moment they spent together.

Paint night hosted at the Muse Paint Bar at Commonwealth Landing seemed like the perfect adult date for early September. Jonah had scraped together the money and, with their generous student discount, was able to pull it off. They arrived a half hour early, as suggested on their website.

"I'm impressed," Marissa said, stepping into a large room of brick, glass, and copper, "and I'm also surprised."

"Surprised?" Jonah asked.

She giggled. "You hated art class in high school."

He half-shrugged. "I'm hoping this will be a different experience." He laughed. "If Mr. Brault is the instructor, wearing that raspberry beret of his, then I'm out of here."

Marissa laughed. "I loved Mr. Brault," she said.

"And you were the only one who did," Jonah teased.

She slapped his arm.

The paint, a 16 x 20 white canvas, and an apron were waiting at each easel. Snacks were available for purchase, as was a cash bar. *But we're too young to enjoy a cocktail here*, he thought, chuckling. *If they only knew.*

"Let's face each other," Marissa suggested, as they claimed their workstations, "so neither one of us can peek at the other's work."

He nodded in agreement, realizing, *Now I'll be distracted looking at you the whole time.*

Brian, the earthy instructor, wore torn jeans, a silver skull ring on his pointer finger, and what appeared to be a thermal shirt sleeve on his head as a hat. He was seated on an elevated platform in front of a heavily used easel.

"We're going to have fun together," Brian promised, as everyone settled in.

Marissa looked at Jonah to catch him staring at her. "Thank you for this," she whispered.

His heart fluttered.

"Relax," Brian told his room of victims, "you don't need an ounce of artistic skill to pull this off tonight."

"Perfect," Jonah commented, "we're qualified then."

Along with a few middle-aged ladies seated within earshot, Marissa laughed.

"Okay, let's get started," Brian said.

From the first brushstroke, the pace felt frantic. "Be sure to keep the canvas wet," Brian kept calling out.

As a vibrant lake scene began to appear on the man's canvas, Jonah laughed. *I have my own masterpiece to create,* he decided.

Brushstroke by brushstroke, their trained artist guided the entire room from blank canvases to some of the ugliest landscapes Jonah had ever seen.

"Keep the canvas wet and use those filbert brushes," he continued to yell out.

Marissa looked over at Jonah again.

"The filbert is your friend," he joked.

Although she laughed, she still followed every one of Brian's instructions, painting a gray dock on a blue lake; a wood line and mountain range on the horizon, with a giant pine tree jumping out from the right side of the canvas—*as though it were waiting to be climbed.*

As Brian made his way through the room to check on everyone's progress, he stopped at Jonah's station. "What on earth are you doing?" he asked, shaking his head.

"My best," Jonah fibbed, making Marissa giggle.

Brian lingered for a moment.

"I'm trying to capture a masterpiece," Jonah added, earning an unexpected pat on the shoulder.

Marissa stole another peek over her canvas.

"Brian reminds me a lot of Mr. Brault," Jonah teased.

She laughed again.

During the big reveal, when they exchanged paintings, Marissa gasped—realizing that Jonah had painted her face. "Oh my God," she said, holding it up to the light to take it in. "It's absolutely... awful!"

He nodded, proudly. "I know, right?"

"And I absolutely love it!"

"When you have a gift like I do," he joked, "you need to share it with the world."

She hurried to kiss him. "I'm going to hang it up in my bedroom, where I'll treasure it forever."

"Oh, I'm sure your parents are going to love that."

"I'm serious," she said, kissing him again. "I love it, Jonah."

He thought about that. "If that's the case, then I should have probably tried harder."

She kissed him. "It's perfect," she whispered. "I can feel the love that you put into it."

"I love you," he told her, "I really do."

"I love you more," she said.

◊◊◊

Through a blur of deep slumber, the weekend whipped by. It was late Monday morning when Jonah found himself sitting on the college's Student Center concrete steps, unsure whether he should attend Biology 101. Putting down his *Retro Gamer* magazine, he scanned the vast college campus before him. *This place sucks so bad.* He continued to peruse the college quad. *But wanting to play video games for a living is probably not the most realistic career path*, he thought, *no matter how bad I want it.*

When finalizing the college logistics, he couldn't decide whether to experience dorm life or just commute to campus—which was only six miles away. He quickly decided to stay home where there was guaranteed free laundry service, as well as three square meals a day—saving his parents a bundle. He took as many online courses as he could, allowing him the daily luxury of sleeping in.

Some kids his age were dying to get out on their own, but not him. His mother cooked for him. *And Dad does everything else.* Jonah Earle might have been young and dumb, but he wasn't so stupid that he didn't realize he had it made.

Quinn, Jonah's childhood best friend, spotted him and hurried over to take a seat beside him on the cold concrete. "No class right now?" he asked, swinging his backpack off his shoulder. Quinn was clean-cut and handsome, lacking the acne-scars that many teenage boys his age tried to conceal with patchy goatees.

Jonah shook his head. "I'm already done for the day, bro." Compared to his vertically-challenged friend, Jonah was a tall glass of water, with dark short hair, tapered in the back. With his mother's hypnotizing light eyes and his father's thick hair, he'd inherited some stunningly good genes. He was even able to enjoy a swimmer's ripped physique without putting in all that much effort.

Quinn nodded. "I hear that." He scanned the campus. "This place is lame. I'm still not sure I belong here."

"Me either," Jonah thought, nodding. "The struggle is real."

"It definitely ain't high school, brother."

Jonah snickered. "You can say that again."

"It definitely ain't high school, brother," Quinn repeated, continuing to play the role of jackass.

Jonah stood. "You want to go grab some lunch at the Grille?"

"Are you buying?" Quinn asked, getting to his feet.

"I am," Jonah said, surprising his friend, "for myself."

The Somerset Grille was one of their favorite haunts for greasy burgers and fries. Although Jonah preferred fast food—fried chicken, burritos, tater tots—over his mother's bland cooking, he could hardly afford to eat out.

They were just starting to check out the sticky menus when Jonah started laughing.

"What?" Quinn asked.

"Remember this past May, a few weeks before prom when you and I were the only two in the Boys Room between classes. I finished first, hurried out and began screaming. 'Oh my God, that was so gross!' A hundred students stopped in the hallway. 'What happened?' they asked. I pointed toward the bathroom door and told them, 'I just caught a perv in there playing with himself!' Not three seconds later, the door opens and out you walk, adjusting your belt."

Although Quinn laughed, his eyes turned to slits. "I still haven't squared up with you for that one, have I?"

"Are you crazy? That was the only time I've ever gotten you good! You've been pranking me since Kindergarten."

Just then, a beautiful young waitress—Amber—stepped up to their table. "Hi boys," she said.

Quinn leaned into her, as if he were about to share a secret. "This poor guy right here," he whispered in his lisp, gesturing toward Jonah, "he's a bit on the slow side and it's really not his fault. When he was young, he split his head open while drinking from the toilet and he suffered some serious brain damage because of it."

And it begins again, Jonah thought.

"It was so bad he had to have a plate put in his head," Quinn added.

"Oh no," Amber said, playing along.

Quinn shrugged. "His parents couldn't afford metal, so the doctors went with a paper plate." He shook his head. "I don't think it works that great, though." Amber looked at Jonah again. "Every time we go swimming, the plate gets wet and Jonah starts stuttering."

Although she obviously tried to hold it in, she looked at Jonah and began to laugh.

Jonah couldn't help himself and laughed along with her.

"How did you guys meet," Amber asked, "in school?"

Quinn shook his head. "We raised hamsters for a while together. To be honest, they're tough to herd, and they kind of freak me out." Leaning in even closer, he lowered his tone. "Did you know that the harder you squeeze their bellies, the more their eyes bulge? It's insane."

Amber studied his face for a moment. "You're kind of insane, huh?"

Jonah nodded. "You have no idea," he confirmed.

Quinn smiled. "A little, I guess."

After giving Amber their usual orders, she walked away. They looked at each other and laughed.

"You are insane," Jonah said.

"We've had some wild times, brother," Quinn said, "which I wouldn't trade for the world."

Jonah nodded. "Me either."

"Remember the night Jeremy drove his father's car into the pond?" Quinn said.

Jonah laughed hard.

"And he wasn't even drinking," Quinn added.

"And of course, there was sophomore year," Jonah said, "when you took that vicious beating from a girl. Do you remember that?"

"That was just a bad breakup," Quinn explained, "and she was a lot bigger than me."

Jonah laughed. "We've been through quite a bit together," he added, his tone turning nostalgic and bittersweet.

Quinn's eyes drifted off, as he thought aloud. "...all the basketball games and the Friday night dances..."

"...stealing the History final and getting caught," Jonah interrupted, "and the food fight we lost to the underclassmen, those angry little trolls."

"...blowing every dollar we ever made on stupid shit like trading cards."

"...and singing at the top of our lungs."

"...without even knowing the lyrics."

They both laughed.

"Yup," Jonah said, thinking about his current situation, "we're a long way from there now, Quinn."

The jokester offered his signature grin. "It's just one of those things that stinks about having to grow up, I guess?" He shrugged. "But at least we're stuck in college together."

"Good point. It would have really sucked had we been separated."

They sat in silence for a few minutes. "By the way, how's your sister doing?" Quinn asked.

"Layla's doing good, thanks," Jonah reported. "According to my mom, she's loving Montenegro, wherever the hell that is."

"Damn, bro, I'll never forget how blown out she was at your graduation party."

Jonah shook his head. *Me either*, he thought, his mind's eye picturing that legendary night. "Layla's good, bro," he repeated.

"Glad to hear it," Quinn said.

Returning to the table, Amber looked at Quinn's leftovers. "Do you want a box for that?" she asked.

"Well, I'm not a great boxer," he answered with a straight face, "but I'll definitely wrestle you for it."

She laughed it off. "Anyone up for some dessert?" she asked, through the chuckles. "Ice cream fills in the cracks, you know."

"No, thanks," Jonah said.

"Are you sure?"

"I'm sure," he said, shaking his head, "it's a budget thing."

She placed the check on the table. "When you gentlemen are ready," she said. "No rush."

Quinn stood and grabbed for his backpack. "Listen, I need to roll."

"Not before paying half the tab, you don't."

The grinning clown fished a brown leather wallet out of his back pocket, removed a crumpled ten-dollar bill and threw it on the table.

"Is that your first communion money?" Jonah asked, implying that his friend was cheap.

Quinn dismissed the comment. "Are you going to Matty's party tomorrow night?"

"What do you think?"

Quinn nodded. "I haven't seen you miss one yet."

Jonah laughed.

"Are you bringing Marissa?"

"If she wants to go." Jonah's girlfriend was very attractive and equally sexy, a real head turner.

"How are things going with her?" Quinn asked.

"Great! Why?"

"Well, if that ever changes, please let me know. I'd like a shot at the big leagues."

"You couldn't handle Marissa, bro." He shook his head.

"A wildcat in the sack, huh?" Both of Quinn's eyebrows stretched for his hairline.

"Relax, Pervus. Have some respect."

"Seriously, between us, is the sex good?"

Jonah only shook his head in response.

"I hope you're using protection," Quinn said, chuckling. "A serious scholar like yourself doesn't need any distractions."

She's on the pill, you dumbass, Jonah thought.

Quinn shook his head. "You guys have been inseparable since high school. If you're not partying, then you're with her."

"And what else is there?" Jonah teased.

"How about your friends?" Quinn fired back.

"I believe that's covered during the partying portion of the program."

They bumped fists.

"I'll see you tomorrow night at Matty's, then?"

"I'll be there."

"I'm told that there's going to be a contest that includes shots. Unless you've turned into a chicken shit, then—"

"I've never backed down from a challenge yet, have I?" he quickly replied, smiling.

"Nope, you have not! Later, bro."

"Later."

◊◊◊

Jonah returned home to find his parents engaged in another heated argument that could never be won. *Here we go again,* he thought, realizing that the kitchen door that separated them wasn't nearly thick enough to allow for privacy.

"You love playing favorites with our children," his mom accused his dad in a scream. "You always have."

"Different kids have different needs," his dad yelled back, "and our daughter has always been much more resourceful and responsible than our son."

Jonah cringed. *Ouch...*

"And I wonder how that happened?" his mom barked.

"I wasn't alone in raising them, Ginny," he roared, defending himself.

"Well, that's a first," she said, her volume one notch down from a screech.

"How's that?"

"This might be the first time you've ever admitted that we've worked together on anything."

"Come on, Ginny, that's just not true!"

"But it is, Oliver! I don't blame Layla for wanting to live halfway around the world."

"She traveled halfway around the world to better herself, Ginny; that's why she left!" he yelled. "And if she did leave because she wanted out..." He paused. "As far as I'm concerned, everything that's wrong here—and we both know there's plenty—you're on the hook for half of it."

"I...I..." his mom stammered, her audible rage stealing away her words.

"But you're as accountable as you are understanding," his dad yelled.

Jonah shook his head. *Damn, that's cold.*

With a huff, his mom stormed past the kitchen door, through the living room and out of the house—never making eye contact with Jonah.

The bickering never ends, Jonah thought, before approaching his angry father seated at the kitchen table. "If things are that bad, Dad, then why don't you and Mom just split up? I mean, if you're both that miserable..."

"That's not going to happen," his father said, his eyes bloodshot from rage.

Jonah gawked at him. "Why not?"

"Because we're a family, Jonah, that's why. And families need to stick together."

Jonah remained silent. *That's some twisted logic, right there.* He studied his father like he was gazing into a crystal ball; he could plainly see the pain and frustration in the man. "It's going to be okay, Dad."

His father's face changed from furious to calm before he nodded his appreciation. "Don't worry about your mother and me, Jonah," he told him. "I'm not going anywhere, and neither is she. We made a commitment to each other a long time ago and we're both going to honor that commitment."

"That's just great, Dad," Jonah mumbled, thinking, *So the nightmare continues.*

Jonah was happy to head down into the basement. His bedroom could have been—and normally was—a condemned site. Over the summer— between high school and college—he'd claimed the finished basement as his own, setting it up as a bedroom and decorating it to the taste of someone who was young, immature—and without any budget. *If Mom or Dad throw a Pop Tart down the stairs every couple of days, they may never see me again,* he thought. The real upside—there was a separate door where he could sneak Marissa in and out.

He usually had to climb over the landfill of dirty clothes to reach his bed. But today, it was clear. *Mom's the best!* he thought.

He grabbed his cell phone and texted Marissa. *Hey sexy, are you coming over?*

I'd like to. Are your parents home?

My mother just left the house. My dad's upstairs, but he's distracted...trust me. It doesn't matter either way. They never come downstairs.

But what if we get caught?

We won't. We'll just be quiet.

Yeah, right.

A minute went by without any further detail. It was too long.

So are you coming, Marissa?

I'm on my way.

Jonah smiled wide, thinking, *Maybe college life isn't all that bad after all.*

CHAPTER 4

When they'd first met, Ginny was a stunning beauty—like a Ferrari driven straight off the showroom floor—gleaming brightly. As of late, Oliver suffered from buyer's remorse.

He wondered what had happened with his wife that broke their thermostat, plummeting their marital temperature down to freezing. *Maybe Ginny's indifference is because she's having an affair? A fling?* He pushed the thought out of his head as soon as it appeared. *If it is happening, I'm not even sure I want to know.*

Yawning, he closed his eyes, thinking, *I'm not sure I could handle it.*

"I think we need a vacation, badly," Oliver told his wife the following morning, not revealing that he'd begun the planning weeks before.

"I couldn't agree more," she said, perking up.

"Really?"

"Of course."

He was taken aback and trying not to show it. "What do you think about you and me in Aruba for a whole week—alone?"

"I think that sounds perfect."

"Maybe we can spend the week working on the lack of physical love in our relationship?" he suggested, raising a hopeful eyebrow.

"Or maybe we can start by working on our terrible lack of communication?"

Whoa... He thought about it.

"Our lack of intimacy is not the biggest problem in our marriage, Oliver; it's the result." She rose to meet him. "You don't want me just going through the motions in bed, do you?"

He gave that some thought as well—this time, wearing a grin.

"Well, I'm not going to do that. I'm sorry if I need to feel close to you in order to—"

"Don't apologize," he said, halting her. "Maybe Aruba will give us both what we need?"

"I hope so," she whispered, kissing his cheek.

◊◊◊

Feeling like he was suffocating, Oliver was startled from his sleep—his toes spread wide like a chicken hawk landing on a branch. Sitting erect, he ripped the plastic CPAP mask off his face and began hyperventilating. *What the hell?* he thought. Heavy rain and winds pounded off his bedroom window. The alarm clock was blinking red. He sat up straighter, trying to collect his wits. *What the hell?* he thought again when the truth hit him. *The power must have gone out in the storm.* He looked over at his CPAP machine and then back at Ginny. *Trying to kill me, huh?* He thought, grinning. She was lightly snoring. *There's no way she could have made it to the breaker box downstairs and back in time.* He nearly laughed at the thought.

Checking his cell phone, he corrected the time on the alarm clock before resetting it for an early morning wake up. *We don't want to miss our flight*, he thought, glancing back toward the window at the angry storm. *If a week together in paradise doesn't help us, then I don't know what will.* He looked back at his slumbering wife. *God, I hope it does.*

◊◊◊

The flight to Aruba was delayed. *Shocker*, Oliver thought, shooting a smile to his yawning wife.

"It's a good thing we got up early," Ginny moaned, returning the grin.

He nodded. "It'll be worth it," he said. "We need this time away."

Matching the nod, she yawned again—making him do the same.

Oliver grabbed his cell phone and called Layla. It went straight to voicemail. *Her phone must be turned off because she's in class*, he thought. *Either that, or she just screened me.*

He texted her, *Layla, I hope you're doing well over there, and staying safe. Mom and I are at the airport, getting ready to take off on our second honeymoon.* He smiled. *Talk to you in a week.*

As they settled into the flight, Oliver asked, "Do you want to play gin rummy?"

Ginny shook her head. "I was hoping to catch up on some of the sleep we lost, so we can hit the ground running when we land."

He nodded. *Makes good sense.*

While his wife passed out, Oliver watched the flight map on the screen in front of him. He closed his eyes a few times trying to nap, but it was no use. Plucking the tourist brochures from his carry-on, he reviewed the research he'd feverishly conducted.

Tamarijn Aruba All Inclusive Resort: With one and a half miles of beach, you will enjoy what feels like your own private oasis. Featuring spacious lobbies, open-air seating at on-site restaurants, and guestrooms spread out among low-rise buildings, the resorts are designed to give you the space you need to truly unwind and disconnect.

Goosebumps swept across his arms. *I haven't felt this excited since...* He couldn't remember.

For the most part, the flight was uneventful until they were a half hour from their destination. Oliver had just accepted a tiny plastic cup of Diet Coke when the plane felt like it dropped twenty stories, spilling the drink on his shirt, and nearly tossing the flight attendant into the cabin's ceiling.

Ginny's eyes flew open. She immediately reached for Oliver's hand. "What the..."

He'd just finished interlocking their fingers when the plane plummeted again, firing Oliver's heart into his throat.

"Folks, this is the captain," the intercom called out. "We're currently experiencing a small patch of turbulence."

Small patch of turbulence? Oliver thought. *I'm surprised we're still airborne.*

"I've turned on the seat belt sign and ask that everyone please remain in their seats, buckled up."

As the flight attendant scurried toward the rear of the plane, Oliver looked at Ginny. Her eyes were wide with terror.

"We'll be fine," he told her. "Just take deep breaths and try to relax."

Nodding, she squeezed his hand.

It may not be the way I was hoping, he thought, *but at least we're holding hands. It's been a while.*

Hand-in-hand, they walked from the island taxi into the gorgeous resort foyer. Oliver tightened his grip on his wife's hand and smiled. *Now we're holding hands for the right reason*, he thought. *Layla and Jonah would be thrilled to see this.*

Their oceanfront room was ideal for beach lovers who were looking for some real privacy. *This place is perfect*, he thought, pleased that he'd put in the time to research it. They were on the first floor of the low-rise building, where they could walk out of their room a few feet from the beach and Caribbean Sea. He opened the slider and stepped out to suck in a lung full of fresh air. *This view is—*

"I'm going to take a shower," Ginny said, standing behind him. "Do you want to join me?"

He nearly took his fingers off closing the slider door.

At the sight of his naked wife, Oliver became fully aroused. They were on vacation, with time and privacy they hadn't enjoyed in years, so they engaged in extended foreplay—kissing, touching, tasting.

Oliver stopped her. "If we don't slow down, I'm going to finish and we—"

"...don't want that," she said, completing the sentence for him, "at least not yet."

As they began to make love, rocking back and forth in rhythm, Oliver couldn't believe it; he could feel himself starting to go soft. *What the hell?* Panic struck his heart. *No...no...no!* But the fear had already overtaken him, making his mind race out of control. *Maybe this is a side effect of the Lyme disease I dealt with a couple years ago, or the heart arrhythmia issues I've had since?*

Ginny opened her eyes. "Is everything okay?" she asked.

That was it; the starch was completely washed out of him. He went flaccid, thinking, *That new medication, Losartan, is probably contributing.*

"Are you okay?" Ginny asked again.

Rolling off her and laying on his back, he stared up at the ceiling in disbelief. "I'm sorry, Ginny, I don't know what..."

"It's fine, Oliver," she said, placing her head on his heaving chest. "There's no need to apologize."

"It's me," he said, his brain scrambling for the right words without betraying his inner-terror. "It's not you," he assured her.

She choked on a chuckle. "Please tell me you're not using that tired old line on me?"

"I'm sorry," he repeated, unable to reconcile her nonchalance over the horrific situation.

She lifted her head to look at him. "Oliver, don't make this something it doesn't need to be. We're getting older. It happens."

"But it doesn't happen to me!" he shot back, defending his manhood.

After shaking her head, she placed it back on his chest. "It's fine."

He was absolutely devastated. *This vacation was supposed to—*

"It's okay," she confirmed, "really, it is." She hugged him. "We'll try again tomorrow."

But is it okay? he wondered, feeling defeated—even crushed. *This was supposed to be the romantic vacation that brought us back together.* In the middle of paradise, an overwhelming feeling of dread consumed him.

Aruba was a beautiful island, with incredible food and friendly locals. The setting was heaven on earth, every ingredient required to enjoy an unforgettable vacation. *We should have done this a long time ago,* Oliver thought, trying hard to get beyond the previous night.

Their late breakfast at the Palm Grille was going well; they were even able to find topics of conversation other than Layla and Jonah—and Oliver's difficulties in bed.

"I signed us up for the newlywed game this afternoon," he announced, nibbling on a slice of fresh mango.

From the look on Ginny's face, she wasn't completely thrilled about the idea. "But I wanted to get my hair braided."

"You what?" he asked, taken aback. "I thought it would be fun for us to show the young kids how it's done."

"We're hardly newlyweds, Oliver."

He could feel his face drop. *After last night's shit show, she may have a point.*

She shook her head. "I already booked time to get my hair braided."

"So you'd rather get your hair done than have some fun with me?" he asked, half-teasing; his fears about the future of his marriage were always bubbling just beneath the surface.

She searched his face to see if he was serious. "If you want me to cancel, I will."

"I'm just playing with you," he said, opting to let it go. "Get your hair braided. We have all week to be together."

"That's right," she said, "we do."

"Shopping for you and snorkeling for me," he listed, excitedly. "The whole week hanging out on the beach, reading some good books and taking nice, long walks in the sand every day."

"I'm looking forward to all of it." She stood, threw her pink linen napkin onto the table, and gave him a kiss. "I'll catch up with you later, okay?"

"Okay."

That night, they dined at *Pelican Terrace* at the *Divi, Tamarijn's* sister resort only a short walk down the beach.

"I wonder how Layla's doing?" Ginny said. "Maybe we should figure out the time difference between here and there, and try to give her a call tomorrow?"

He nodded. "Sure."

They ate in silence for a while.

"I hope Jonah's still alive," she commented. "We left enough food for him, but with his appetite—"

"Can we please try not to talk about the kids?" he asked, cutting her off.

She looked at him.

"I want this week to be about just you and me."

She nodded. "Okay," she said, "then let's talk."

There was silence for an extended moment.

"This is exactly what scares me the most, Oliver," she whispered.

"And what's that?" he asked.

"That we both want to talk about something other than the kids, but neither one of us knows what to say." Her eyes misted over. "That maybe there isn't a whole lot left for us to say?"

Oh my God, he thought, *she has the same fears I do.* The kids had been their combined purpose for years. *But we're wrapping up our job as parents,* he thought, *and if we're being honest, any common ground between us is shrinking by the day.* He and Ginny were hardly standing on a postage stamp, threatening to fall off. "I love you very much," he blurted.

"And I love you too, Oliver," she vowed, "but that's not the issue, is it?" She shook her head. "The problem is that we've forgotten how to communicate with each other, which has created some real distance between us."

"And that's my fault?" he asked, defensively.

As her eyes softened, she reached across the table to grab his hand. "This isn't about blame," she whispered. "Although I wish it were." She half-shrugged. "It might be easier to figure out, if it were."

Oliver's blood turned to ice water. *Shit,* he thought, *she's right.* Many couples their same age were waiting for the last birdie to fly the nest so they could put the house up on the market, split the profit, and put an end to the cruel charade called marriage. "Oh Ginny," he whispered, squeezing her hand.

She held on tight.

"So you're not happy?" he asked; it was a rhetorical question.

Although it took a moment, she shook her head. "Not the way things are between us, no," she admitted.

He felt like someone had socked him in the gut, emptying the air from his lungs.

"You're not happy either, Oliver," she said. "Admit it."

He surrendered with a nod.

They each took a long drink, neither one able to consume enough alcohol to soothe the sharp sting.

"Why won't you come to therapy with me, Ginny?" he asked. "I don't understand."

She began to cry, taking him aback. "Because when my parents— who fought all the time—finally agreed on marriage counseling, they learned things about each other that neither one of them could take back." She shook her head. "After a couple of sessions, both of them came up with a list of reasons to call it quits." She squeezed his hand harder. "I'm terrified of that, Oliver."

Oh my God, he thought, *I had no idea.*

They drank more.

"I was hoping we could just get past this rough stretch," she confessed, shaking her head at the foolishness of it.

"Just get past it?" he repeated.

"I don't know, Oliver," she said. "I really don't."

His heart sank into his leather sandals. *Me either,* he thought, before ordering two more drinks. "And give us the strongest you have," he told the waiter.

Back in their room, they undressed—going through the motions of what a romantic getaway called for.

"Relax," Ginny whispered into his ear. "See, he works just fine," she teased, as she began massaging him to orgasm. "You just need to get last night out of your head."

My mind is empty.

Without engaging in intercourse, he then returned the effort, endeavoring to satisfy his wife more than he had in years. From Ginny's moans, she thoroughly enjoyed the extra attention.

"Now that's great sex!" she announced before they nodded off in each other's arms.

They lay together in the darkness—in the silence—for a while.

"I hope we can fix this," he whispered, and he wasn't referring to their sex life.

"Me too," she whispered back.

At that very moment, all the anger and rage Oliver had felt toward his wife bled into sheer melancholy—sadness.

Hours turned into days. There were no salsa dance classes or hysterical limbo contests, like Oliver had imagined. "They're having karaoke at the beach bar tonight," he said during their buffet lunch. "What do you say we—"

"The way I sing?" she said, immediately dismissing the suggestion.

"Who cares, Ginny? We don't know anybody here."

She shook her head, offering her final answer. "Go, if you want to, Oliver. Have fun. I'm planning to finish my book tonight."

"But I don't want to go alone," he said. "I'm tired of being alone." He felt bad as soon as the words left his lips.

"It's not a big deal," she said. "I'm not sure why—"

"You're right," he said, quickly dismissing the idea, "it's no big deal."

They finished their lunch in silence. As they prepared to leave, Ginny said, "We can do karaoke tonight, if you want."

He shook his head. "No, it's fine."

That night, a few extra cocktails eased Oliver's worries and removed his inhibitions. But he discovered that it also kept his flag at half-staff. *Damn it!* he thought, as he lay with his eager wife. Like a man on a life-or-death mission, he was hell bent to make love to her.

Although Ginny's enthusiasm waned when she realized he was just trying to finish, her patience was beyond admirable. Somehow, he was able to seal the deal.

He rolled onto his back, thinking, *Now that, was anything but great sex.*

Fearing that they might cause even more damage between them, they remained quiet for the rest of the week. The silence was deafening. Every romantic dinner table they occupied was darkened by the shadow of the big pink elephant following them around. Whether it was at *Tamarijn's Cunucu Terrace* or *Ginger* restaurants—or the *Red Parrot* and *Pure Lime* at the *Divi*—they dined listening to the competing conversations around them.

The lack of conversation at their own table made Oliver turn to internal dialogue, which boiled his fears into complete panic. *It's as though we're given a certain number of happy days together, and we've already used them up,* he thought. He'd hoped they'd make new memories together during day excursions like bicycling through town or dining on a sunset cruise from a catamaran. Instead, Ginny did yoga on the beach while he camped out in the resort's fitness center—climbing their rock wall once and jumping in on a game of pool volleyball without the company of his sunbathing wife.

When they were on the beach, getting their money's worth from the open bar, they sat side-by-side. It didn't matter. They could have been miles away from each other and it wouldn't have made a difference—both of them lost in their own novels.

Each night, they attended whatever event the resort hosted—movie night, live bands—wherever the drunken mob landed. Although they sat together, they remained imprisoned within their own frustrations.

Oliver and Ginny's comfortable king-sized bed now served as a demilitarized neutral zone, each of them dangling an arm off their own side of the giant bed to create as much distance as they could between them. Oliver couldn't decide which was less painful—anger or sorrow. *Erectile dysfunction is the least of our problems.*

On the last night of the vacation, Oliver lay on his back, sickened by their terrible stalemate. *This was supposed to be the magical getaway that brought us closer.* Instead, the second half of the week had turned dreadful; a stark reminder that things could still get even worse between them. He looked sideways at his snoring wife. *We didn't have to travel thousands of miles or waste an absurd amount of money to confirm that our marriage is in big trouble.* He continued to study her beautiful face in the moon's soft light. *It doesn't make any sense. How can I miss her when she's lying right here beside me?*

◊◊◊

They were buckled into the plane seats when Ginny turned to him. "I'm sorry this week didn't go the way we were both hoping, Oliver," she said.

We? he thought, strangely surprised by this. "We both need to put in effort, Ginny," he said. "I don't know much, but I do know that."

She nodded in agreement.

"Just be honest with me," he said, getting choked up, "be honest with yourself." He shook his head. "If we're both done trying, then maybe it is time that we throw in the towel. Is that what you want?"

"What?" she said. "That's not what I want. You know that."

He stared into her eyes. "I do now," he said, interlocking their fingers; there was no need to be inspired by bad turbulence this time. *At least it's something,* he thought.

They'd just exited the shuttle bus in the long-term parking lot. Rolling both of his wife's heavy, over packed suitcases, Oliver walked ahead of her when it dawned on him. *I've never walked ahead of Ginny in my life.* Oddly enough, his legs kept moving.

"Oliver," he heard her call out behind him.

He stopped and turned to her, his heart and mind so filled with fear.

"I'm sorry," she said again, and meant it. These were not words used often between them.

"I am too, Ginny," he replied, realizing that this was not the type of apology he ever wanted to offer. With a sorrowful nod, he turned around and kept right on marching to the car. The failed vacation had left such a bitter taste on his tongue that he couldn't manage another word.

◊◊◊

"Nice tan," Dr. Borden-Brown said.

"Thanks," Oliver told her.

"How was the vacation?"

He shrugged. "Better than being at work, I suppose."

The doctor made a note in her trusty pad. "Did you ask Ginny to join us today?"

Oliver shook his head. "Ginny's never going to come here," he snapped, his voice filled with as much sorrow as anger.

"Okay, why?" the doctor asked, calmly.

She has her reasons, he thought, feeling defensive of his wife. He remained silent.

"Even after having the time away, things aren't great at home?" she asked.

"We're working on it," he said, thinking, *Though our vacation certainly didn't help.* He shook his sorrowful head.

"What were you thinking just now?" Dr. Borden-Brown asked. "Can you share it with me?" Her pen and notebook at the ready. "Whatever you say in this room remains confidential."

At this point, I don't even care, he thought. "During our week away, I had a problem with erectile dysfunction...for the first time in my life," he said, surprised at how difficult it was to admit to Dr. Borden-Brown. "It rocked me pretty hard and I barely recovered from it all week."

The compassionate shrink never batted an eye. "It's very common for men your age, Oliver. I'm not sure what the statistics are but they're not low. And from what I understand, different factors can contribute to this. Age, weight, certain medications..." She paused. "...and stress."

He nodded, thinking, *And I check every box.*

"But I think this problem can be easily remedied with a visit to your primary care physician." She half-shrugged. "I can't watch a TV show without seeing two or three commercials about those little blue pills." She smiled.

He shook his head. "I don't like taking medication unless I absolutely have to."

Although it was slight, her head cocked sideways. "I'd say it beats the alternative, and I'm guessing that your wife might feel the same way."

He sighed heavily. "She kept telling me not to worry about it, but I couldn't help it. I felt so humiliated, you know—consumed by it."

"It sounds like Ginny was very supportive, though?"

"She was."

"Then think about that, Oliver...how it's so much more valuable than some orgasm."

She's right, he thought, *Ginny was amazing, acting like it was no big deal.*

"Sex can be very different for men and women. While it's basically all physical for you—which is how males are wired to feel love—women are seeking an emotional connection beyond the physical pleasure." She paused to let the explanation sink in. "There are many different ways to view the same situation, Oliver. Maybe this is the perfect opportunity for you to reconnect on an emotional level with your wife?"

Oliver's head was spinning. *Maybe,* he thought, unconvinced.

"You might even have fun working on the issue together."

"Yeah, real fun," he said, shaking his head. "Sex isn't something I've ever had to think about. It's just something I did...and enjoyed more than anything else in the world."

She nodded. "Then stop thinking about it."

◊◊◊

Oliver arrived late to work again, nearly tiptoeing to the day's assigned desk. The company had recently gone agile, which meant staff shared space while the company saved a bundle on real estate costs.

The cubicle walls had been taken down, creating an open corporate tundra, exposing the entire floor. A sea of desks and bobbing heads—intended to fulfill the company's new initiative—created a cacophony of the most dreadful sounds. Even with these new distractions, the company perpetually boasted about their three-pronged mission—the second prong being collaboration. *This new feng shui concept must have earned some executive a nifty etched-glass award,* Oliver guessed, *while we worker bees suffer his or her success.* The concept was fantastic on paper. In reality, Oliver and his disgruntled colleagues couldn't hear themselves think, never mind host an effective meeting.

This new initiative drove Oliver nuts, having to book a new desk each morning; and that was only if he was the first to submit the request, which wasn't always the case—like today.

Oliver prided himself on riding the river when it came to change, keeping his legs up so they didn't get smashed on the rocks below. *But this is absurd,* he decided, *possibly life changing. I can't even display a framed photo of my kids anymore.*

When taking calls or facilitating meetings, everyone used a headset. The only way to guarantee privacy was to book a conference room. And his beloved office chair—*the one I spent months adjusting to the perfect position*—was lost in a sea of identical chairs. Each day, someone else used it, readjusting it over-and-over. As small as it sounded, it was infuriating— promising to kick off every new day on the wrong foot.

Don approached. "Just getting in?" he asked.

Oliver only looked at him.

"Maybe paying some special attention to the old lady this morning?"

Oliver was about to tell him to leave, but the ignorant man kept right on talking.

"Not me, I'm not even on my wife's radar anymore," Don confessed. "Yup, I'm condemned to live the rest of my life as a celibate monk." He shook his head. "That seems like a lot of power to give to another person, don't you think?" He looked to his left to see their boss approaching. "Talk later," he said, hurrying off.

I hope not, Oliver thought.

"Nice of you to join us, Oliver," Sadie said, as she drew nearer.

"That's a new one," he countered.

"Have you completed your self-assessment for the Annual Performance Review?" she asked, ignoring his comment. "I'd like to meet with everyone next week and get them wrapped up."

"I'm almost done, Sadie," he reported, struggling not to roll both of his eyes completely out of his head. The Annual Performance Review was a flawed rating system that bordered on lunacy. *Regardless of what I report,* he thought, *I'm guaranteed to receive the same rating as the pieces of driftwood in this group.* Other than one's own sense of honor and work ethic, there was no real incentive to "get the job done." *To earn an 'Exceeds,' a team colleague must score a 'Doesn't Meet'—and that's never going to happen.* Everyone gets the same rating. The whole process is an HR debacle that is hardly worth the fight.

"I'll get it finished today," he confirmed.

Sadie nodded, turning to head off.

"Oh Sadie," he called out to her, "I wanted to ask, is there any truth to the recent acquisition rumors?"

She stopped, turning on her red heels. "And what rumors are those?" she asked, smirking.

My God, he thought, *does everything have to be a frigging game?* He forced himself to wear his best fake smile. "Word has it that the company is about to be acquired by a much larger company." If this were the case, Oliver's professional life would become even more unstable—with a possible demotion or even the threat of being let go shimmering on his horizon.

Sadie shrugged, unconvincingly. "I don't know anything about it, Oliver. And if I did, I wouldn't be able to discuss it with you anyway." Without another word, she turned and marched off.

"Thanks boss," he muttered under his breath, "that's super helpful."

◊◊◊

Oliver's cell phone rang, startling him from some broken sleep in the recliner. In the darkness, he looked at the caller ID. *It's Dad's friend, Peggy,* he thought, and quickly answered.

"Have you recently talked to your dad?" she asked. Even through Oliver's mental haze, he could still detect a hint of concern in the older woman's voice.

While Oliver switched the cell phone to his other ear, he squirmed his way out of the recliner. "Actually, I haven't. I called him a few days ago and haven't heard back. That's not like him." Something churned in Oliver's gut.

"It's not like him at all," Peggy said. "He hasn't returned my calls either."

Something's wrong, Oliver thought, the sick feeling in the pit of his gut getting stronger. "Let me try him again," he said. "I'll call you right back."

"Okay."

Oliver ended the call and quickly dialed his father's number. It rang five times before he was forwarded to a computer-generated, automated voice messaging system. "The person you called is not available. At the tone, please record your message. When you've finished recording, you may hang up or press one for more options."

I'd better go check on him. There was no other choice, and he knew it. As he headed for his bedroom to throw on a pair of jeans and a fresh shirt, Ginny looked up from the bed. "What's up?" she asked.

"I'm going to head to Westport to check on my dad," he told her. "Peggy just called, and she hasn't heard from the old man either."

Ginny sat up in bed.

"Something might be wrong," he finished, unknowingly picking up his pace.

"He might be sleeping already," she said. "Maybe he's..."

"I'll let you know as soon as I do," he told her, giving her a quick kiss—without thinking.

"Do you want me to go with you?" she asked, sincerely concerned.

He shook his head. "No. I appreciate it, though."

"Call me," she said, as he hurried out of the room.

"I will."

In the car, Oliver called Peggy back. "I tried calling him again and he still hasn't picked up," he reported. "I'm heading over there now."

"Really?" she said, nervously. "Maybe he's just dozed off early for the night?"

"Ginny just said the same thing." Oliver backed out of his driveway, put the car into drive and pressed down hard on the accelerator. "My gut tells me differently."

There was a pause. "Okay," she said, "I'll meet you over there."

"It's fine, Peggy," he told her. "I can—"

"I don't mind," she interrupted.

"Really, I appreciate it, but there's no need. I'll keep you in the loop. I promise."

"Okay then, thanks," she said before hanging up the phone.

What's up with Dad and Peggy anyway? Oliver wondered. *Are they really just friends, or is Dad keeping another secret?* He jumped on the highway and over the bridge, speeding off to his father's house two towns over. *And why won't that old man record his own voice mail message? It's really not that hard.*

He arrived in record time.

Before Oliver even reached his father's front door to give it a knock, he knew his instincts had been correct. *Oh shit,* he thought. Luna, the elder's partner in crime, was barking. No—she was wailing, and it wasn't because she was being cordial in greeting him. *She's screaming for help,* he realized. *Something's definitely wrong.* He steeled himself for the unknown.

He turned the doorknob to find that it swung open. *Of course, it's not locked.*

Luna met Oliver in the living room. She continued to wail, spinning in circles a few times at his shins. He bent to pet her, but she took off running, making a beeline toward the closed bedroom door.

Oliver took a deep breath. *Please God,* he thought, *let him be okay.* He knocked. There was no response. *Shit,* he thought, *I should have checked on him sooner.* He knocked again, this time louder. Still nothing. *Shit!* He pushed the door open to find his elderly father laying in his tighty-whities, rolled into the fetal position on his bed. "Dad," he called out.

The old man didn't budge.

Please God, he thought, *not here...not like this this.* "Dad!" he yelled.

His father never flinched.

Oliver yelled for him twice and, as he approached, his dad's eyes slowly opened. "I'm in trouble, Ollie," he said, coughing. "I'm messed up pretty bad."

"I'm calling an ambulance," Oliver told him.

"No...no ambulance," he said. "I don't want to go to the hospital. We both know that once they get the hood open and start poking around, I'm never leaving that place."

"Well, you're going to the hospital—whether it's by ambulance or I have to carry you out to my car and drive you there myself."

The old man looked at him, his eyes softening.

"Can you get up?" Oliver asked him.

His dad slowly sat up and swung his feet onto the floor. Even more slowly, he stood and grabbed for his pants at the foot of the bed.

"Why didn't you call me or Peggy and tell us you were sick? We've been trying to call you."

"I didn't feel all that bad until recently," he replied in a hoarse whisper. "I was hoping it was just a passing thing."

Passing thing? Oliver shook his head. *Stubborn Swamp Yankee,* he thought. "How long have you been feeling sick, Dad?"

The slightly hunched patriarch slid on a yellow, short-sleeved shirt, fastening the bottom two buttons. "A couple of weeks, I guess."

"Jeez Dad."

"Don't give me a hard time, Ollie. I feel bad enough," he reminded him. "Besides, I was gonna go get myself checked out this week, if it didn't clear up."

Clear up? Oliver repeated in his head. The white-bearded free-spirit was usually deeply tanned from riding around all day with the convertible top down; he now looked yellow. "What are you feeling?"

"I'm wiped out," his father reported, although anyone with eyes could have seen that. "I've been spittin' up green phlegm and I can't lay flat."

"Damn," Oliver said, grabbing his father's arm to steady him.

"Been pissin' orange too."

"Have you been drinking enough?"

The elder shook his head. "I haven't had a beer in almost a week," he quickly explained.

"Water, Dad." And then it hit him. *He hasn't had a beer in a week? This is bad.*

Allowing for the hands-on escort, his dad walked to the car, panting like an overweight dog with each baby step he took.

Oh God, Oliver thought, buckling him in. His father was wheezing like he was struggling to take in air through a straw.

Oliver started the car, threw it into drive and stomped on the accelerator.

"I...I.." the old-timer began.

"Relax, Dad. Save your energy," Oliver said, his heart matching the car's firing pistons. "We'll be there soon."

His father opened his eyes. "If you don't kill us first," he mumbled.

The ride to the hospital was driven at better than at 100 mph.

Oliver stole several glances at his distressed father. *His skin color definitely looks off*, he confirmed. It wasn't the usual tone of rich Corinthian leather. Instead, it had a light yolkish tinge, the blotching and ancient scars making his skin look like a weathered road map—every line earned. "They're going to patch you up good," Oliver promised, speaking to his father in a calm, even voice. "Don't you worry."

The old man looked sideways at him. He parted his chapped lips to reply, but not a single word escaped. Instead, he inhaled deeply—taking in small gasps of air.

Oliver pressed down harder on the gas pedal. "Relax," he repeated, speaking as much to himself as to his ill father.

In record time, they pulled up to the red neon *Emergency* sign. Oliver jumped out, ran over to the passenger side door and helped his father out of the car. "Can you just hang here for a minute, while I park the car?"

The old man's face said everything his words couldn't. *Are you daffy? Where the hell am I going to go?*

With a single nod, Oliver hurried to park the car.

Hustling back toward the hospital's red neon, Oliver's mind commenced a brutal set of mental gymnastics. *What if he's really sick? If he'd called me earlier, maybe we wouldn't be in this situation right now? I can't remember the last time the old man went to see a doctor.* He searched his memory. *I don't think he's ever seen a doctor—not in my lifetime, anyway.* He picked up the pace. *This isn't good!*

His dad was hunched over in the exact spot he'd been deposited. Oliver lost his breath, realizing that his once-larger-than-life father now looked like the skeletal version of his former self. *Damn,* he thought, picking up the pace to shorten the distance between them.

Grabbing the old man's flaccid arm, he escorted him in. "You're gonna be fine, Dad," he said, his words lacking the tiniest hint of confidence.

His father shook his head. "I hate these damn places," he said. "I always have."

Which is why we're probably here right now, Oliver reasoned.

Immediately, an EKG was performed. "Any chest pains, Mr. Earle?" the first nurse asked.

"Nope," he said.

"Numbness in your right arm?"

"Nope." He shook his head. "Just feeling exhausted and weak." He paused to breathe. "I'm having trouble breathing when I lay flat."

Or sitting up straight, Oliver thought.

Blood was then extracted for a full lab workup. "As soon as we get the results back," the nurse explained, "the doctor will be in to discuss them with you." As she stepped out of the curtained room, she shot the old man a compassionate smile.

I wonder if she already knows something? Oliver thought. The smell of rubbing alcohol competed with pine cleaner. He looked at his father, who was already fidgeting on the white-sheeted bed. *Dad must hate this place more than any other in the world.*

"I've always hated hospitals," his father blurted.

Concealing his grin, Oliver felt grateful that he was allowed to sit with his dad in the exam room—even though there was no cell phone service. *I need to get word to Ginny and Peggy.*

Straight out of a horror movie, the curtain swung open again and Peggy appeared; she was disheveled and panicked. *She looks like she should grab the open bed across the hall,* Oliver thought.

"Robert, why didn't you call one of us?" she asked, her wrinkled face etched in worry.

"Because you would have made a fuss and blown it way out of proportion." He shook his head. "Like you're both doing right now."

She looked to Oliver to see whether it was true.

Oliver shrugged. "We're waiting for the test results to come back."

Peggy turned her attention back to his father. "You should have called someone," she scolded in her gruff smoker's voice, "Who knows whether—"

"I'm here now, aren't I?" he asked, putting an end to the reprimand.

The curtain parted again. The Emergency Department resident physician, Dr. Cheryl Berube, was standing there, holding Robert Earle's chart. Her face looked somber.

Oh shit, Oliver thought, sliding to the edge of his plastic chair to hear the sobering news.

"I have a lot of information to unpack," Dr. Berube said, pausing to inhale.

Oh shit, Oliver repeated in his head, getting to his feet.

"Mr. Earle, you have bi-lateral pneumonia, with significant fluid built up in your left lung," she explained.

Oh my God, Oliver thought, *he's been slowly drowning.*

"You're a very sick man, Mr. Earle," she added, turning a page before flipping it back. "It appears that as a result of your body struggling to take in oxygen, you've strained your heart and have suffered a mild cardiac arrest."

Shit, shit, shit...

Eyes wide, the old man looked to Oliver.

"You've had a heart attack, Dad," he translated.

The man's sapphire eyes turned fearful. "I'll be a son-of-a-bitch," he murmured.

Dr. Berube nodded. "We've given you some medication to make you comfortable, but we'll obviously need to admit you. We need to conduct more testing and—"

"Admit me?" he asked, cutting her off. He sounded like a small, frightened boy. Clearly, the old Yankee had only planned—and hoped—to get checked out and then sent home. "What about my fundraiser?" he mumbled under his breath.

Oliver distinctly recalled his father's disdain for doctors and hospitals. *"If they ever got a hold of me, Ollie,"* he'd say, *"I'm a goner."* Oliver cleared his throat, hoping to put more bass into his words. "Let's just see what they find, Dad," he told his father. "You'll be here for only as long as it takes for them to fix you up."

"I always knew it," the elder said, shaking his head; "once they pop the hood open, they're gonna find more damage." He looked at the doctor. "Too much wear and tear, ya know?"

She smiled compassionately at him.

"Dad, you're exactly where you need to be right now," Oliver confirmed. "You're in the best hands."

Nodding, Dr. Berube jumped in when she was sure their exchange had ended. "We'll need to drain your left lung, Mr. Earle, and then give you a good once-over to see what's really going on with you, okay?"

"I called it," his father mumbled under his breath, still nodding his gratitude for her care.

"We're just waiting for a room to open up, and then we'll transport you upstairs where you'll be a lot more comfortable,"

"Thank you," Oliver told her for them both.

As the curtain closed behind her, his dad sighed heavily. "Where I'll be more comfortable, all right," he complained. "I've got things to do, Ollie. That fundraiser isn't gonna plan itself."

Oliver turned to Peggy. "Do you mind sitting with Mr. Sunshine for a few minutes, so I can go check in with my wife?"

"Of course," she said, "take your time."

Ginny picked up on the first ring. "What's going on?" she asked. "I've been worried sick."

Taking a deep breath, he filled her in on the details. The novelty of the news was wearing off and starting to hit home.

"Oh, Oliver," she said, the worry thick in her voice. But there was also love and, oddly enough, he was happy to hear it.

"I'm sorry I didn't call you earlier, but I couldn't," he said. "There was no cell service, and I didn't want to leave him. He's not all that comfortable with being here."

"Please don't worry about that." She paused. "What do you need me to do?"

"Nothing for right now. But I'm going to stay with him until he gets in his room upstairs and gets comfortable."

"Of course."

There was silence. Oliver felt overwhelmed and didn't want to say anything further, anything that might strike a crack in his strong facade.

"Do you want me to tell the kids?" she asked.

"Not yet," he said, "not until we know what's really going on with him."

"Okay. How are you doing?"

"I'm okay, I guess. In shock, maybe." He shook his head. "I just need to be here for him...to..." Emotion stopped him.

"I know," she whispered. "Your dad's very lucky to have you."

"Thanks."

"Call me when you know more. I don't care what time it is."

"I will," he said, pausing. "I love you too."

"I love you," she said.

Flipping it had always been their thing, and had been for years. He'd always tell her, "I love you too," and she always replied, "I love you."

I've forgotten how much I've missed that, he thought. When he got off the call, he couldn't believe it—but he was actually smiling.

On their way up to his father's new bedroom, Kay, the new nurse, asked, "Who is your primary care physician, Mr. Earle?"

The old man looked at her, blankly.

"You haven't seen a doctor since you were six years old, right Dad?" Oliver said, coming to his aid.

His father grinned. "Maybe five, five and a half."

"Actually, he served in the military during Vietnam," Oliver offered. "They might have some records on him from then."

Kay looked bewildered. "Nothing since?"

Both men shook their heads.

Although it was subtle, Kay shook her head. There was no medical history, no baseline available for the deep woods Yankee. "Have you had all your shots, Mr. Earle?" she asked, refusing to surrender.

"Nope, no shots for me," he said. "Beer drinker only."

In spite of the moment's terrible weight, Oliver laughed.

"Okay," she said, "I think I get the picture."

"I need to beat this thing, whatever the hell it is, and get up out of here," his father vowed with enough anger to pucker Oliver's backside. "People are depending on me, Ollie—especially one little boy in a wheelchair."

"But you need to think about yourself right now, Dad."

He shook his head. "That fundraiser isn't gonna plan itself, Ollie," he repeated. "This year, I'm raising money for a kid named Dylan who needs a wheelchair ramp to get in and out of his house."

How much could that cost? Oliver wondered.

"He's only got his mom and she can't afford it." He shook his head.

I'll make sure they get the ramp, Oliver silently promised.

"It's not about a handout," his dad said, now looking at him; "it's about giving someone a hand-up. The small event I run every year gives people an opportunity to help someone in their community." He nodded. "And that's just as important."

"I get it, Dad," Oliver said, hoping to change the subject. Although he and Ginny bought tickets every year, they'd only attended once. *There was always one reason or another to miss it.* He shook his head. *I never realized how much this means to him,* he thought, suddenly feeling guilt slug him in the jaw. "We'll make sure they get the ramp," he blurted.

His father searched his face. "We will?"

"We will," Oliver confirmed, making the old-timer smile.

Tucked in like a child, his dad required two teaspoons of applesauce to swallow his pills. This made Oliver think about his own children. *Man, do I miss those days.*

He watched as his dad slowly began to doze off, the covers tucked up under his bearded chin. *The old man's returned to the beginning,* he realized. For the first time in his life, Oliver saw his father as fragile. It was absolutely terrifying. *He's always weighed around 200 pounds,* he figured. *He's now maybe 175.* Terrifying or not, Robert Earle was only a fraction of the blue-collared workhorse he'd once been.

Propped up straight in the bed, his dad finally fell asleep. While medication ran through IVs in both of his tanned, tattooed arms, he started mumbling in his sleep. "Uhhh...you people are way off. You got it all wrong."

"That's what you think, Dad," Oliver whispered to no one. It was comical and he couldn't help but chuckle.

"No doubling back..." the old man muttered, pausing for a long stretch. "Not on this one."

I hope you're wrong there, Dad.

There was silence for a while, just the buzz and whirl of the machines that were hooked to the sickly man; there was also the rhythm of the heart monitor, proof that he was still in the game.

"Come hell or high water..." his father yelled out, actually sitting up straighter. "Never again, Ollie, never again!"

Oliver stood and took a step forward, but his father never fully woke. Instead, he slipped deeper into his sleep.

That's good, Dad, Oliver thought, *get some rest. You need it. It's how you're going to heal.* Once the old-timer remained silent for a few minutes, Oliver approached him. "I'll be here first thing in the morning," he whispered, before kissing his forehead. It was the first time he'd kissed his dad since he was a boy. Although he hated to leave him alone, he quietly slipped out of the room.

I need to call in sick for a few days, Oliver thought, feeling completely exhausted. *I'm sure Sadie won't like it, but who gives a shit what Sadie likes.* By the time he reached the elevator, he realized, *Well, at least we have something new to add to Dr. Borden-Brown's weekly hit list.*

By the time Oliver approached the parking lot, he was filled with a strange sense of hope. *Maybe once they figure out what's wrong with him, he'll be cruising with Luna in that convertible again?*

Reaching his car, he texted Layla. *Sweetheart, it's Dad. When you get a chance, please call me. I have some news that you need to hear. Love you!* He hit send before checking the time and doing the math. *I won't hear from her until tomorrow.*

CHAPTER 5

Robert awoke early in a bed that felt as unfamiliar and uncomfortable as his first night in Vietnam. *I'm in the hospital,* he confirmed to himself, a ball of angst throbbing in his gut, *the one place I've been trying to avoid my entire life.* It had been decades since he'd been filled with such fear and uncertainty. *Oh God, I hope I'm not...* The whole situation made him as angry as he was scared. Considering his upcoming fundraiser, he shook his head. *The timing of this bullshit couldn't be any worse!*

He'd just finished picking at his breakfast when Mark, a bearded nurse, entered the room and threw on the overhead lights, suspending the start of some very dark thoughts. "Good morning," Mark said, carrying his plastic box of torture devices.

"Mornin'," Robert said, squinting under the room's bright fluorescents. "Are these tanning bulbs?"

"Should I turn them down?"

"Either that, or get me some sunblock," the old codger teased.

Mark didn't crack so much as a grin. "I need to draw some blood, Mr. Earle."

Oh boy, tough audience, Robert thought when he spotted the long needle. "Whoa," he said, "there's no need to hunt rabbits with an elephant gun, is there?"

"You'll be fine."

"Please go easy on me," he told the guy, half-joking—as the long spike searched for a good vein.

Mark hit it on the first try.

"I'm proud of you," Robert said, pausing, "and this time I mean it."

Mark laughed,

Finally, Robert thought.

Not twenty minutes after Mark left the room, nausea got the best of Robert. He was violently throwing up when he heard Oliver enter the room. Looking up from the bedpan, he attempted a smile. "Ollie, good news," he reported, wiping his mouth with the back of his large hand, "the nurse thinks I might have either gingivitis or halitosis."

Reaching for some paper towels, Oliver shook his head. "You'll never change."

Robert shrugged. "Physically, maybe...but that's all they're going to take from me." He nodded with conviction. "Nothing more."

"Good for you," his son said, "positive thoughts, Dad." He helped his father lay back in the bed. "Not a great breakfast, I'm guessing?"

Robert smirked. "Terrible by third-world country standards. The maple syrup tasted like it came from a telephone pole."

Oliver chuckled. "Have they run any more tests?"

"Blood and urine. I'm told that they'll be taking me downstairs later today for a full work-up, whatever that means."

"It means that they're going to find what's wrong with you and make you feel better."

"Is that what it is?" Robert asked, skeptically. "Why aren't you at work?"

Oliver's eyes narrowed. "Because I'm here with you, where I should be."

"You don't need to—"

"Please stop. I'm not going to argue with you about this." His son nodded. "I'm taking a few days off to be with you."

"Ummm, okay," he said, realizing those two words should have been followed with a thank you. "How's Luna? Is my girl okay?"

"She's fine, Dad. She's staying at our house."

"With Sophie?"

Oliver chuckled. "They're best of friends now."

"Sure, they are."

Mark entered the room again. "Mr. Earle, have your stools been loose?"

Robert nodded. "Ahhh, the joys of diarrhea." He grinned. "Giving food all the taste without the calories."

In spite of the heavy situation, Oliver laughed. "Jeez Dad, you don't have to give the poor guy such a hard time."

"Hard time?" He shook his head. "Why would I give my best friend a hard time?"

Mark grinned. "So, I'll take that as a yes, then?"

He nodded.

"Just to confirm, you haven't taken any drugs in the past few weeks?"

"Are you kidding me?" Robert said. "I used to think NyQuil was a gateway drug."

"If you count beer as a drug," Oliver chimed in, "then he's been self-medicating for quite a few years now."

"But not lately," Robert snapped back. "I told you that, you stool pigeon."

Reaching for his patient's IV stand, Mark banged his own hand. "Ouch!"

"It could have been worse," Robert said, the little devil on his forearm getting the best of him.

"Oh yeah, how?" Mark asked, rubbing away the sting.

"It could have happened to me."

Mark laughed. "You're gonna be a tough one, aren't you, Mr. Earle?"

"Oh, you have no idea," Oliver volunteered.

"That's okay," Mark said, "I like a challenge." With a smile, he headed for the door. "Someone will be up soon to grab you for your testing."

"Looking forward to it," Robert said.

"I bet you are," Mark replied before leaving the room.

For a few minutes, Robert and his son sat in silence. "So how are the kids doing?" he asked.

"Layla seems to be really enjoying Montenegro."

"Monte Carlo?"

"Montenegro," his son corrected him.

He smiled. "Where the hell is Montenegro?"

"Near Bosnia, Serbia..."

He shrugged.

"Yugoslavia, Albania..."

He shrugged again, enjoying every second of the exchange.

"North of Greece," Oliver said, concluding the geography lesson.

"Oh..." He fought off his grin.

"What's the time difference there?" he asked; it was his first legitimate question.

"They're six hours ahead of us."

Robert whistled. "What's that in travel time?"

"It's a ten-hour flight, Dad, one-way."

"That's a hike," he said, whistling. "She's teaching there?"

"Yup, she's on a scholarship as an English Teaching Assistant."

"For how long?"

"The grant period is for ten months, from September through June."

Robert thought about it. *Good for her,* he thought. *It's important to go see the world while you're young.* "And Jonah?" he asked. "The last time we talked, he was giving you some trouble over—"

"Kids are just different today than the way we were," Oliver quickly interrupted, shaking his head. "Lazy, completely entitled...."

One of Robert's eyebrows stood at attention.

"You don't agree?" Oliver asked.

He half-shrugged. "If I'm being honest, Ollie, I think kids are what they're expected to be. And as parents, we set those expectations. That's what I think."

Oliver was immediately silenced.

Robert put his hand on his son's forearm, leaving it there. "Jonah's not a little boy anymore, Ollie. He needs to start being responsible for his own actions."

"Yeah, I know, Dad," Oliver said, dismissively. "You sound a lot like Ginny. She believes that being a parent is a lot like flying."

Robert was surprised his son was willing to stay on the subject. "Oh yeah, and how's that?"

His son snickered. "She thinks she should put on her own oxygen mask before helping anyone else—even her children."

"Sounds to me like she gets it."

"What?" Oliver gasped; he obviously couldn't believe his ears.

"The way you think, Ollie, both you and your kids would be in big trouble."

"But..."

"Unless you're happy, healthy and whole," he went on, "how can you possibly expect to be helpful to someone else, never mind being able to provide the support they need?" He nodded. "It's taken me too many years to figure it out, but I think it makes the most sense to love ourselves before we can share that love with others?"

It was rare, but Oliver was finally at a loss for words.

"And let's not even get into discipline," Robert said; "you and I are worlds apart on that one."

"I agree."

They were both right. The idea of discipline—even the need for it—differed greatly from one generation to the next. While Robert could be heavy handed—believing physical discipline was an expression of love—Oliver never even raised a hand to his children. *Even when they needed to be awakened from their self-absorbed comas*, Robert thought.

I don't think it matters what generation you come from; parenting is just plain hard. It was insane the incredible power that parents exerted over their children. Phrases like "I'm ashamed" or "you've disappointed me" could cut deeper than any knife and Robert was never shy about wielding that blade. He looked sideways at his son and grinned. *I must have done something right, though*, he thought. *Ollie's one of the best men I've ever known.*

They sat in silence again; it was probably best that they did.

"You look good with a tan," Robert said. "I never got a chance to ask about your vacation. Did you lovebirds have fun?"

Although Oliver nodded, he remained tight-lipped.

"How are you and Ginny getting on lately?" he asked. He couldn't help it; he'd never experienced so much nervous energy in his life, and he needed to burn some of it off.

"I could've bet my life that this was coming next," Oliver said. "Even when you're sick..." He stopped.

Without a reply, Robert waited for the update.

"What do you want me to say, Dad? The truth is my marriage is so draining that I usually feel like I'm swimming against the current." He shrugged.

"Well, that's not good."

"Well, you asked."

"And I'm still listening," Robert confirmed.

"Love is a game for two, right? Or it just isn't all that much fun. Remember when you told me to make a list of the top four or five traits, characteristics in a mate that I could not compromise or do without?"

Robert nodded. "I do."

"Well, people change. They become bitter, angry. Priorities change. And sometimes those four or five traits have become so diluted that they hardly exist."

"I see. Have you tried talking to her about it? Being up front and honest about how you really feel?"

Oliver sighed heavily. "More times than I can count."

Robert cringed. *I'm almost sorry I asked.*

"Ginny and I are in a bad place right now, Dad."

"Ollie, be honest with me, have you really tried to make things better with your wife?" He shifted in his hospital bed to get more comfortable.

"I have," Oliver vowed. "It's why I insisted that we go on that vacation together, just the two of us."

"And you never answered me when I asked you how that went?"

Oliver looked into his father's eyes. "I'm still wondering whether that trip was the beginning of the end for us."

"There is no end, Ollie, not when you share children together."

"I know that. I'm talking about Ginny and me, not me and the kids."

Robert shook his head. "It's all connected, son." He paused to take in some much-needed air. "What have you done to try to make things better since the vacation?"

Not made love, Oliver thought, becoming annoyed, *although that one's on me.*

Robert smirked. "Maintaining a good marriage is one of the most difficult jobs you'll ever have, you don't know that?"

Oliver's eyes narrowed. "Give me a break, Dad. Of course, I know."

"Even at its best, marriage is hard work, son." He paused. "It takes effort and real commitment. For better or for worse, in sickness and in health, remember?" He half-shrugged. "I know I still remember my vows, and your mother's been gone for quite a while now."

"Your logic's spot on," Oliver replied, "but in practice..."

Whether it's the mundane daily grind; the bills; or all the resources it takes to maintain basic survival, marriage is nothing more than one decision after the next, Robert pondered. "It's work, Ollie," he repeated, "and the only real question is whether you care enough to put in that work."

"It's not that easy, Dad," Oliver blurted.

Robert grinned. "Ahhh, so we're finally in agreement." He nodded. "It's as easy as getting a raw egg back into its shell."

Oliver shut up, appearing as though he wasn't going to come out of his own shell anytime soon.

"When's the last time you said something nice to your wife? Complimented her?" Robert asked. "Said a few simple words to let her know how much you love her?"

Oliver remained statue-like.

"Well?"

"It's been a while," he finally admitted.

"On the day you got hitched, what did I tell you?"

"That you wished it was open bar?" Oliver joked.

Robert laughed hard, making his son do the same. "No, I told you to make sure that you say two nice things to your wife every day...and to be sure that they're genuine."

Oliver nodded. "I remember."

"It still applies, son," he finished.

Tommy, a grinning orderly, entered the room, saving them from further torture. "I'm here to take you downstairs for some testing, Mr. Earle."

Fear suddenly took hold. *My damn stomach's all tied up in knots*, he realized. He looked toward Oliver and feigned his bravest face. "Don't waste your time hanging around here. I'm guessing it'll be..."

"When will he be done?" Oliver asked, looking directly at Tommy.

"It looks like they're on schedule in radiology, so it shouldn't be any more than an hour."

Robert looked at Tommy, his face serious. "I'm holding you to that."

Tommy smiled.

"I'd rather you steal money from me than my time," Robert said. "Now that's something we can never replace."

Oliver shook his head, so the orderly could see it. "I'll be back before then," he told his father.

Robert nodded. *Good*, he thought. "Are you sure you don't have work that needs to get done?"

"I'm sure," Oliver said, nodding. "And please be on your best behavior when you're down there."

As Tommy prepared to take him downstairs, Robert joked, "I can't wait to show you guys my new tramp stamp. But I think it might be infected." He shrugged playfully. "I got the tattoo from some guy in a van parked just off the highway." His smile grew. "He seemed like a nice fellow."

"I can't wait," Tommy said.

Robert could still hear his son laughing when he was being wheeled out of the room. For him, the low brow humor was nothing more than a defense mechanism. In reality, he was nearly paralyzed from the bolts of terror that struck his already-failing heart. *And I'm pretty sure that everyone else knows it too*, he decided. *But it doesn't matter. The laughter still helps.*

Exactly one hour later, Oliver stepped back into the room. "They finally made you take a shower, huh?"

"They didn't make me do anything," Robert insisted.

Oliver laughed. "Yeah, sure."

"Are you kidding me? The water pressure's so good here that I wanted to do a handstand and get a good scrubbing of my undercarriage."

"Oh God!" Oliver said. "How'd the testing go?"

Robert shrugged. "It was okay, but I have a strong suspicion that the bastards aren't done with me yet."

Dismissing the comment, his son waited to hear more.

"They have me scheduled for a cardiac cath tomorrow, whatever that is."

"Good," Oliver said, "the more testing, the better."

"Easy for you to say."

"Don't you want to know what's going on with your health?"

"Not really," he admitted, quickly changing the subject. "Listen, you know I appreciate you being here with me but are you sure you can afford to take so much time off from work?"

"It's fine, Dad, really. Stop worrying about it."

"And how is work?" he asked his son, scrambling to discuss anything other than his health.

"Honestly? It sucks," Oliver said, pulling no punches. "I hit the ceiling a long time ago in the job I'm at."

Robert shook his head. "That's too bad," he said, thinking, *Reaching for success is a lot like being in a bucket full of crabs, where all they do is try to pull you back down.* He shrugged. "Not everyone's going to cheer for you, Ollie, but there are some who will." He plunged his thick thumb into his chest.

Smiling, Oliver nodded his appreciation.

"I spent forty years with the same company, when everyone took their vacations in the first two weeks of July." He smiled. "It was a different deal back in my day, I guess...when loyalty was a two-way street. Although I lived a comfortable, predictable life, I was proud to put in an honest day's work for an honest day's pay." Over the years, he'd worked more double shifts than he could count—especially when he was saving for the family's summer getaways in New Hampshire or for Oliver's expensive Christmas presents.

"It sure was different," Oliver said. "Today, we're obsessed with co-ordination and facilitation; efficiencies and streamlining; initiatives and performance goals."

"What? That sounds like a bunch of gibberish to me."

"That's because it is," Oliver said. "Believe me!"

Robert shrugged off the foolishness. "My real job was to provide for you and your mother," he said, "and I took my job very seriously." Every night, on bended knees, he thanked God that he'd received his father's steel backbone—never asking for more than being able to get up in the morning and provide for his family again. To him, there was no greater expression of love. "If I'm being honest, it really never mattered to me what I did, as long as I kept you and your mother clothed and fed, with a decent roof over your heads."

"Maybe I was born in the wrong time?" Oliver suggested.

Damn, Robert thought, *Ollie's unhappy in his marriage and at his job.* He could feel the extra weight his son was carrying. *He might be in worse shape than I am.*

◊◊◊

Days passed, some incredibly worrisome days, when Dr. Godin, the cardiologist, entered the room. He was a middle-aged man with kind eyes. "Here we go," Robert blurted, his mind drunk on fear. *I'm betting dollars to donuts that this ain't gonna be good.*

Oliver got to his feet and stood as close to Robert's shoulder as he could.

"So, what's the verdict, doc?" Robert asked.

The white-jacketed man opened the thick folder but paused before speaking.

Oh God, Robert thought, just as his son audibly gasped.

"Mr. Earle," Dr. Godin began, "unfortunately, the diagnosis is not good."

Robert felt his son's hand rest on his arm.

"You have a rare disease called ATTR-CM, which is short for trans-thyretin amyloid cardiomyopathy."

"Oh, that doesn't sound great," Robert said, his voice shaky.

"It's not," Dr. Godin admitted, "the disease can weaken and stiffen the heart muscle and is often overlooked as a common cause of heart failure. It's a protein misfolding disorder, where amyloids—which are made by the liver—are deposited in the heart where they clump."

"So, what does all of that mean?" Oliver asked, sounding like a young boy.

His son's tone scared him even more.

"Is there a cure?" Oliver asked.

The doctor looked up from the folder. "I'm sorry, no. Newly developed treatments can help reduce symptoms, improve quality of life, reduce heart failure hospitalizations, and prolong life, but..."

"But?" Oliver squealed.

"But given your father's age and the progression of the disease, I'm very sorry to tell you that the prognosis is fatal," he said, now speaking directly to Oliver.

Fatal? Robert repeated in his head; the meaning of the word was yet to click. He tried to slow his thinking, so he could approach the moment rationally. *This man has obviously looked at my case very closely,* he thought, feeling strangely relieved to receive such a confident diagnosis. *No more wondering.*

Oliver appeared to be wobbling.

"At least we have answers," Robert announced, shocking even himself.

"But it's a fatal disease, Dad," his boy reminded him.

He nodded. "You don't think any of us are getting out of this world alive, Ollie, do you?"

His son collapsed into the plastic chair, where he momentarily stopped breathing.

"You should also know that ATTR-CM is caused by an inherited gene mutation," Dr. Godin added, his eyes betraying sorrow.

Robert's head snapped sideways. "Everyone needs to get tested, Ollie...you and the kids. I won't be able to forgive myself if—"

"Stop Dad," Oliver told him, sucking in some air, "We'll all get tested." He shook his head. "Let's just worry about you for now."

"There's nothing to worry about anymore," he said; "we know the outcome."

Oliver hung his head to conceal his emotion.

"I'll leave you two alone," Dr. Godin said, heading for the door. "Again, I'm very sorry."

Both men sat in quiet reflection, Robert in shock.

I've been playing with house money for years, anyway, he thought, trying to convince himself to accept this fate. "It's the oddest damn thing," he said, breaking the silence. "I actually feel at peace now that I know I have no chance of winning this battle."

"What?"

He nodded. "When I first got here, I was so angry, promising myself that I wouldn't go down without a fight. I figured there are too many people that still need my help, you know?"

Oliver snickered. "Oh, I know," he mumbled under his breath.

"Now I can focus on the people that mean the most to me."

Oliver's head whipped up.

"I may be feeling the pain," Robert said, "but I'm not suffering alone." He winked. "And I have you to thank for that."

With a nod, his son bowed his head again to hide his emotions.

No need to get all knotted up over this foolishness, he thought; it was more for himself than his son. "It's okay, Ollie. It really is," Robert said, noting that his son had never once left his side. *I could've learned a lot from him earlier in my life.*

CHAPTER 6

The house was eerily quiet when Jonah's mom announced, "Your father and I have decided to separate, and he's moving out."

"No way," he said, feeling conflicted.

"I'm sorry, Jonah," she said.

Me too...I think.

The next thing Jonah knew, he and his father weren't ten miles down the road when his dad asked, "So how's your mom?" Before he could answer, his dad added, "Still miserable, I'm guessing?"

I knew it! "See, that's why I don't want to talk about her with you."

"I'm sorry," his dad said, "that was wrong of me. It won't happen again, I promise."

No, it won't! Jonah took a few deep breaths before summoning the courage to confront his father for the first time in his life. "Do you think Grandma was perfect, Dad?"

The weary-looking man was clearly taken aback. Although his dad had kind eyes, the man's gaze was the only deterrent anyone ever needed to hold their tongue around him. He didn't reply.

"Well, I don't want to talk about my mother either," Jonah said, defensively. After the recent breakup, Jonah's body locked up at the mention of his mother.

"I'm sorry," his father repeated.

A few more miles down the road, Jonah studied his dad's face. *Maybe he really does want to know?* "She's good," he said, shrugging, "working now."

"I'm glad she's doing good," his father said, "truthfully, I am." There wasn't a hint of sarcasm or negativity in his voice.

Jonah searched his dad's eyes once more, finding nothing but sincerity. He suddenly felt grateful. He'd been dreading the topic coming up again, but his father had finally removed the weight from his shoulders. The rest of his anxiety floated away. "So, how are you?" he asked.

His father's distant eyes confirmed that something had already changed between them. "Good, I guess." He half-shrugged. "Still trying to get used to all the silence."

Jonah didn't know what to say.

"But life goes on," his dad added, saving them from another awkward moment. "No matter what happens, life always goes on." He offered a hideously fake smile.

◊◊◊

Waking from the nightmare, Jonah was catapulted to a seated position. He gave the awful scene some thought. *It was only a dream,* he realized, *but I'm betting that scenario's not that far from reality. It could happen at any time.* He then thought about why.

From what he surmised, his mom was the typical neurotic housewife that endured each day in a mutually dismal marriage—*unwilling to make a move. Unfortunately, Dad's also reluctant to end their marriage and spare me and Layla any more pain.* To most of the world, the Earle's were a traditional family. But behind closed doors, those traditions cast long shadows of darkness on everything they touched.

I know how to forget about that nightmare! He thought about calling Quinn to come over but decided against it. *Should I play League of Legends or Fortnite?* he wondered. It was an easy choice. He selected Fortnite, putting it on competitive game mode.

For the next two hours, Jonah engaged in a Fortnite Battle Royale, where a hundred players were dropped into the match. Immediately, he began to locate the weapons and building materials that he needed to fight to victory. *Last one standing wins,* he thought, *and I hate to lose.*

As he sprayed down walls and took the high ground, one player after the next was knocked down—and then knocked out. *I'm good,* Jonah thought, referring to his game skills, *but am I good enough to win real money?* Once again, he couldn't lie to himself. *I'm not.* The truth continued to sting. *So, I need to find another path.*

Jonah was lying on the living room couch, chomping on a banana and skimming through a copy of *PC Gamer* magazine when his father entered the room.

"Sit up and eat, or you'll choke!" the man warned.

As if on cue, he began to gag.

Jumping into emergency mode, his dad pounded on his back, traumatizing them both in the process. Neither one of them was sure whether he was trying to send the wedged banana piece down Jonah's throat or back up.

While the magazine went flying, the banana chunk finally dislodged and came up.

"Damn it," his father barked, "you just took two years off my life!"

"And you just took five years off of mine," Jonah replied.

"Why don't you get up and do something?" his dad suggested.

"Because there's nothing to do, Dad."

"Really? Because there are dishes in the sink, the grass could use a trim, and the basement—which you're obviously claiming as your new residence—looks like a tornado hit it." His father sighed heavily. "Don't tell me that you're starting to use a bucket as a toilet down there?"

"What? No! It's just that there's more privacy down there," he said, sidestepping the real issue.

His father shook his head. "There's plenty that needs to get done around here."

Jonah stared at him, blankly.

"You don't work, Jonah, not even a part-time job," his dad yelled, "and God knows you don't do a damn thing to help out around this house." He shook his head. "If I'm being honest with both of us, you've always been expected to do nothing...and you've always met those expectations."

"It's my job to get good grades," Jonah claimed, volleying back.

"And how are you doing at your job?" his dad asked.

"Good!"

The disappointed man's eyes slid sideways, landing flatly on him.

Even Jonah knew that making sense of his logic was as easy as putting toothpaste back into the tube.

"Jonah, with all the competition that you're going to face, *good* is never going to be good enough. You know that, right?"

Jonah did what he could to avoid further eye contact.

"I swear, you'll be living in my house until you're forty."

Jonah snickered to himself. *You have no idea what you're talking about, old man!*

"Shit," his dad said, "your grandfather's right. You're completely ill-prepared to head out into the world."

"Whatever," Jonah said under his breath.

"And speaking of your grandfather, he's sick in the hospital. Why don't you go see him before you end up regretting that too?"

Regretting that too? Gee, thanks Dad.

Jonah loved his brutally honest grandfather, even though the crass man had no filter. *Sometimes, it's for the good, though,* he thought, his mind returning to the perfect memory to prove it.

◊◊◊

When he was young, Jonah played baseball. Actually, it all began with tee ball. Since day one, his father had been his coach. Tee ball was, by far, the most dangerous sport for coaches, given the number of injuries caused by impatient bats.

From the first time Jonah stepped up to home plate, he hated everyone gawking at him. But he'd never seen his father so excited or happy—not to mention all of the positive comments he received from his seemingly visually-impaired dad.

"You're good, Jonah," his dad told him, "especially for someone who just started playing the game. You really are!"

Even with all my strikeouts and errors?

"After today's game, I can't even imagine how good you're going to get."

Jonah couldn't believe his young ears. *Why is he lying to me? Is he just trying to make me feel better? I suck. He was there. He saw me play. I'm terrible.* Jonah couldn't understand why his father would lie to him.

His dad, however, was the greatest coach. He was kind, patient, and fair. *He's perfect for all the other kids who love this stupid sport. Unfortunately, he's too excited about coaching for me to be honest and tell him that I hate it.*

On the way home, Jonah and his dad stopped for ice cream.

"It looks like we've found the right sport for you, son," his father told him.

In shock, Jonah ate his cone of soft serve twist with rainbow sprinkles.

Jonah later confessed his secret to his grandfather. "I hate baseball, Grandpa," he reported to the big man. "I really do."

"Then why not be honest with your father," his grandfather asked, "and just tell him how you feel?"

"I can't."

"Why?"

"Because he loves it too much and it would hurt him."

The patriarch nodded. "Do you want me to tell him?"

"No! Please don't, Grandpa."

"Okay, I won't." There was a pause. "But you should. He's your dad. He'll understand."

"No, he won't. You don't know him, Grandpa."

The old-timer nodded in agreement. It was unexpected. "Does he take you for ice cream after the games?"

"Yes, after every game."

"Even when you play bad?"

"Yup."

"Does he let you order whatever you want?"

"Yes."

"Even sprinkles?"

"Yes."

"Ugh..." his grandpa groaned.

"What?"

There was a dramatic pause. "Only winners should get sprinkles," he teased, chuckling.

"That's not funny."

"No, Jonah, what's not funny is that you don't feel comfortable enough to be honest with your own father."

Jonah thought about it. "Do you think my dad's always been honest with you, Grandpa?"

This time, the blue-eyed sage took pause. "From the mouth of babes," he mumbled.

◊◊◊

Returning to the present, Jonah considered how much he detested the sport of baseball. From what he could remember, baseball was the start of a litany of exaggerations and embellishments that his father strung together. These weren't necessarily lies, but they were less than truths. *For years, Dad tried to make me feel better about myself,* he thought, shaking his head, *which would have been awesome...if he'd had any credibility at all.*

Shaking off the memory, he fired up his newest video game, *Into the Breach*; it was designed to be a series of realistic military missions. He'd become obsessed with the new game, playing it until his eyeballs actually itched.

Finally pausing the game to preserve whatever eyesight remained, he called Quinn.

"Hello?"

"Hey, have you checked out *Into the Breach* yet?" Jonah asked him.

"Not yet," he admitted. "I heard that it's the bomb, but my gaming partner's too busy spending time with his girlfriend so I haven't—"

"It's good," Jonah reported, interrupting him. "Really good. You start off with a full squad of soldiers; each one has his own skill set—a weapons expert, scout, medic..."

"I get it," Quinn said.

"But here's the kicker, when one of them gets ghosted, they don't return to the game. No new lives."

"Damn."

"The main player is the squad leader, who has only three lives to finish the game."

"Wow, how far have you gotten?"

"I'm pretty deep into it," Jonah said, "enough to have discovered a few subtle bugs in the game."

"For real?"

"Yeah. The algorithm seems off, though. Two of the levels are caught in a loop that you can only break if you travel through them twice in the same sequence of moves."

"Maybe that's the design?" Quinn suggested.

"I thought the same thing at first. But I'm starting to doubt it," Jonah said. "There's also a glitch in the system when the machine gunner tries to restock his ammo."

"Hmmm..." Quinn mumbled.

"I'm thinking about writing a product review and submitting it to Electronic Gaming Monthly and Game Informer Magazine."

"Really?" Quinn said.

You know what, Jonah thought, *I'm definitely going to submit a review.* "Really."

Jonah and Marissa sneaked into Howland Beach for their monthly picnic. It was Jonah's turn to host. As they walked side-by-side into the deserted dunes, he carried an old Igloo cooler, as well as the blanket that normally covered his car's backseat. She carried the bunch of flowers that he'd picked from his backyard for her.

Dinner consisted of foods Jonah had snatched from his refrigerator or picked up from the gas station convenience store at the top of Marissa's street: A bag of Bugles, two boiled eggs, one banana, two bottles of water, and an unopened package of strawberry Pop Tarts. He'd also scraped together enough change to purchase two chicken sandwiches from the drive-through's dollar menu.

As they ate, they discovered that the sandwiches had grown cold and inedible.

"This is so gross," he said.

"Maybe we should feed them to the seagulls," Marissa suggested, her face contorted in disgust.

"That seems cruel to me, considering that they were probably cousins," Jonah teased.

She stood. "How about we walk away then, so we don't have to witness the cannibalism?"

Wearing sweatshirts to ward off an early chill, the conversation immediately turned emotional. "I love you," Jonah told her, just out of the reach of the lapping surf.

"And I love you," she said.

He grabbed her hand. "No, Marissa," he said, stopping in the sand. "You need to understand how I really feel about you." He lifted her hand to his lips and kissed it. "I never stop thinking about you. Even when we're not together, I feel like you're with me."

She opened her mouth to speak.

"The only thing I ever think about is making you happy," he added.

Marissa became emotional. "I love you so much," she whispered.

"I love you more."

They watched as the sun dropped behind the shimmering horizon. *I need her to know how much she means to me*, he thought, kissing her, *and it's going to take a lot more than a walk down the beach to pull that off.*

Back at the house, Jonah and Marissa had just finished making love in the basement when she lay still, listening for Jonah's parents' footsteps coming down the stairs. After a few minutes, she relaxed.

"You worry too much," Jonah told her, laughing. "I'm telling you, they never come down here."

"And you don't think they know what we've been doing down here?"

"Well, they're not stupid, that's for sure. But we're both in college and I think they'd rather have us hanging out here than at some crack motel."

She slapped his arm. "You're so lucky to have the parents you do."

He nodded. "Most days."

"You have it made here."

"I won't argue with that," he said. "Just don't tell them I know, okay?"

She laughed. "You're not enjoying college, are you?" she said, out of the blue.

He shook his head. "I'm really not...though I wish I was. I know college is a necessary evil to get to where I need to go. I'm just not sure where that is yet. And to be honest, it's starting to freak me out."

"You must have some ideas?"

"Power Ranger is probably a stretch, but I think I could be very happy as a button maker."

She slapped his arm.

He smiled. "I'm pretty sure I want a career in the gaming industry. I've been dreaming some big dreams about it my entire life, but I'm not sure..." He stopped.

"I think a lot of people don't really know how to get where they need to go—for a while, anyway," Marissa reasoned, trying to make him feel better.

"But you know who you want to be," he reminded her.

"I already know who I am," she teased.

"You know what I mean."

She nodded. "Sure, but I've wanted to be a lawyer since I was a kid."

He nodded, feeling envious.

"So, what are your options in the video gaming industry?" she asked, tackling the subject in her signature rational approach.

"What do you mean?" he asked, buying time to consider a career path other than player.

"It's obviously a huge industry," she said, "even bigger than the film and music industries, from what I understand—and not all those people are actors or singers." She grinned. "There must be lots of other options to consider?"

A bolt of excitement shot from the top of his head to the tip of his toes. *Yes,* he thought, *of course!* He'd always been well-aware of the countless supporting roles in the gaming industry, but he'd never considered one of them for himself. *I've always dreamed of being a player, but...* He sensed that this new perspective had the potential to be life changing.

"Well?" she prodded.

"Programmer. Research and development. Marketing." He couldn't rattle them off fast enough. "Game reviewer..." He paused there, remembering, *I haven't told her yet.* "And speaking of that, I wrote a pretty smoking review on some new game and submitted it to Electronic Gaming Monthly and Game Informer Magazine."

"Really?" she said, excitedly.

"I haven't heard anything back yet though."

"I'm surprised with how well you write," she said, being sincere.

He nodded, thinking, *I'm kind of surprised too. It's clearly a tough industry to break into.*

"Okay, answer me this then," she said, "where do you see yourself in ten years?"

He grabbed her naked waist, pulling her closer to him. "I have a good idea."

"No, really," she said, "I'm trying to be serious."

He twisted up his face. "I honestly don't know yet."

She settled onto his chest again. "So, what *do you* know, then?"

"I know I love you and that I have since the moment I saw you," he said, sincerely. "I also know that wherever you are, that's exactly where I want to be." He kissed the top of her head. "I know that."

She lifted her head to kiss his lips. "That sounds like the perfect plan," she said, looking into his eyes, "and maybe that's all you need to know for now?"

He nodded "Maybe," he said, "but I also know that I'll be discussing my options with my college advisor as soon as I get back to school." It was the first time he'd felt excited about school—*maybe ever.* Kissing her deeply, they started in on round two.

It wasn't long before Jonah announced, "I hate to say it, beautiful, but I need to get some sleep."

"What...why?" Marissa asked.

"I have to go see my grandfather in the morning. He's been in the hospital and I haven't been over to see him yet."

"Oh, I'm so sorry," she said, "what's wrong with him?"

Jonah thought about it but could only offer a shrug. "You know what, I don't really know. My dad only said he was sick." He shrugged. "But if I don't go visit him before he gets released, I'll never hear the end of it. That much, I do know."

"Okay, if you don't want me here anymore," she teased, "then I'll just get dressed."

He pulled her into his arms. "Maybe we have a little more time."

◊◊◊

The hospital smells made Jonah's skin crawl. As he stepped into the old man's room, he stifled a gasp. *He looks so old,* he thought, *and sick.* "How are you feeling, Grandpa?" he asked, getting in close for a kiss and a hug.

"How do I look?"

"You look good."

The old-timer chuckled. "You lie as bad as your father does."

Jonah wasn't seated by his grandfather's bedside for two minutes when the usual interrogation commenced.

"Are your parents still fighting?" he asked, cutting straight to the chase.

Jonah could picture it, thinking, *As much as I love Marissa, I have to question marriage. It obviously doesn't work.* He offered his grandfather a half-shrug. "They still fight sometimes, but not nearly as much as they used to."

"That's good." The old man matched his shrug. "It's wise to keep clear of it." He smiled. "I've always believed that when the giants are fighting, it's best to stay out of the high grass."

Jonah laughed. *That's a good one.*

"Can you please explain something to me, Jonah?" he asked.

"Sure, anything."

"Can you tell me why you don't cut your mother and father's lawn?"

While his heartbeat sped up, he quickly responded, "Because my dad wants to do it."

His grandfather's left eyebrow rose.

Jonah nodded. "It's true, Grandpa. He likes doing it."

"Is that right?" He shook his head. "And you have no problem watching your old man out there on the weekends, sweating his ass off?"

Jonah was smart enough not to respond. *I know a trap when I see one.*

"For someone who doesn't pay any room and board, I'd think you'd want to pitch in and carry some of your own weight?"

Room and board? What the hell is that?

His grandfather glared at him.

"I'll start doing it," Jonah said, and meant it.

The old-timer smiled. "Oh, I'm sure your dad would really appreciate that! I know I used to."

"Yeah, but you used to pay me, Gramps."

The ailing man snickered. "Boy, you've never cost me a fraction of what you've cost your father. I got off cheap, believe me."

Jonah thought about how, on Saturday mornings, he hated being awakened by the sound of a lawn mower roaring outside of his basement window. *So rude,* he thought. *I have to wake up early all week to go to school.* He figured that the least he deserved was to sleep in on the weekends. *So annoying!*

There were times he'd lay there, contemplating getting up and going outside to help his dad. Although the thought was rare, it did occasionally strike him. *Nah...* The thought was always quickly dismissed.

It doesn't matter, he thought, *Dad will just tell me, "It's okay, Jonah. I got this. Go relax. You've had a long week."*

When he thought about it, it did seem peculiar coming from a man who left their house each morning before Jonah even got up and didn't return from work until he had already played a dozen video games in the afternoon. *Yeah, I do need to start helping out more at home,* he thought, before looking over at his grandfather.

The old-timer was still smiling at him.

"I do need to help more," he admitted.

"I know you do, but it's good to hear that you finally agree."

Even sick, he's still as sharp as a straight edge razor, Jonah thought.

"You also need to stop focusing on the next time you'll get your private parts tickled," the brutally honest man said, "and start thinking about your future, and what you should be doing with your time."

"Wh...what?"

"Don't tell me that I've figured it wrong," he said, "because we both know that I'm spot on."

Jonah was stunned into temporary silence.

His grandfather peered at him, never breaking eye contact—waiting.

"Until recently, I've felt stuck," Jonah finally confessed.

"Stuck how?"

He shook his head. "I've always known that I want to be successful and really make something of my life, but I wasn't sure which direction to move in."

"It doesn't matter."

"Doesn't matter?" The answer surprised him.

"Just start moving. Eventually, you'll find the right path." He grinned. "But if you stand still, you won't find a damn thing, will you?"

"No, sir," Jonah said, hearing a small bell ring in his head.

"Just get moving," his grandfather confirmed. "You might be surprised to find yourself exactly where you're meant to be before you know it."

The bolt of excitement returned, leaving his skin covered in goose-bumps. *I can't wait to talk to that college advisor!*

◊◊◊

Jonah had just finished mowing the lawn and was sitting on the front step with a basketball wedged between his legs. He watched as his dad returned home from work, looking exhausted. The weary man walked toward him.

"Did you go visit your grandfather?" his dad asked.

"I did."

"Good. How was he?"

"He looks pretty rough, but he's still as feisty as ever."

"Thank God."

"You know what, that's a lot of gray hair, Dad," Jonah teased, pointing toward his father's head.

"Yup," his dad replied, taking a seat beside his son and running his hand across his scalp, "and I earned every single one of them."

Jonah chuckled.

"You won't understand this for a long time, but on the inside, I still feel like I'm 25 years old," he said. "My body, however, lets me know every day that I'm twice that. The creaky knees, the swollen feet..." He shook his head. "And I'm not sure I'll ever get used to being called *Sir*."

"I get it," Jonah muttered.

"No, you don't—not even a little," his father said, without any judgement. "Scars on the battlefield of life—both inside and out—have to be earned; most of them unrecognizable to the human eye." He nodded. "And you'll suffer the same in your time, Jonah." He looked directly at him. "I'm sorry to say."

"So, are you admitting that you don't have a chance at beating me on the basketball court ever again?" Jonah teased.

His dad smiled. "If I play fair, probably not," he said, "but when you get to my age, what you lose physically you gain in experience and wisdom."

"So, are you saying that you don't plan on playing fair?"

"That's exactly what I'm saying."

"I'm still not sure that all that experience and wisdom is going to help you on the court, old man," Jonah quipped.

"There's only one way to find out, isn't there?"

"Yup." Jonah palmed the basketball and stood.

"Good, I've got enough time to beat you before I have to get over to the hospital."

"Maybe we should make this interesting, Dad?" Jonah suggested.

"How do you mean?"

"We should place a wager."

His dad started laughing. "You don't have a job, son. Whatever money I do win will be my own."

"Ouch, that hurts!"

"Then get a job," his father said. "I guarantee it'll help to heal that wounded pride of yours." This time, his dad did the laughing.

"Let's play to twenty-one," Jonah suggested.

"Eleven sounds better to me," his father countered.

Jonah bounced the ball to him. "Age before beauty."

Without a comeback, his dad immediately took a shot and swished it. "Do you think that was wisdom or experience?"

"Neither," Jonah said, laughing, "I think that was pure luck."

◊◊◊

It was late when Jonah lay in his bed, wishing Marissa was snuggling beside him. *That girl drives me crazy*, he thought, *I wish—*

Suddenly, he heard a bang; it was a fist pounding the kitchen table, followed by some loud screams.

Mom and Dad are at it again, he thought, *playing their favorite blame game.* He slipped out of bed and headed for the stairs.

"If you were around more instead of being at work all the time," his mom screeched, "then—"

His dad screamed at the top of his lungs; there were no words, just a warlike wail. A moment later, the front door slammed shut.

Jonah carefully stepped into the living room and looked at his mother, expecting her to explode. Instead, something much worse happened. She smirked; it was the kind of grin that announced she was no longer capable of being hurt by her husband's words—because she no longer cared. *So that's what indifference looks like?* Jonah thought. Deep down, he wished she'd just continue yelling, but she only smirked. And that's when Jonah knew that his parents were in another place in their relationship, at a different stage. *And it isn't a good place,* he decided. *Maybe I should go crash at Quinn's place for a while?*

CHAPTER 7

U nable to accept his father's fate, Oliver conducted his own research online. He was surprised that the internet was teeming with so much information about a disease deemed "rare."

Amyloidosis refers to a disease caused by a buildup of an abnormal protein, called amyloid, in the body's organs and peripheral nerves. These protein deposits can cause organs to not function properly and lead to nerve damage. Often, symptoms of amyloidosis are not specific or may seem similar to symptoms caused by other conditions. ATTR-CM primarily affects the heart and its ability to function properly.

Medical issues leading up includes nerve issues in the hands, specifically carpal tunnel syndrome and trigger finger; diagnosis of congestive heart failure (CHF); problems with sciatica—a nerve condition that causes pain, weakness, numbness, and tingling that starts in the back of the thigh and travels all the way down to the sole of the foot.

He paused, thinking, *Dad's had trouble walking for a while now, and he even mentioned suffering from sciatica.*

As Dr. Godin had reported, there was no cure for ATTR-CM.

He read on. *Treatments exist to slow the development of the amyloid protein and manage symptoms. A liver transplant may treat the disease for certain types of hereditary amyloidosis. New therapies are known to slow the production of the abnormal protein TTR. For ATTR-CM patients should be referred for evaluation for enrollment in one of the ongoing clinical trials. Cardiac management primarily involves diuretics and rhythm management.*

Oliver shook his head. *We're heading toward the end,* he realized, accepting the ghastly truth of it.

Picking up his cell phone, Oliver called his daughter. After one ring, it went straight to voicemail. *She just screened me,* he thought before leaving his message. "Layla, it's me. Your grandfather's sick, and it's worse than we thought. Please call me back so I can fill you in. I love you." He hung up.

He wished he could tell her that her parents were no longer fighting. *But I'm not lying to her. Even if it costs me, I refuse to tell my children anything but the truth.*

◊◊◊

"Any more issues with erectile dysfunction?" Dr. Borden-Brown asked, having no issue ripping off the festering scab.

Oliver shrugged. "No idea," he said, "we haven't gone near each other since then."

She took a long note in her book. "Do you want to get into it?" she asked, without looking up.

"I don't," he said.

"Okay," she said, "then explain the relationship differences between you and your two children."

"Well, that one's complicated," Oliver said.

She grinned. "They usually are."

"Jonah has always been a handful, but Layla—if I'm being honest, I never really worried about her." He half-shrugged. "She was born mature."

"Born mature, huh?" The therapist took a note.

Did I say something wrong? he wondered.

"What kind of relationship did your parents have, Oliver?" she asked.

He felt perturbed, unable to hold back. "Maybe it's just me, but these venting sessions are starting to feel a bit redundant," he complained, sorry to have used the corporate phrasing.

"How so?" she asked, calmly.

He snickered. "Just like that. You ask a question and I rant for twenty minutes or so until we move on to the next topic."

She nodded. "Oliver, you need to get it all out and hear it for yourself before you can develop logical strategies to address your problems. You've pent up lots of resentment—years of it, in my opinion—and you need to get it all out into the open before you can start making it better."

He nodded in surrender. "My parents had a good relationship, as far as I can remember. My mom passed away when I was just a kid, and my father is probably what you'd best call a free spirit."

"Tell me about your father?" she asked.

"My father?"

"Yes." She paused. "Is he still with us?"

"Physically, yes." He tried to laugh the comment off, but it sounded contrite even to him.

She took a note. "What kind of relationship do you have with him?"

"With my father?"

"That's the one."

"I don't know. The usual, I guess."

"And what does that mean—the usual?"

"He could be rough on me when I was growing up, and now he has selective memory about a lot of it."

"How so?"

"I remember when I was in the fourth grade," Oliver explained without hesitation. "I came home from school and had to report that I'd been in a fight. I'd been challenged by the schoolyard bully and had a decision to make. Either turn tail and run, or fight."

The doctor listened attentively.

Oliver went on. "Either risk being ridiculed by all the kids at school or face my father's black leather belt when I got home." He cleared the emotional debris from his throat. "I chose the latter." He paused to take in a few breaths. "When I got home and told the old man about the fight, he went off. He kept screaming 'We don't hit! We don't hit!' while he whipped his leather belt across my backside a half dozen times." Shaking his head, he smirked. "That's when I learned the true meaning of a mixed message."

"I see," the therapist said, writing as fast as her fingers would allow.

Oliver exhaled, long and slow. "Oh, and he's currently dying in a hospital bed."

"What?" Her head whipped up.

Oliver nodded. "I'm guessing it won't be long now."

"Oh, I'm so sorry to hear that."

Me too, he thought, *more than I would have ever imagined.*

◊◊◊

Oliver was grabbing a coffee in the office's kitchen area—the modern-day water cooler—when his twisted coworker, Don, approached. "Well, it looks like my wife's finally healed me from having a normal, healthy sex drive," he half-joked. "Fourteen years ago today, she called me a moron and then accepted my marriage proposal to prove it."

I don't care how bad it gets in my marriage, Oliver thought, shaking his head, *I'd never disrespect Ginny like that.*

Rebecca stepped into the area, silencing Don.

Thanks Rebecca, Oliver thought.

"Did you guys get your performance ratings from Sadie yet?" she asked, whispering.

Oliver nodded. "Yup, and no surprises. We all got the same, I'm sure," he said, comfortable using his normal voice.

"What a waste of time," Don added.

"You've got that right," Oliver said. He had no problem ranting and raving with the rest of the disgruntled staff. It was beneath him and he knew it. *But it still feels good.*

"I need to start looking for a new job," Rebecca groaned.

Don nodded. "Good luck with that. The job market's not what it was. Believe me, I've looked."

Oliver checked his cell phone. *Still nothing from Layla.* He then noticed the time. "I gotta get going guys," he said. "I have a pandemic planning meeting in ten minutes, and I need to open the call."

"Another waste of time," Don said.

Oliver looked at him.

"When will we ever use that?" the buffoon complained.

"We don't want to find out," Oliver told him. "Just a simple virus could turn this entire world upside down." Although he rarely missed an opportunity to join in on the visceral banter, he still cared about his work.

"I disagree," Don said.

For years, Oliver was at the top of the food chain and had no problem sinking a few extra teeth into every debate. He didn't have the time nor the interest for this one. "Whatever, Don."

"It's true, Ollie," Don said, "the chances of us ever having to—"

"It's Oliver," he interrupted, quick to correct him.

"What's that?"

"My name's Oliver, not Ollie." For as long as he could remember, he hated the nickname, Ollie. *Only my father can call me Ollie and get away with it.* Everyone else was promptly corrected.

"What's the big deal? I was only—"

"Listen, I'm not a cartoon character, or half of some slapstick vaudeville act. My name is Oliver. Do you want to debate that too?"

"Umm okay, Oliver..." Don muttered in surrender.

"Good," Oliver said, nodding, "now I need to go waste my time building a plan that might save lives."

◊◊◊

Returning home from work, Oliver could smell the marijuana from the moment he stepped into the house. *Damn this kid!* He hurried downstairs.

"You've got to be shitting me," he screeched, walking in on Jonah who was smoking pot beside an opened window, "in my own house?"

"Relax, Dad," he said, "it's legal now."

His son's look of apathy instantly burrowed under his skin, sending a chill down the length of his spine. "Not in this house, it isn't," he roared, "and it never will be, Jonah!" He shook his head. "My God, you know better!" he said, hearing his own father's disappointed voice spewing from his mouth. "Besides, it's not legal for someone your age!"

"Layla smokes too," Jonah blurted.

For many reasons, this wasn't nearly as concerning to Oliver. *Layla can handle anything and find the right balance,* he thought. *She always has.* He shook his head, thinking, *And she's not a snitch.*

"I'm sorry," Jonah muttered.

"You're sorry?" Oliver screeched, trying to calm himself. The last thing he wanted—or needed—was to push his son away the same way he had his daughter. He took a few deep breaths, clasping his trembling hands together—and wondering if he was scoring a contact high.

"I screwed up, Dad," Jonah confessed. "I'm sorry. I won't do it again."

As he stood there, Oliver was at a complete loss at how he should handle the situation. "Is something wrong, Jonah?" he asked, instinctively. "Is there something going on with you that you need to—?"

Jonah shook his head, cutting him off. "It's not like that, Dad," he said.

Oliver nodded, gratefully.

They stood together in terrible silence for far too long.

Jonah finally shook his head. "I'm sure you never did anything stupid or irresponsible when you were my age, right Dad?" he commented.

By this point, Oliver had calmed himself, realizing that he was at a crossroads—*to either gain my son's trust or push him away.* He picked the former. "Are you kidding me?" he said, his mind sprinting back in time. "When I was young, I was just as stupid as you are right now."

Jonah dropped his gaze.

"Maybe even more so," Oliver added. "Let me tell you a story." His mind went back. "I was young, maybe a year or two older than you, when I bought a new Dodge 4x4 custom convertible. It was an awesome ride. It had the ruggedness of an off-road vehicle, with the amenities of a high-end, convertible coupe."

"That does sound awesome," Jonah said, trying to focus his squinted eyes.

"The only problem was that when you took the top off, it was almost impossible to snap it back into place. The thick fabric needed time to stretch." He shook his head. "But even at twenty years old, I was not what you might call a patient man—or even a smart one—so I just kept the top off. Within a month, three days of torrential rain left about four inches of water on the new vehicle's floor. The entire interior was destroyed."

"Holy shit!"

Ignoring the comment, Oliver forged on. "But I was unfazed and contacted the dealership, letting them know that I'd left for a week and returned to find that the roof had collapsed on my new ride—that the interior is totaled."

"Damn Dad," Jonah said, his grin widening, "so what did they do?"

"They agreed to have the entire interior refinished. But this wasn't good enough for me, though. Nope. I told them that I needed a rental while I was waiting."

Jonah whistled.

"I never understood why, but they loaned me a brand-new pickup truck. So, what did I do? I picked up my friends and we took it four wheeling." He shook his head, wondering whether he should go on. Although he'd laughed about the stupidity for years, hearing it aloud now made him feel embarrassed. *And should I be sharing this with my son, giving him more bad ideas?*

"Well," Jonah prodded impatiently.

"We beat on that truck so bad that we basically destroyed it," he said, making the very long story short.

Jonah started laughing.

"Sure, it's funny now," Oliver said, "but the dealer threatened to have me charged with malicious destruction and intent to defraud an insurance company."

Jonah whistled again; this time, the tone sounded different.

"Your grandfather got involved and saved me." He shook his head again. "That's a whole different story altogether." He looked back at his son. "The point is, one wrong choice, one bad mistake at this point in your life, Jonah, and you can easily change the trajectory of your future—and not for the better."

His teenage son contemplated this before nodding that he understood.

"So, as you can see," Oliver added, wrapping up his irresponsible past, "I was once a jackass too."

Jonah was clearly taken aback. "Wow, Dad," he said, "I would have never guessed. Grandpa must have been pretty teed off."

"Teed off is one way to put it," he said. "The truth is, he was furious—and he had every right to be."

His son sat still, while the story took root.

"See Jonah," Oliver added, "you're not the only one to be young and stupid." He placed his hand on his son's shoulder. "But at some point, I had to grow up." He met the boy's eyes. "And so do you, before you jeopardize your future," he said, sliding his hand down to grab Jonah's forearm, "really jeopardize it so that it becomes irreversible."

"But Dad..."

"No buts, Jonah. You need to wake up. And I'm guessing that smoking marijuana isn't going to enhance your work ethic either?"

Jonah silently pled the fifth.

◊◊◊

Ginny had just returned home when Oliver blurted, "Where have you been?"

She glared at him, clearly trying to decide whether to do battle.

"It would have been nice if you could have joined me at therapy this morning," he said, still tasting the vinegary resentment at the back of his throat, "maybe we could have even—"

"Please, Oliver," she said, upset, "I already told you why I don't go."

"How does that make any sense?" he asked. "Refusing to try because you fear you might lose something...that same something that's already slipping through your fingers due to lack of effort?" He shook his frustrated head. "I just don't get it, Ginny."

She began to cry.

Instinctively, he went to her.

"I'm sorry," she said.

"Stop apologizing," he replied, hugging her. "We both need to start trying harder, or we're in real trouble."

"I agree," she whimpered in his arms, "we *both* need to try, and going to therapy is not the only path."

As though he'd been slapped, he took a half step back. *She's right*, he thought, *whether she goes to therapy with me or not, I need to put in a much bigger effort around here.*

"I spoke to our daughter today," she quickly announced, happy to change the subject.

"You did?" he said, letting it go for the time being. "What's the latest?"

"Although she's upset about your dad, she clearly loves it there. She really does. I was so happy to hear the joy in her voice, but..."

"But?"

"I miss her so much, Oliver. I didn't think I'd cry when she and I spoke but..." She stopped again.

He hurried to hug her again. Although the mechanics were spot on, something felt like it was missing, making him feel even worse.

Although he gave his wife an extra squeeze, he thought, *The old man's window is closing. I hope Layla can get back to see him before it's too late.* He considered telling Ginny about Jonah smoking pot in their house, but quickly decided against it. *There's no way I'm traveling down that dark alley right now.*

"Why don't you come with me to visit my father tonight?" he suggested, breaking their tepid connection.

"I've already been to see him today," she reported.

"You already went?"

She nodded. "Before I talked to Layla."

"You couldn't wait for me?" As soon as he asked the question, he wished he could take it back.

Her eyes narrowed. "Should I have waited for you, Oliver?"

"No, that's fine," he said, attempting to dismiss it.

"I can go back, if you need me to."

Need you to? he thought. *It might be nice if you wanted to.* "No, that's fine," he repeated.

With a nod, she headed for the bathroom to take a shower. "There are leftovers in the fridge," she called over her shoulder. "Chicken and rice."

He snickered to himself. *Lucky me.*

Before he left for the hospital, Oliver made Ginny a hot cup of peppermint tea—her favorite. "Here you go," he said, delivering it to her on the couch. *It's been too long since I've done this,* he thought.

"Thank you, Oliver," she said, surprised by the simple gesture.

He kissed her on the lips. "You're welcome, beautiful." Pausing inches from her face, he kissed her again. "And you smell really nice today."

"Thank you," she repeated. Holding her cup steady, she stared at him.

He was nearly at the door when she called out, "How about I record *Modern Family* and we watch it together when you get home?"

He smiled. *Modern Family* was one of their shared loves. "I think that'll give me something to look forward to when I'm visiting the crotchety old codger."

He could still hear her laughing when he closed the front door behind him. *God, how I've missed that laugh,* he realized.

◊◊◊

Oliver stepped into his dad's hospital room.

"I need to shit, shower, and shave," the old man said, fidgeting in his hospital bed.

Oliver shook his head. *He must have used that same phrase ten thousand times,* he thought, *and I'd live a happy life if I never heard it again,* He stopped, catching himself. *Or not...* Collapsing into his designated plastic chair, he sighed heavily—before reaching for the package of crackers on his father's cluttered bed tray.

"Be careful," his dad warned, "those crackers are almost old enough to vote."

Oliver wisely recoiled. "So how was your day?"

The jokester shrugged. "I heard a loud pop this afternoon," he reported.

This caught Oliver's attention.

"At first, I thought it was my good testicle, but I think it was only a light bulb calling it quits."

Shaking his head, Oliver grabbed the remote. "Do you want to watch the Sox?" he asked, flipping through the channels.

His father shook his head. "I'm all set."

"But you always loved following the Red Sox, especially leading into the post season?"

"Most of my life, I was a die-hard New England sports fan—and it didn't matter which sport—until the hometown players started moving to other teams for better money." He shook his head. "For me, that's when the true rivalries died." He shrugged. "I figured if they don't care, then why in the hell should I?"

"Point taken."

"Your wife came to visit me today," the old man said.

"I heard." He nodded. "I wish she'd visit me," he added, shooting for a laugh. There was so much truth in the statement that neither one of them even smiled.

"It wasn't always that way, I'm sure," his dad commented.

"We're working on it," Oliver replied, feeling hopeful.

"I haven't heard from Layla," his father said, changing the subject. "Does she even know I'm here?"

"She does."

"How?"

"I texted her."

"Texted her?" the ailing man said under his breath. "How personal."

"Ginny just talked to her." Oliver took a deep breath, exhaling his frustration. He opened his mouth again to defend his position when his father raised his hand.

"I don't mean to give you a hard time. I know things are tough for you right now." He paused, offering his first smile.

Oliver stared up at the TV hanging from the ceiling. "I wish this day would just end," he blurted. "From this morning's heavy traffic and all the negative news on the radio to the bagged lunch and the emails that never ended."

The old man chuckled.

"What?" Oliver asked, his attention diverted from *The Andy Griffith Show* rerun.

"I remember wishing the same thing," his father said, stifling another chuckle. "If I can just get to the weekend, past the drop-offs and pickups, the homework and time-outs."

Oliver nodded, his attention heading back toward the TV.

"If I can just get past this month," the old man added, clearly unfinished with his latest spiel, "beyond the weekend chores and the constant worry over unpaid bills."

Oliver stared at him.

"If I can just get to the new year," his dad said, "beyond the hustle and constant chaos, the deadlines and deliverables...the same old, same old." He looked at Oliver. "Be careful what you wish for, Ollie. You may end up wishing your entire life away."

"I get it, Dad."

"I hope so," the old man whispered, "because it'll all be over before you know it, trust me."

Oliver nervously fidgeted with his cell phone. *That kid's gonna be the death of me yet*, he thought.

"What happened?" his father asked. "Something's wrong."

Oliver shook his head, reluctant to share any details. *I just don't want to hear it right now.*

"There's nothing crueler than torturing a dying man," the old man said, trying not to grin.

"I just caught Jonah smoking pot," Oliver blurted, surprising himself as much as his wide-eyed father.

"You what?"

Oliver nodded. "And right in my house."

His father was clearly beside himself; Oliver had seen that same look of disgust before. "That would be the damned day!" he barked, passing immediate judgment on both Oliver and his grandson.

I knew it, Oliver thought. *When will I ever learn to shut my stupid mouth?*

"So how did you handle it?" he asked.

"I talked to him, Dad."

"Talked to him?"

"That's right. I talked to Jonah and let him know that it wouldn't be tolerated under my roof."

The old man shook his head.

"What should I have done, Dad, kicked him out onto the street?"

His father's head was still shaking. "It's like I've always said—if you spoil someone rotten, then how can you be surprised when they act rotten?" he muttered under his breath. The old man loved to break out the saltshaker and season any open wound he could.

The callous comment infuriated Oliver.

"I don't care what you say, Ollie, it's just not right," the old-timer snapped. "Not drugs! Drugs are unforgivable."

"Just like drinking alcohol and gambling?" he shot back, surprised that he'd dared to even mention it.

The big man stared at him for a long moment, his eyes changing to a look that Oliver hadn't seen for quite some time—*maybe even since childhood?* He considered it, deciding, *It's contempt.* "Of course, it's not right," Oliver snapped back, still angry. "Believe it or not, alcohol's also a drug, Dad, and I watched you abuse that since I can remember."

"This isn't about me, Ollie."

"Really? Because it sure seems like you're making it about you."

The old-timer's shaking head began slowing. "At least alcohol's legal, Ollie," his father countered, like he was trying to score the final point.

"And so is pot," Oliver explained, snickering. "It's a different time, Dad."

"It's just not right," the old man repeated. "I don't care what you say." He shook his head. "If you don't think you deserve respect enough to demand it," he added, "then don't expect to receive it."

Whatever, Oliver thought. "You had your opportunities to screw up your son. It's my turn now."

"I had a cousin, Lenny, whose father never cared enough to discipline him," his father revealed. "The kid was always in trouble, but the old man didn't care enough about him to square him away. As he got older, he got worse...and ended up in prison."

"I didn't know you had a cousin in prison." he said, thinking, *Wait a minute, does he think his grandson is going to end up in jail for smoking weed?*

"Because I never talked about him. There was no need to. Lenny was only behind bars for two or three years when he got into a fight. Some other inmate shanked him, putting him out of his misery." The old man shook his head. "I still say it was his father who killed him."

"I get what you're saying, Dad, but that example's a little drastic, don't you think?"

His father shrugged. "It probably wouldn't have been if my uncle had given a shit about his son."

Oliver let it go, still thinking, *I didn't know we had a cousin who was a convict.*

Not even another episode of *The Andy Griffith Show* could slow the old codger down. "Please tell me that you don't pay for Jonah's car insurance," his father said. "Do you?"

Oh, here we go again, Oliver thought, dreading the exchange. "It's a good thing you're not looking to give me a hard time tonight."

"Well?"

"It's cheaper, if I just put him on our policy," he replied, having to defend himself more than his entitled children.

"It sure is—cheaper for Jonah, anyway." His dad grinned. "If there's reincarnation, I definitely want to come back as him." He chuckled; it had a cruel tone to it.

Oliver bit his tongue.

"I'm guessing that you and Ginny bought him that car that he drives around in too," the old man said. "Am I right?"

Oliver sighed. "It's different today, Dad."

The old man shook his head. "I don't care what era you live in; nothing ever changes when it comes to teaching responsibility and independence to teenagers." There was a pause. "You're not putting gas in the kid's tank, are you?"

Ollie remained silent.

"Oh, dear God." His father sighed, shaking his head even more vigorously. "You and Ginny pay for his college and his clothes too, I'm sure. Does the little tyke still get an allowance?"

"Listen," Oliver said, pushing the words out of his chapped throat, "I don't give a rat's ass what you think. I—"

"I just don't get it, Ollie," his father interrupted, clearly uninterested in hearing any excuses. "I never wanted anyone in my wallet, but you have no problem letting your kid set up camp in yours." He was on a roll. "It's not good, Ollie. It's not good for either one of you."

"So now I need your permission on how to raise my kids?" Oliver snapped back.

"I think you probably do."

Oliver glared at him.

"Listen," his dad said, "I'm not worried about you or your money. I'm worried about Jonah."

"Oh yeah, and how's that?"

"He needs to be trained, Ollie. He's not always going to be living under your roof, right?"

Oliver said nothing.

"Please tell me he's not going to live with you forever?"

"Of course not!"

"Then how's he going to know how to pay his own bills, or work for the money that he needs to live?"

"I get it," Oliver said in brief surrender, "but he's still young."

"He's not that young!" his father spewed. "In my day—"

"You had to walk up hill both ways in a blinding snowstorm," Oliver said, interrupting. "I know, Dad."

It was the old man's turn to stare him down. "No need to be a wiseass."

Oliver slid forward in his chair. "You're criticizing the hell out of me about how I parent, and you think I'm the one who's being a wiseass?"

"That's my job, Ollie," the old man said, his face serious. "Don't tell me that you never bust Jonah's balls?"

Oliver thought about it and smirked. "Of course I do."

"That's right. Of course, you do because that's part of your job as his dad. He needs at least one person in his life to keep him honest." He nodded. "Jonah can have a thousand friends, but he'll only ever have one father."

Oliver nodded in agreement. "I know that."

"You're a great dad, Ollie. I'd be lying if I said any different. But Jonah's never going to stand up and become a man until he has to."

Oliver continued to nod, knowing, *There's a lot to download on this one.*

"It's our job to prepare these little monsters for the world," his father said, softening his tone significantly, "and when they've been given everything their entire lives, they're obviously ill-prepared to face the real world or to survive in it. That's all there is to it."

"Got it," Oliver surrendered, knowing that his old man was right and that he needed to do a better job applying the wisdom. "You're tough."

"It's only tough love, son. If I didn't care, I wouldn't bother to waste my breath," he said, grinning, "especially since even those are numbered now."

Oliver shook his head.

"I think you need to start introducing some tough love to Jonah."

"I have, Dad."

"Not enough."

This time, Oliver nodded. *The old bastard's right*, he thought. *My job's been to raise him, not keep him.* Although Layla was easy, bringing up Jonah had been like raising veal. *It was my job to prepare my son for the world, and I've clearly failed at my job.* Few truths proved more sobering or devastating for a father.

"We need to start talking about my spaghetti dinner fundraiser," his father said.

"We will, I promise. For now, why don't you get some rest?"

◊◊◊

It was late when Oliver returned home. He stepped into his bedroom to find his wife already sleeping. "Sorry I stayed so late," he whispered. "Maybe we can watch that *Modern Family* episode tomorrow."

Ginny never budged. Instead, soft beams of moonlight illuminated the contours of her body. *She's so sexy*, he thought, wanting nothing more than to wake her and make love—*or at least try*. But he didn't. *Maybe we'll try again tomorrow*, he thought, remembering Ginny's same words in Aruba. But he knew better than that. *It won't be tomorrow*. He nodded. *But hopefully soon*. Kissing her softly, he took his place beside her, strapped on his CPAP mask, and closed his eyes.

CHAPTER 8

Like the old bull shark he was, Robert Earle needed to keep moving to stay alive. *And now I'm tied to a hospital bed by a tangle of tubes and cords*, he thought. *It's only a matter of time now.* He shook his head. *All that carefree living has finally caught up to me.*

Although the pain was being managed by medication, the fatigue had grown so much worse. *I feel as weak as a house cat now*, he thought, before thinking about Luna and feeling even more depressed.

As he lay in bed, counting off the seconds, he began to consider the life he'd been blessed with.

Just then, Peggy walked into the room for her daily visit. "How's my boy today?" she asked.

"Your *boy*?" he asked, grinning.

"That's right," she said, almost flirtatiously.

He chuckled until a sharp pain in his side made him stop.

"Have you eaten today?" she asked, holding the plastic water cup to his face so he could reach the straw.

"Yes, Mom," he teased, taking a long drink.

"What did you have?" she asked, taking a seat beside him while grabbing the TV's bulky remote control from his lap.

"Poor man's surf and turf," he joked.

"What?"

"They brought me fish sticks and fried bologna."

She laughed, before changing the channel.

"Hey, I was watching something," he complained.

"Of course, you were," she replied dismissively, leaving it on her soap opera and then placing the remote control out of his reach.

"You're something else, Peggy," he muttered, "you really are."

Her grin widened. "Which is why you love me."

He froze.

She watched her show in silence for a few minutes before blurting, "Jackson should just be honest with Victoria and tell her how he really feels."

What? Robert thought, quickly realizing that she was referring to her soap. His eyes climbed up to the TV and stayed there to avoid Peggy's probing stare.

"How are you feeling today?" she asked.

"Physically, I'm wiped out," he said, happy to change the subject. "In every other aspect, I'm not sure I've ever been better."

She folded his hand into hers.

"For an ordinary man," he explained, giving her bony fingers a squeeze, "I've lived an extraordinary life."

"And I get to hear the details?" she said, half-teasing.

"Oh, I wouldn't dare bore you with those."

She squeezed his hand back. "It'll hardly be a bore, I'm sure." Her eyes twinkled with compassion. "I've always been a sucker for a good back story."

"Are you sure you want to miss your soap opera?" he asked.

She shrugged. "I'm betting I'll be just as entertained."

He chuckled. "My parents came to America from Europe in search of a better life, only to survive the Great Depression, so needless to say—there was no coddling."

Chuckling along with him, Peggy nodded, "What folks call tough love today would have been considered mollycoddling back then." She nodded. "We came from the generation where children were seen and not heard."

"And kids were workers, not just more mouths to feed," he added. "From the time my brother and I could walk, we served as two more sets of hands to help put food on the table." He tried to take in even breaths. It was becoming more difficult. "Love wasn't a word we heard from our father—not ever. The old codger kept our bellies full and boots on our blistered feet." He smiled. "That was love—unspoken but shown."

Peggy searched his face, as though she were looking for the root of their conversation.

"Life was hard back then," he said, continuing. "There was no room for softness or weakness. My old man was tough and, if we dared to speak up, we faced his heavy hands—which I truly believe were made of leather."

Peggy nodded sadly. "I remember," she muttered under her breath, confirming she'd taken her beatings as well.

Robert went silent, as sudden glimpses of his life—mental pictures that were captured throughout the years—flashed across his mind. *My brother, Bay, who passed much too early. Georgey Gouveia. Ruthie, my wife. And of course, Oliver—the reason for all of it; for my purpose.* It was like an old projector displaying one still shot after the next, providing hard evidence that he'd been blessed.

"Well, your old man must have done something right," Peggy said, shattering his daydream. "From what I've seen, Robert Earle, you've helped a lot of folks over the years."

He nodded his gratitude, remembering the day he'd experienced his great epiphany: *We're pretty much all in the same boat, most of us carrying one heavy anchor or another.* And that's when he promised himself: *I'll help anyone I can, whenever I can—for as long as I can.* As far as he was concerned, his own family needed nothing; *I was providing it.* His mind flipped back to Oliver. "Now I have the opportunity to help my own son," he said. "I may have no chance of winning this war against the Grim Reaper, but at least the game is not yet complete."

Peggy squeezed his arm again. "Good for you," she whispered.

He nodded again, grateful for the borrowed time. *Maybe I'll find peace if I can really come through for my son at his most critical hour*, he thought, *and finally help the one person I should have been there for all along.*

Not ten minutes passed when Ginny stepped into the room. "Hi Dad, I hope you don't mind that I stopped by, but..." She noticed Peggy. "Oh, I'm sorry, I didn't know you already had company."

Ginny and Peggy exchanged pleasant nods.

Robert turned to his friend, "Peggy, do you mind if Ginny and I have a few minutes alone?"

"Of course not," she said, already getting to her feet. "I can use a smoke, or three."

Both Robert and Ginny laughed politely.

"So how are you, kid?" he asked his daughter-in-law, as she took Peggy's seat.

"Well, you know," she said.

"I don't, actually, which is why I asked." He followed the comment up with a smile, so she knew he wasn't being rude.

"I've had a real tough time of it since Layla left, Dad."

"Well, I can understand that," he said, "but from what I'm told, she's loving it over there in Monte Carlo."

Ginny smirked; she was too clever to bite on that one. "I know that. It's just hard, you know. I don't think I'm ready for the kids to be all grown up and out of the house."

"At least you still have Jonah," Robert said. "He should be with you until he's well into his forties." He laughed.

She didn't. "That's not funny," she said, fighting off a smile.

"I couldn't agree more."

"Jonah will find his way," she said, nodding. "He just needs a little more time."

Robert bit on his tongue, hoping he wouldn't chew it off. "How are things with you and Ollie?" he asked.

Her head snapped up. She thought about it for a moment. "Well, I'm not going to lie to you, Dad. Things have been pretty rough between—"

Robert's chuckle cut her off. "Oh, how I miss that roller coaster ride."

"What?"

"Marriage," he explained, nodding. "When Ruthie and I first got hitched, being with her was like riding a roller coaster without a safety bar." He smiled. "Thrilling, but absolutely insane."

Ginny laughed at the analogy.

"I never knew when the next drop was coming, you know?" He searched her sad eyes. "When I was younger, it was so exhilarating. As I got a bit older, it could be just plain exhausting."

"I know what you mean," she mumbled.

"But can you imagine if you'd never taken that thrill ride?" he asked, raising his voice to drive the point home. "Or not being able to ride it now?"

This time, she dove into his eyes. "I do love your son, Dad."

"I'm happy to hear that."

"I'll admit that Oliver and I have gone through a bad stretch for a bit...trying to figure out who we are again after the kids, you know?"

Although he nodded, he thought, *I wish I did. But my Ruthie passed when Ollie was still young.*

"But I'm on this ride until the end," she vowed, making him smile, "and I know Oliver is too." She shrugged. "We're both starting to put in more effort." She nodded. "We'll figure it out."

"I have no doubt," he said, feeling more weight slip off his shoulders.

"Oh," she added, excitedly, "I put a deposit down for a couple's week in Aruba...to make up for the last one we screwed up." She smirked. "We need to make some better memories on that island."

He smiled. "Does Ollie know?"

She shook her head. "I wanted to surprise him with—"

"Don't!" Robert blurted. "Don't keep it a surprise, Ginny. Let him know." He nodded. "If my guess is right, your husband needs to know what you've done for him more than taking the trip itself."

"Okay Dad," she said, reluctantly, "but it's on hold for now." Her eyes turned sad.

"You'll both be in Aruba again before you know it," he said, smiling wide. "But for now, let him know, so he has something to look forward to." He winked at her. "The anticipation is half the fun in life, right?"

She nodded in agreement. "I'll let him know," she said. "Thanks." They sat for a moment when Ginny said, "It just dawned on me that we've talked about everyone except you." She grabbed his hand.

"What's to talk about?" he said. "I'm dying."

She spread her lips to reply but decided against it.

"It's the natural course, Ginny," he said.

She stayed for a while longer before giving him a kiss and heading for the door.

"Thanks for coming by today," he told her.

"Of course, Dad. I'll see you in a few days, okay?"

I hope so, he thought, nodding.

Smelling like a casino ashtray, Peggy stayed for the remainder of her usual two hours, most of the time staring up at one TV rerun or another. When she stood to leave, she kissed him on the cheek. "Have you told Ollie that you're sorry you only took him fishing once?"

"Not yet, but I will."

"And that you love him?"

"He knows that," Robert said, too defensively.

"Tell him again," she said, before starting for the door. "I'll see you tomorrow?"

He half-shrugged. "Not my call."

With a smirk, she nodded. "I'll see you tomorrow."

Oliver and Jonah arrived soon thereafter, making Robert happy.

"So how are you feeling?" his son asked him.

"The same, like shit."

"Any more tests?"

He shook his head. "Nothing new to discover," he said, not shooting for crass—just realistic. He sized them both up. "Glad you guys came together."

"Big news, Dad," Oliver announced, "Jonah cut the lawn!"

"What?" Robert said, adding a whistle. "Well, isn't that something?" He was happy to jump in and help bust the kid's chops.

His grandson grinned. "If I didn't, then he was going to beat me," he teased, pointing toward his father.

Oliver shook his head. "Maybe him," he said, pointing toward the bed, "but not me." He then turned to Jonah. "Your grandfather used some really antiquated methods on me when I was growing up, and I promised myself that I'd never do the same with my children." He snickered. "Evidently, his tough love was inspired by a cousin who got murdered in prison."

Jonah's head cocked sideways, his eyes resembling a seagull's. "Huh?"

"Antiquated methods?" Robert repeated, taken aback. He stayed focused on Jonah, hurrying to defend himself. "When most kids are young, they listen. As they get older—like your age, Jonah—they suddenly know everything, or at least they think they do."

"Kids have to make their own mistakes," Oliver said, "even if it is more frustrating."

Jonah scratched his head. "Wait a minute, are we talking about me?"

"Your grandfather loved to shower me with tough love when I was a kid," Oliver repeated, also talking directly to Jonah. He attempted a chuckle, but it came out as anything but.

What the hell? Robert thought, not expecting this sudden bend in the road.

"I remember when I was in the fourth grade," Oliver said. "I came home from school and had to report that I'd been in a fight."

Jonah grinned. "Really?"

"I don't remember that," Robert said.

"Oh, I do," Oliver said, nodding. "I had a decision to make. Either face the schoolyard bully or my father."

"That was a long time ago," Robert muttered.

Oliver looked at his father. "When I got home and told you about the fight, you took your leather belt to my backside."

"I did?" Robert mumbled; it felt like he'd gone from holding all four kings to having no face cards—and he was ready to fold. "I barely laid a finger on you," he added, defending himself. "Only when you really needed it."

"Well, I must have needed it a lot then."

"That's not true."

Oliver looked at him. "What's this, the onset of dementia too?"

Robert glanced at his grandson and then back at his son. "Oliver..."

"You're the one who brought it up," he said. "You're the one who wanted to talk about—"

"I only struck you when you needed it, son," Robert repeated, his guilt and shame suddenly more unbearable than the physical pain.

An odd moment hung between all three men.

The conversation's change in direction was as awkward as playing frozen tag in a wax museum. Robert wanted nothing more than to change the subject, and skirt as far away as possible from his son's harsh memories. He looked at Oliver, preparing to apologize.

"It's all water under the bridge, Dad," Oliver said, saving him with a soft pat on the arm. "Like I've said before, different generations have very different ideas on how to best parent." He shrugged, before looking at Jonah. "Trust me, Grandpa did the best he could with me and I'm grateful for it."

He's not talking to Jonah, Robert realized. *He's talking to me.* His eyes filled. *And he's letting me off the hook.*

Oliver shrugged. "At least he cared enough about me to try to teach me," he said without a hint of judgment or anger—only gratitude.

"Of course, I cared," Robert said, his voice sounding gravelly.

"I know, Dad," his son said, easing him further off the hook. "You only struck me when I needed it."

Robert nodded.

"It's what you knew," Oliver said, "what you'd learned."

Jonah was absorbing every detail.

"What was Papa like when you were a kid?" Oliver asked him. "From what I remember, he was a nice man."

Robert felt a hundred pounds slide off his shoulders. He chuckled and meant it. "Of course, he was to you; he was your grandfather. That was his job."

"He wasn't always like that?"

Robert looked at Oliver, thinking, *Have you completely lost your mind?* "Not even close, Ollie. He was my father, and he was a mean prick most of the time."

Jonah snickered. "Just like you, Dad," he joked.

Robert glared at him. "Not even close, Jonah!" he said. "Trust me, you have no idea."

Oliver nodded.

"That's how it works, right?" Robert said. "Dads take all the heat because it's their job to keep their children honest and respectful. It's their responsibility to discipline their kids. But when you become a grandfather," he said, grinning at Oliver, "which you're gonna love by the way—"

Jonah gagged. "Maybe Layla's gonna have kids, but—"

"Layla and Jonah are still too young to have children," Oliver said, cutting them both off. "I'm happy to wait." He grinned. "Although I do sometimes imagine how wonderful being called *Grandpa* would be."

"And when you become a grandfather," Robert repeated, "all of the difficult responsibilities that come with being a father are gone, and all that's left is the good stuff."

"I can't wait," Oliver mumbled under his breath.

Robert grinned. "It's a wonderful thing, Ollie; you just wait and see. In my opinion, the good Lord saves the best for last."

Both Oliver and Jonah smiled.

They sat in silence for a bit until Oliver repeated his question. "So, Papa was tough, huh?"

Robert's eyes squinted to recall his past. "Your Papa was a hard man, Ollie," he said, shaking his silver mane. "He could be mean as hell and physical and..." His words trailed off. "Maybe it's a family tradition that was passed down?"

No one commented. No one flinched.

"My old man was tough, even when he didn't need to be," Robert added before pausing again to breathe. "But I learned how to survive him." He looked up to meet Oliver's eyes, and then Jonah's. "That's what we do as children, right? We learn how to survive our parents."

"Dad, I never..." Oliver began.

"I know I wasn't perfect, Ollie," Robert hurried to say, "and I need you to forgive me for all the mistakes I made." His eyes misted over. "Just know that I always had your best interests in mind. I never wanted to hurt you, son—not ever. I only wanted to..." He stopped from the emotion overload.

"I know that, Dad," he said, "and there's nothing to forgive."

"Sure, there is, and I'm guessing the list is fairly long too."

Jonah's face dropped. He stayed silent, taking it all in.

Oliver struggled to keep his own emotions at bay. "All forgiven, Dad," he muttered. "Trust me, as far as I'm concerned, all that bullshit's been left in the past."

There was an even longer pause, with Robert studying his son's face. "Thank you, Ollie. I believe you," he finally said, sighing heavily. "You have no idea what that means to me."

Oliver turned to Jonah. "Oh, I'm sure I have some idea," he said in a whisper. "My best guess is that I'll be asking for the same forgiveness from my kids at some point down the road."

"Dad, I don't think you'll ever have to..." Jonah began.

"It's inevitable," Robert said, with conviction in his voice, "we do our best as fathers, and then we still have to ask for forgiveness in the end."

Silence took hold again.

"Listen, Dad, we're going to run to the cafeteria to grab a bite to eat," Oliver said. "Do you want us to bring you back something?"

Robert smirked. "And miss my pureed beef? Oh, I don't think so."

He could still hear their laughter after they'd left the room.

At this point, there's no use walking on eggshells, he thought. *I need to speak my mind, and they need to do the same.*

The guys returned a half hour later. Oliver pulled a wrapped sandwich out of a paper bag. "We got you a tuna sandwich," he said, "do you want it?"

"Thanks, but I usually don't eat cat food," Robert replied.

"It's actually not half bad with mayonnaise."

"Fine, you sold me." He grabbed the sandwich and quickly unwrapped it. "Believe it or not, the beef puree was not as good as it sounded."

"Shocker," Jonah said, laughing.

Robert took a bite. "You were right, Ollie. This isn't half bad." He smiled, mischievously. "But going forward, it's probably not the best investment to buy me green bananas."

"What?" Jonah said, confused.

"Don't say that, Dad."

"But it's true." He maintained his grin. "It doesn't mean I don't like bananas, though. Just make sure they're ripe."

Oliver and Jonah shook their heads in sync.

"Don't lose your sense of humor now, boys," he said. "We need it now more than ever." He smiled wide. "And stop worrying. I'm on my way to where all of the broken things are made whole again, that's all."

"You're too much," Oliver mumbled.

As Robert ate, he asked his son, "Do you still remember the top ten knots I taught you?" Although he'd served in the Navy during Vietnam, he rarely spoke of his service. *It was hell on earth.* But he knew and loved his knots, something he'd always been proud to pass down to his son.

"How could I forget," Oliver said, chuckling, "you grilled them into my brain for years."

"Okay, let's hear them then," Robert said, talking with his mouth full.

"Is this a test?"

"It is," he said, "your final one on this subject."

With a nod, Oliver turned to Jonah—as if to teach his boy what he knew. "According to your crazy grandfather, although there are thousands of knots, a person can get by with about ten good knots committed to memory."

"That's right," Robert said, proudly.

"Knot tying can make your life easier, and it might even save your life or someone else's someday."

"But it has to be rope," Robert added, "not nylon cord or that bungee cord crap."

Oliver's head snapped his way. "Am I taking this test, or are you?"

Robert laughed. "You may proceed."

Oliver returned his attention to Jonah. "There are three knots to make a loop, four hitching knots, and three ways to join two ropes together which are called bends."

Aside from the pain, Robert's body felt warm. *At least I gave him something,* he thought.

Oliver began counting off on his fingers. "The bowline forms a secure loop, and the clove hitch is a simple knot to tie a rope to a post."

"I could probably handle that one," Jonah commented.

"The constrictor knot ties up bundles of things, while the double fisherman's knot—also known as the impossible knot—joins two ropes together." He paused to look at his father. "That one's your Grandpa's favorite."

And you have no idea why, Robert thought, nodding, *but you will.*

"The figure eight is the strongest knot for a loop at the end of a rope," Oliver continued, "while the half hitch is a basic overhand knot. A sheet bend joins ropes of unequal size. The square knot secures non-critical items." He paused to look at his father. "It's a quick and easy knot for temporarily joining two ropes together, right?"

Robert smiled wide. "Most good sailors would never use it, though."

Oliver nodded. "See, I still remember."

"There have probably been more lives lost because some knuckle-head's used a square knot as a bend," Robert added, speaking directly to Jonah. "A square knot will slip if it isn't under tension, and if you're foolish enough to use nylon rope, then it's pretty much a guarantee."

Oliver chuckled. "If you can't tell, your grandfather isn't that fond of nylon."

Clueless about what he was hearing, Jonah nodded.

Jonah looks just like his father, hoping the lesson will end soon, Robert thought, grinning. He turned to Oliver. "You're at eighty percent. Two more to go."

"The taut-line hitch is an adjustable knot, while the trucker's hitch is used for securing loads."

"Excellent," Robert called out, proudly, "you did it!"

"How did you learn all this?" Jonah asked his grandfather, trying to get in on the conversation.

"Because I joined the Navy when I was younger than you are right now." He smirked. "In fact, I'd already been working and making my own way for a few years when I joined the Navy." He paused. "Speaking of that, how are you making out with your job search, Jonah?"

"I'm going to school," Jonah fired back.

Oliver kept his mouth shut; for once, he appeared pleased with the conversation.

"So, no plans on getting a job while you're in college?" Before the boy could answer, Robert snickered. "Generation X and Millennials," he said, happy to poke fun at their different generation's stereotypical attributes. "While I worked hard and saved my entire life, Jonah, your father's generation preferred to work smart, not hard."

"How did I get dragged into this?" Oliver teased.

Robert chuckled. "And your generation is upset that you even have to work at all," he told Jonah.

"Yeah, okay Boomer," Jonah muttered under his breath.

Robert was going to laugh when Oliver turned on his son. "Hey, have some respect, smart-ass!"

"Even when he doesn't show any respect to me, Dad?" the teenager asked.

Robert watched on in silence. *Go get him, Ollie.*

"He's your grandfather, Jonah. I won't tolerate you disrespecting him—not ever."

Jonah shook his head.

"I'm your father," Oliver said. "Would it make you feel good if you heard someone shitting on me?"

"Okay, I get it," Jonah surrendered, "I get it."

Robert grinned. *Good enough.*

"I didn't say he was in the right, but he's your grandfather."

Robert's grin disappeared. "You guys know I'm laying right here listening, right?"

"And that gives Grandpa a pass?" Jonah mumbled under his breath again, ignoring his grandfather.

Oliver glared at him. "As far as I'm concerned, it does." He pointed at his father. "If it wasn't for this crusty, old bastard, neither one of us would be here."

"Well, thanks...I think," Robert said.

Oliver and Jonah shared a smile.

Oliver turned to his father. "See, I told you I know what I'm doing."

"You're a smart man, Ollie," Robert replied, "but you still don't know everything."

Jonah snickered.

"Oh, I don't know about that, Dad," he teased, shrugging, "I'd say the jury's still out on that one."

This time, Robert snickered. "I'm still not sure where I went wrong with you, Ollie."

"Yeah, *Ollie*," Jonah said, stressing the name.

"What's that?" Robert asked.

"Nothing," Oliver said, glaring at his cocky son.

Jonah smirked. "Why not just tell him, Dad?"

"Tell me what?"

"Nothing," Oliver repeated, turning to stare down his son.

"He hates when anyone calls him Ollie," Jonah announced.

Robert's eyes turned to confused slits. "I didn't know that." He looked at Oliver. "Why didn't you tell me?"

"Because I don't mind when you call me Ollie." He nodded. "That's who I am to you, Dad." He shrugged. "If you called me anything else, it would feel wrong."

Robert scanned his face. *He's telling me the truth.* He finally nodded.

After returning the nod, Oliver's head snapped back toward Jonah. "Maybe you don't know everything either, smart-ass?"

"But you've always corrected anyone who's ever called you Ollie," he said, trying to reconcile this new information.

"And how many times have you heard me correct your grandfather?"

"None." The teenager dropped his gaze to the floor, where it stayed.

Robert and Oliver continued right on talking, both knowing there was precious little time to spare.

Finally, Robert announced, "Well, this crusty, old bastard has a hankering for some fresh tapioca pudding. Who wants to head back down to the cafeteria to grab me..."

Jonah stood. "I guess this lazy bum will go," he quickly volunteered. "I just hope I can handle such a big, important job."

"We'll see," Robert said, his face serious.

Oliver laughed.

An hour later, his son and grandson were starting to fidget, preparing to leave for the night. "Listen, before you go," he told them, "I was hoping to talk to you about the fundraiser."

Oliver and Jonah exchanged a look and laughed.

"What is it now?" Robert asked.

"We were planning to do that as soon as we got here," Oliver said, "until you ambushed us with your latest rant."

Jonah snickered.

"We went over a few things in the car, Dad, and wanted to get you up to speed."

Robert tried to sit up in the bed. Oliver helped him get there. "Well, let's hear it," he said, already feeling grateful. "I'm all ears."

"We'd like to host a comedy fundraiser event to help Dylan get that wheelchair ramp," Oliver said.

"And then some!" Jonah added, smiling.

Comedy fundraiser? Robert thought.

Oliver nodded. "I have a buddy, this guy Joe Holden, who does stand-up. He can emcee the event and book the talent for us. We can probably get the hall donated and—"

"Run some raffles and even an auction," Jonah said, jumping in, "and make the kid the money he needs."

Overwhelmed with unexpected emotion, Robert held his tongue—fearing that he would burst out in tears.

Oliver pulled out a paper from his pocket and unfolded it. "This will take a lot of planning," he said, reading from his list. "We're going to need four or five comedians, raffle prizes for a pick-and-pull raffle, a Grande raffle, and a silent auction."

"We're also going to need to book the hall soon," Jonah said.

"And maybe even get some snacks donated?" Oliver said. "Ginny doesn't think we should serve a sit-down meal. It'll cost too much to feed two hundred people."

"Two hundred people?" Robert asked, shocked. *And Ginny's already in on it?* The thought made him smile.

"Go big or go home, right Gramps?"

Robert chuckled. "I just hosted a small spaghetti dinner," he said, "but this works for me too." He took a deep breath in the hopes of keeping his emotions restrained. "Thank you, guys," he whispered, "this means more to me than you could ever know."

As Oliver and Jonah bid their farewell for the night, Jonah commented, "This was quite the visit, Grandpa. We covered a lot of ground." He kissed his grandfather's cheek. "I'll never forget it."

Robert's heart skipped three beats. "I really hope that's true, Jonah."

As the boys opened the door, Robert called out. "Ollie, bring me a dozen lengths of rope, each one a foot long. That should do it."

"What do you need a dozen of—"

"Just bring me the rope, son, okay? And no nylon."

"Okay, Dad. Never nylon, I got it," he said, "I may not be able to get over to the hardware until—"

"As soon as you can," his father interrupted. "Please bring them to me first chance you get, okay?"

He nodded. "Okay, Dad. I'm on it."

"Good man." He grimaced in pain before closing his eyes.

◊◊◊

Before shutting off the lights for the night, Hen Zannini, the second-shift nurse, wrapped Robert's shins in a pair of edema compression pumps. "We don't want you forming any blood clots that might travel to your heart," she said, a slight smirk resting in the corner of her mouth.

The constant motion on Robert's shins drove him nuts, so as soon as Hen exited the room, he freed his feet from the annoying restraints, put them on top of the inflated wraps, and then covered them with a sheet.

Minutes later, Hen stomped back into the room to catch him. "Nice try, Mr. Earle," she said, "but I wasn't born yesterday."

"And neither was I," he said, smiling, "although my birthday is coming up soon." He lowered his tone. "Maybe as an early birthday gift, you can look the other way on this one?"

"Not on my watch," Hen said, wrapping his shins even tighter this time.

Oh, we can do this all night, he thought, before catching the twinkle in her mischievous eyes. *And I'm guessing Hen's thinking the same damn thing.* He laughed aloud. *I really like this lady!*

CHAPTER 9

After a full day of hiking in the Blue Hills, Marissa and Jonah were back in the basement bedroom—her head on Jonah's chest.

"Today was fun," she purred.

"Every day with you is fun," he said.

She sighed. "I love when we can spend the whole day together," she said, "especially when it doesn't cost all kinds of money that we don't have."

"Which is why we do things that don't cost money," he teased.

She slapped his belly. "We always seem to end up back here, though, don't we?"

"I hope that's not a problem?" he said.

"Oh, I'm not complaining. I'm just pointing out the obvious."

"Honestly, Marissa," he said, positioning himself so he could look into her eyes, "it's because there's no other place in the world I'd rather be than in bed with you," he vowed. This was not intended in a nasty way, and she somehow understood that. "It's not just about the sex. It really isn't." He wished he had the right words to explain. "I feel closest to you when we're being physical together."

She kissed him. "Good answer."

"I love you," he said, "and that'll never change, no matter where we are."

"I love you more," she purred.

They lay quietly for a while, content to be in each other's company while awaiting another surge of energy.

"Do you think we have a chance at making it," she asked, "being high school sweethearts, and all?"

"Of course, we do," he said, "my parents did." He cringed. "Although it might be nice if we did more than just tolerate each other."

She giggled. "I wouldn't mind fighting with you for the rest of my life."

"What?"

"It would still mean that we're together, right?"

"Wow, I like that," he said, "although I'd rather live in peace, if we can." They both laughed.

"I love you so much," she said.

"Ditto, beautiful," he told her, "and we can stop being physical with each other for a while, if you're wondering how much I really—"

"Are you crazy?" she said. "Why would you suggest something so awful?"

He laughed for a moment, and then kissed her passionately. The time for talk was over.

Marissa had just tiptoed out of the house when Jonah thought, *I really do love this girl. I wonder if she really is the one.*

◊◊◊

The following morning, Jonah headed upstairs, surprised to find his father sitting in his recliner, reading a book. "No work today?" he asked.

His dad shook his head. "I can only take so much at one time. I'm playing hooky." He looked up from his book and smirked. "You know what that is, right?"

Jonah was smart enough not to answer that one.

"Marissa left late last night," his father commented.

Jonah nodded.

"I could hear you two from here. I hope you're using protection?"

"We are," Jonah said, comfortable talking to his father about such things. "I think she's the one, Dad."

Placing the book into his lap, his dad smiled. "Jonah, let me give you the same advice my father gave me about finding the right woman when I was your age. Make a list of the top five things that you absolutely need in a mate. Loyalty, integrity, sex—whatever you think you can't live without. Nobody's perfect, but if you can get those top five things, then..."

"That makes sense to me," Jonah said.

His father nodded. "It sure does, until you realize that people change and that relationships are constantly evolving."

Jonah's smile disappeared. *Damn.*

"Although the nature of who we are doesn't change all that much—a snake is a snake, you know—relationships change over time." He shrugged. "Priorities change. Wants and needs change." He sighed. "And it's a tormented life, son, if you ever need someone to change in order for you to be happy." He nodded. "Relationships ebb and flow." There was a long pause. "What starts out as a nice compromise can sometimes end up as a complete surrender."

Jonah searched his father's eyes. "Are we still talking about my future, Dad, or yours?"

"Both, I think."

Jonah nodded that he understood. "So maybe you need to figure out what you can't live without?"

In spite of the heaviness of the moment, his dad chuckled. "Sure, I can kick it around all I want but I realized long ago that the one thing in this world that I can't live without is your mother."

Jonah's smile mirrored his father's. "I could have told you that one, Dad." He placed his hand on his father's shoulder. "And if helps, she couldn't live without you either. Trust me."

"That's nice to hear," his dad said.

"If it wasn't the truth," Jonah said, shrugging, "I wouldn't have said it." Heading for the kitchen for a bite, he thought about his father's advice. *I realize Dad's always trying to teach, but he might actually be on to something this time.*

◊◊◊

"Did you butt dial me?" Quinn asked.

Jonah shrugged. "I usually carry my cell phone in my front pocket, so..." He laughed.

There was a pause. "That's nasty."

"It's not my fault," he said, gesturing toward his crotch, "you know he's always had a mind of his own."

"Are we partying tonight?" Quinn asked.

Jonah shook his head. "I have plans with Marissa."

"Plans? You mean you're having sex." He shook his head. "Do you ever take her anywhere but your basement?"

You have no idea, bro. Jonah thought, remaining silent; he was unwilling to share the details of his and Marissa's relationship.

Quinn laughed. "So, I'll see you in class tomorrow?"

"Maybe."

"Why don't you just withdraw then, if you're done with school?" Quinn asked, perturbed.

"Relax, bro. I was joking. What's your problem, anyway?" Jonah asked, not understanding the sour attitude.

Quinn snickered. "I don't have it like you do, bro. I'm paying my own way through college."

Whatever, bro, Jonah thought. *You need to stop tripping.*

◊◊◊

Jonah picked up his father from work.

"I appreciate this," his dad said, jumping into the passenger side of the beater.

"No worries," Jonah told him.

"My car's at Keith Tripp's shop. He says it should be done in a week."

"Doesn't he always give that same timeframe?" Jonah noted.

His father laughed. "That's true." He thought about it and shrugged. "I may need a few rides before that long week is up."

Jonah chuckled. "I got your back, Dad."

Just then, a pretty lady wearing a red power suit walked in front of the car. She was somewhere between Jonah's age and his dad's. "Who's that?" he asked.

"That's my boss," his father reluctantly answered.

"Shouldn't you be her boss?"

"I probably should," he said, "but it has a lot less to do with age than a lot of other factors."

"And what are those?" Jonah asked, watching the lady in red jump into her white BMW and race out of the parking lot.

His dad opened his mouth to speak but held his tongue for a moment. "It doesn't matter, son. I've made my choices, and she's making hers."

As Jonah pulled out onto the street, he thought about that. *This mediocrity is exactly what I don't want!* He stifled a snicker. *I'm still not completely sure which branch of the gaming industry I'll end up in, but what I do know is that I'm going to climb as high as I can.* He'd recently switched his college major to business, but still had his eye on marketing. He looked sideways at his father and felt real sorrow for the man. *I'll never be afraid of heights like Dad is,* he thought. *I can't wait to climb.*

"Listen Jonah, I'm glad we have this time alone," his dad said. "I've been doing a lot of thinking lately sitting in that hospital room with your grandfather and...and I realize I've been wrong."

Jonah nearly crashed into the car in front of them. *Wrong? My father?* He was going to respond but decided to await the rest of the explanation.

"This isn't easy for me to admit to the two of us, Jonah," his father confessed, "but I know I wasn't the best dad I could've been for you."

"What?" Jonah blurted, not expecting to hear any of this. "You can't be serious?"

"I am." The man nodded. "It's true, son. I should have been much stricter with you. I should have set higher expectations." He shook his head.

What?

"All I ever wanted to do was give you and your sister everything, Jonah."

"And you did, Dad."

"Which is precisely the problem, son. I've recently realized that my approach has been detrimental to your development and, unfortunately, much of the damage has already been done." His eyes misted over, taking Jonah even further aback.

Jonah opened his mouth to speak. Only hot air escaped.

"I helped you do your homework, recalling how I used to have to struggle through it on my own. I coached your sports teams and, remembering the dejection I'd felt when I played, I made sure everyone made the team. You worked hard in school all week, so I decided not to trouble you to cut the grass—like I had to for my dad when I was your age. And you know what, I still gave you an allowance because what the heck, I'm your dad and that's what dads do, right?"

What the hell is going on right now?

"I rode my bike or walked everywhere. But not you, I'd never let that happen to you. So, I drove you everywhere. When you had a problem, I solved it for you. When you had a need, I filled it. And wishes, well, I made sure they came true—every one of them. And unlike my parents—my mean, slave-driving father—I gave you *everything*..." he paused, shaking his head, "everything but the wings you need to fly on your own."

What the hell? Jonah repeated in his head, feeling totally ambushed.

"People don't give you free rides in the real world, Jonah—they just don't. In fact, you'd be lucky to get the right directions if the GPS app on your phone shits the bed. And..." He paused again. "The world will undoubtedly throw curve ball after curve ball at you."

This time, Jonah nodded. It seemed like the right thing to do.

"I've allowed you to relax on the couch and play your video games from the safe little haven that your mother and I have provided." He shook his head. "But those days are done, son."

"Okay, Dad, okay," he finally blurted, the tone of his voice crying out for mercy. "I'll go find a job, okay?"

"When?"

"Today!"

His father grinned. "That's my boy!"

The rest of the way home was driven in silence.

◊◊◊

Several missed sunrises came and went, with Jonah keeping the same delightful schedule. In most respects, he didn't have a care in the world, and he loved it. Life was good—*almost perfect.*

He called Marissa. "Hey, babe," he said, as soon as she answered. "I know it's getting cool out, but what do you think about going on a canoe trip down the Westport River this weekend? It'll cost a few bucks, but no big deal. We can pack another picnic, a good one this time, and start at the Head of Westport. From there, we'll—"

"I'm late, Jonah," she said, cutting him off.

"No problem," he replied. "We can get together later. But the canoe trip could be—"

"No, Jonah, I'm late with my period."

As reality penetrated his thick skull, every cell in his body went straight into panic mode. "No way," he squealed, unable to conceal his fear. "We used protection, Marissa!"

"I know we did, Jonah," she said, "but that doesn't mean it worked."

He felt sick to his stomach, the rest of the world and everything in it disappearing—at least for the time being. *Oh shit!* he thought. "It can't be," he told her; "you haven't missed taking the pill, right?"

"Of course not."

"Good, then we should be all set then." His mind continued to race. "I'm sure you'll get it any day now."

"We'll see," she whispered. "I'm going to buy one of those home pregnancy tests."

"That might be a waste of money."

"I'm not really worried about fifteen bucks right now, Jonah."

But I don't want to know, he thought.

Marissa sighed.

Jonah wasn't sure, no matter how great sex could be—*and it can be great*, he thought—that it was worth the angst that could accompany it. If only his raging hormones agreed.

Marissa might be pregnant, he told himself, even though the truth of it—and all its life-changing details—was yet to truly sink in. *We might be having a baby?* He held his breath. *There's no way! I'm nowhere near ready to be a father.*

"But you want to be a lawyer, Marissa," he reminded her. "You've always wanted to be a lawyer. How are you going to do that if we have a kid right now?"

"I'll do it," she said, convincingly. "Either way, I'll do it. It might not be the path I expected to take, but I'm still going to do it!"

When the call ended, the same questions kept repeating in Jonah's throbbing head. *When? How? Why?* He jumped in the shower, hoping to cleanse his mind of the maddening loop. It was no use. *When? How? Why?*

Hours passed, some long grueling hours, when Marissa called his cell again.

"What did the test say?" he blurted.

"It was positive."

"But..."

"I took two home tests, Jonah, and they were both positive."

"Ummm...okay. Let me call you right back, Marissa."

"What? Call me back?"

"I think I'm going to be sick," he confessed, before ending the call and hurrying to the bathroom to kneel before the toilet, where he alternated between vomiting and saying his prayers.

After cleaning his mouth, Jonah caught his reflection in the bathroom mirror. He looked like he'd just traveled a hundred miles of bad road—*and I feel even worse.* Anxiety had a vicious way of stealing all positive energy. It was exhausting. *And it's only been a few hours.*

His cell phone beeped. It was a text from Marissa. *I just called my doctor's office. I can't wait to know for sure. They scheduled bloodwork for me this afternoon. I'll call you when I get back and we'll talk more.*

Jonah called Quinn.

"Hey stranger," his friend said, breaking his back. "We have a long-time listener, first-time caller on the line. Go ahead, sir."

"Hey bro," Jonah said, "do you think it would be cool if I came over and hung out for a bit?"

"Of course. What's up?"

"I need to talk."

"What's going on?"

"I'll fill you in when I get there."

Quinn snickered. "How bad?"

"Not bad...but definitely life changing."

"Make it quick then. I have a six pack of tall boys waiting on ice."

◊◊◊

After three of the longest days in his life—and more than a dozen nervous conversations with Marissa—Jonah's cell phone rang. He looked at the caller ID. *It's her.* With his heart in his throat, he immediately picked up. "Hello?"

"Jonah," she said, "I have news. Do you want me to come by?"

"Of course, I want you to come by. But what's the news? There's no way I can wait." He could hardly breathe.

"The bloodwork just came back," she reported.

"And?" he gasped.

"It's positive," she announced. "We're going to be parents."

We're going to be parents? There's no way! Jonah stopped breathing. "But we used protection, Marissa!" he countered, retrying an earlier argument.

"I know we did, Jonah," she said, "but..."

"But?" The word came out as a mouse's squeak.

"But I've been on antibiotics and the doctor just told me that antibiotics can wipe out the pill."

"Are you serious?"

"Yes."

Oh God, Jonah thought, *antibiotics can wipe out the pill?* "Are they sure, Marissa?"

"What do you think, Jonah? They took blood at the doctor's office. I'd say they're pretty sure."

"So, what are we going to do?" he asked.

"What do you mean, what are we going to do? We're going to have a baby!" Whatever excitement or joy she'd had in her voice was now completely gone.

"There...there are other options, Marissa," he stuttered.

There was a dreadful pause. He could hear her starting to cry on the other end of the phone. Although he felt bad, he whispered, "Have you even considered that?"

"No, I haven't, Jonah, and I won't! This could be the best thing that's ever happened to us." She tried to calm herself. "There are no other options, Jonah! This is our baby." She took in a few more calming breaths. "Can you imagine if your dad thought the same way when your mother got pregnant with you?"

"I'm sorry, babe," he whispered. "I didn't mean it. I'm just..."

"We're having this baby, Jonah," she repeated matter-of-factly; "that's what we're going to do." Clearly upset, she paused. "Listen, I know this is a shock. It is for me too, and it's gonna take some time to sink in. But we're definitely pregnant."

He remained silent.

"I love you," she said.

"And I love you too. You know that." He gagged once before covering his mouth. "I just hope I'm ready to be a dad," he said, wondering whether he should begin keeping his fears to himself.

"I'm not sure I'm ready to be a parent either," she said, "but I don't really think that our baby cares whether we're ready or not."

Our baby, he repeated in his head, fighting off the acid swirling around in his throat. *Oh God, why did this happen now?*

"Do you still want me to come over?" she asked.

"What do you think?" he said.

"I'm honestly not sure."

"Of course, I want you to come over. I love you, Marissa."

"I love you more," she whispered.

He spent the next half hour with his face buried in his hands, forcing himself to think. *There's no way I can cut and run. That would be the most cowardly thing I could ever do, and I'd never do that to Marissa.* He considered what it might be like to accept his role as a father. *But I don't even know what I want to be when I grow up, never mind having to take care of another human at this point in my life.* He shook his head so hard that it hurt. *I need some time to accept this,* he thought, *some time to think.* He looked toward the stairs. *The one thing I do know is that I'm not telling Mom and Dad—not yet anyway.*

The world—and everything in it—became a surreal blur. A hurricane of emotions battered his heart and mind; it was so overwhelming that he didn't know what he felt. Physically, he was numb—as though someone had drugged him and taken away any control he'd once had over his life. *I'm not ready for this,* he thought. *How could I be?*

Minutes felt like hours. Hours turned into days. *I'm going to be a father,* he kept repeating in his head, *a dad.* He couldn't think of anything else, yet he couldn't comprehend the truth of that either. *When? How? Why?* he wondered, over-and-over-and-over again. *When? How? Why?*

◊◊◊

Jonah and Marissa sat out on his back deck, carving two giant pumpkins—and clinging on to any sense of normalcy. Although it was only early October, Marissa had insisted. Her jack-o-lantern looked perfect, well thought out—each cut surgical and accurately proportioned. His was a deformed mess, appearing as though a visually-impaired zombie missing both thumbs might have created it.

She got up to look at his hideous creation. "Are you kidding me, Jonah?" she asked. "You're not even trying."

He forced a grin. "Be careful you're not too critical. You know who my favorite muse is."

Her gorgeous eyes went wide. "That had better not be me!"

He laughed—for a moment—until remembering the difficult situation they were in. "So how are we going to break the news to everyone?"

She shook her head. "It's not going to be easy," she admitted, polishing up her work.

"I'll tell my parents in a few days when the time is right," he said.

She nodded. "If you want me to be there when—"

"And I'd like to be with you when you tell your parents," he added, cutting her off.

"You've met my father, Jonah," Marissa said, abandoning her carved pumpkin, "but you don't know him. He's old-school Portuguese. Trust me. He's going to freak out."

"I want us to tell him together," he confirmed.

"I'm not sure that's the best idea."

"And why is that?"

"Because I honestly have no idea how he's going to react. I've only seen him violent once, and it wasn't pretty."

Violent? Jonah thought, swallowing hard. "If I don't go with you and face him now, babe, then he'll never have any respect for me. And I need him to respect me. My child is going to be his grandchild. Whether he likes it or not, we're connected forever now." He nodded. "I'm not saying that I'm not dreading it, but it's something I need to do." He grabbed her hand. "Please don't take that from me."

"But Jonah, you really don't know how bad this could—"

"I'll accept whatever he wants to give me," he interrupted. "This is a long-haul deal, babe, and I have no intentions of hiding in the shadows just because it's going to be uncomfortable for me to face him."

"Uncomfortable. All right," she said under her breath.

He gave her a hug. "We're going to be fine," he said, as much for himself as for her.

"Okay, Jonah," she said in surrender.

He pulled her to him and kissed her forehead, realizing that it was the first difficult promise of many.

◇◇◇

It took every ounce of courage he had—and some he didn't—to approach his parents with the news. "I need to talk. Do you guys have a minute?"

"Always," his father said, shutting off the TV and offering his undivided attention.

"What's going on?" his mom asked, closing her book.

"I have something to tell you." He thought he was going to throw up.

"What is it? You can tell us anything," his dad said, "You know that."

"It's Marissa," Jonah said, intentionally sparing his girlfriend from the awkward scene, "she's..." He stopped, burping back the horrible sensation just behind his tongue.

"What is it?" his mom repeated, her voice now panicked. "What happened to Marissa?" She slid to the edge of her seat.

"She...she's pregnant." Jonah held his breath and waited.

Instantly, his dad's face turned from worried to terrified.

"Oh, my God," his mom said.

"You have got to be shitting me?" his father roared. "Do you realize what you've just done to your future? To your girlfriend's future? Life is hard enough, Jonah." His eyes grew distant, glossed over in pain. "You're both just kids...and now you're having *a kid?*"

He felt totally panicked.

His mother was taken aback. "Is she sure?"

Jonah nodded. "She took two home pregnancy tests and they were both positive."

"Well, that sounds pretty sure to me."

"She's also seen her primary care physician who had her do some bloodwork." He looked toward his mother for help. As she shook her head, tears filled her eyes, making Jonah want to cry.

"What does Marissa think about the pregnancy?" his dad asked.

"She's scared, but she wants to have the baby. We both do."

His parents gawked at him like they were looking at a dead man. The look frightened him.

"Do her parents know?" his mom asked.

"Not yet," Jonah admitted. "We're going to tell them together."

His dad huffed. "Good luck with that," he said. "I'm sure they're going to be thrilled." He kept shaking his head. "You were supposed to reach further than I did, Jonah...accomplish more," he mumbled, as though he were talking to himself. "It's the natural order of things."

"It happened, Dad," Jonah said, breaking the old man out of his trance. "It's happening. Marissa's pregnant. What can her parents do?"

"What can her parents do?" his mom repeated. "They can worry about their daughter, knowing that her life's path just became so much more difficult and challenging." Her voice rose with each word. "They can lose sleep because their daughter's options and opportunities have just been reduced to one."

"Mom, that's not—"

"There's a lot they can do, Jonah," the hurt woman said, cutting him off, "and none of it will bring them a second of peace."

Jonah realized that his mother wasn't only referring to Marissa's parents.

"It's a baby," he said, raising his own voice, "It's our baby. And I'm sorry for all the trouble this has caused, that it will cause, but we're having this baby!" Fighting off the urge to dry heave, he hurried out of the room.

When? How? Why? he continued to wonder.

CHAPTER 10

Oliver had only written one poem in his life; it was for Ginny when he was auditioning for the role of husband. He thought about that. *Maybe I should start writing again.*

Only the Best?
(for Jonah)

On the day an eagle was born; a legacy,
feathered in gold and cradled
tightly in his father's strong wings,
a curious promise was made:
"Your life will be better than mine—
for I will give you—only the best."

Nurtured and coddled, as he grew, Daddy:
Wiped his behind,
then all of his fears away.
Picked him up when he had fallen,
and later when he was sad.
Chased monsters from the night,
and soon bullies from the yard.
Filled every star-struck wish,
then every other hope conceivable.
Only the best.

Season-after-season, Daddy:
removed all worries,
fought all battles,

solved all problems,
met all wants, while
providing protection
from the harsh world.
As promised—only the best.

Alas, the dawn had arrived
when the young bird would fly the nest.
But taking the great leap from innocence,
he plummeted straight to the earth.
Shaken, he sat up to find his father
hovering over him, weeping mournfully.
"Don't cry Daddy, it's not your fault,"
he said, "you gave me—only the best."
"No," replied his father, "I gave you everything but wings."

Putting pen to paper had a funny way of allowing Oliver to work through his angst. He read over this new piece a few times, only to find that it caused him even more distress. *And now Jonah's going to be a father?* He decided to keep the poem to himself.

Oliver was facing a one-two punch and he knew it. As if his dad's terminal illness wasn't enough, his teenage son's shocking news was costing him even more sleep. His instinct was to immediately go into crisis mode and fix everything—*which might destroy it all instead,* he decided. His life was no longer a take-it-one-day-at-a-time situation. *It's more a take-it-one-hour-at-a-time kind of deal, even minute by minute at some points.* He focused on his breathing. *I don't know how much more I can handle.* It was all he could do to keep it together and not break into a million jagged pieces.

Fortunately, he'd been presented with the perfect distraction to immerse himself into.

As accurately predicted, the preparation for the fundraiser was immense. With only weeks to put it all together, he secured the Liberal Club in Fall River.

"You can use the hall free-of-charge," the manager said, "just as long as it's on a night in the middle of the week." He grinned. "And we get the bar." A Thursday was chosen.

With the help of Ginny and Jonah, Oliver made over 300 phone calls and sent out even more emails and letters to solicit donations for raffle and auction items, as well as for snack food.

They also called local businesses to solicit cash donations that would cover all expenses. In total, they took in nearly $1,000, or enough to fund the entire show. *Every penny we earn from ticket sales will go straight to Dylan now*, Oliver realized.

Ginny contacted the local printer, talking him into donating the tickets to be used for admission and the raffles. At work, Oliver discreetly created signage for everything: tent cards for reserved seating, flyers to be placed under one seat per table for another fun giveaway, and table cards for the pick-and-pull raffle items.

The Pick-and-Pull Raffle is guaranteed to be the highlight, Oliver predicted. With twenty-five items to win, there would be a labeled cup for each prize. Attendees could purchase twenty tickets for ten dollars and then place as many tickets as they wanted within the prize cup that they hoped to win. While some folks might place one ticket into different cups, others would place all twenty tickets into one cup—greatly increasing their chances of winning that one prize.

Finally, Oliver drafted a press release to promote the event, ready to be sent to every local media venue. *Wait until Dad sees this*, he thought, excitedly.

◊◊◊

"No Ginny again this week?" Dr. Borden-Brown asked, dressed in her brown and tan power suit.

"Nope."

"Did you ask her?"

"Weekly," he said, playing their customary game.

"This week?"

"Every week." He cleared his throat. "Listen, Ginny has her reasons for not coming here and I have to respect her for that." He still felt defensive of his wife, realizing that it was a positive sign.

"Can we talk about that?" she asked, nodding. "I'd really like to focus on your marriage for this week's session."

"Well, there are some other things going on, some pretty heavy—"

She nodded as though she understood. "I think we've avoided your marriage long enough, Oliver. What do you say we finally get into it today?"

Oliver took a deep breath before taking the plunge. "I've recently come to the conclusion that our timing with each other has been atrocious over the past few years."

"What do you mean?"

"Every time I reached out to Ginny, she wasn't there." He shook his head. "She was either hurt or frustrated from something thoughtless I'd said or done. And the times she'd reached out to me, I wasn't able to hear her because I was so angry or hurt."

"This is good," the doctor said, unable to write fast enough.

"Good?"

She looked up from her pad. "I'm sorry, I meant that you sharing this information is good."

He nodded.

Dr. Borden-Brown waited for him to go on.

"At one point, I became angry because Ginny began treating our house like she was staying at a bed and breakfast," he explained. "She started to expect that everything would be done for her."

"Like she was one of your kids?" the doctor commented.

"Exactly!" Oliver replied, when it dawned on him that this might be an indictment. He hurried to go on. "For the longest time, I couldn't tell whether things were falling apart with us, or falling back into place," he explained.

Dr. Borden-Brown took a note. "Have you made any real attempts toward making things better?"

"I have." He shook his head. "I booked that tropical vacation for just the two of us."

She nodded. "Right."

As Oliver's mind flew back to the island, both eyes filled with tears. *And that went wrong in so many ways!*

She caught something in his face. "So, if you're that unhappy, Oliver, then why do you continue to endure it?" she asked, nonchalantly. "Have you ever asked yourself that?"

"A thousand times and it always comes back to the same two answers," he said. "The first is that I don't want to disappoint everyone."

"Disappoint who?"

"The kids. My father."

"Your father?" She took another note before allowing her notebook to fall into her lap. "And the second reason?"

Oliver snickered. "Because I still love my wife."

They stared at each other, neither one flinching.

Oliver finally broke. "Although it's been hard to be with Ginny at times, it would be impossible to live without her. I may not be the smartest man in the world, but I know that much at least."

The therapist's subtle nod complemented her grin. "I understand."

"And we've each started taking small steps back to each other," he added.

"That's good," she said, with no need to explain it this time.

They stared at each other for nearly a full minute; it felt like an eternity.

"Okay then, it looks like you're done," Dr. Borden-Brown finally said, wrapping up the weekly session.

"Oh, and by the way," Oliver said, getting to his feet, "I just learned that I'm going to be a grandfather."

"What?"

He nodded.

"Layla?"

He shook his head.

"Oh..." she said. "Are you okay with the big news?"

"Let's just say we have plenty to talk about next week."

◊◊◊

After giving his wife two sincere compliments, a cup of hot peppermint tea and a passionate kiss, Oliver entered his father's hospital room to find an empty bed. Two seconds later, he heard a toilet flush and then turned to find the old man slowly hobbling out of the bathroom.

"As I'm sure you're starting to learn, Ollie," his dad said, "gravity is not our friend."

Oliver laughed. "Someone seems like he's in a better mood today?"

He shrugged. "What choice do I have?"

Oliver nodded.

"I'm trying to get in as many bathroom runs as I can before they shackle me to a catheter," his dad said, "I'm not sure how much longer I can hold them off."

Shaking his head, Oliver handed him a clear plastic sleeve of Sam's Syrian meat pies. "Without the yogurt, just the way you like them."

The old man licked his lips. "Great job. I'm proud of you," he said, his face remaining stoic.

Oliver thought about the comment for a few moments before his father's sly grin appeared. *He's still busting my balls.* "Just eat them, so I don't catch any flak from the nurses."

Oliver also handed him the lengths of rope he'd requested.

"I appreciate it," his father said, sliding up in bed.

"Hey, did you see that new nurse on the floor? The older one?" The old man chuckled.

Oliver nodded. "I did. Why?"

"I think she's wearing a wig."

"That's not a wig, Dad. Stop."

"It's definitely a wig," he whispered. "I swear I saw a chinstrap." Opening the steaming bag of meat pies, he quickly tore into his contraband lunch.

Oliver laughed. "Be nice, Dad."

"I'm always nice. It's the only thing I have left."

"Then be nicer. She might end up being my future stepmom," Oliver joked.

They both laughed.

"I have about seventeen comebacks for that one, but I'd rather leave the low-hanging fruit on the tree for someone who's a bit shorter than me."

"Shorter, huh?"

"Shorter on wits, yes." He paused to study Oliver's face. "What's going on?"

Oliver shrugged.

"What is it?"

"The world still feels like it's spinning out of control," Oliver admitted, shaking his head. "I keep trying to—"

"To control everything, right?" his father finished for him, chuckling. "As far as I know, you don't hold the remote, Ollie. That's God's job."

Oliver nodded. "I know that, Dad."

"Then stop acting like you're in charge. You're not. None of us are." He nodded. "Just learn to ride the river like the rest of us."

Taking a deep breath, Oliver exhaled slowly. *Sure,* he thought, *except I feel like that river's pulling me under, trying to drown me.*

"Stop being so hard on yourself, son. There's no need for it. You do the best you can and leave the rest in the hands of God."

He nodded again.

"Your hands aren't big enough," he joked.

They sat for a bit, staring at the same white wall.

The old man's one-liners aside, Oliver also knew that his father's situation weighed heavily on him. "So, tell me, Dad, what's bothering you the most right now?"

"Besides dying?" Grinning, his dad shook his head. "I sometimes try to imagine how much greater life would have been if the Filet-O-Fish sandwich came with a full slice of cheese." He looked at his son. "Can you just imagine?"

"I'm being serious," Oliver said, peering into his father's sapphire eyes. It was amazing that after all the tragedy and pain, the wear and tear of life, the old man's baby blues had never dulled. *Even now, they're still as bright and sharp with mischief as they've ever been.*

"And so am I." His father shook his head again. "I mean, if you've gone to the trouble of catching Alaskan pollock in the wild, the least you can do is crown it with a full slice of orange government cheese." His face remained serious. "I mean, how much more could it cost?"

Unreal, Oliver thought. This time, he was the one shaking his head. *Why would I believe he ever could be serious—even now?* "Dad, for once, will you please just be serious?"

The old man nodded. "Fine," he said. "I'll make you a deal."

"And what's that?"

"I'll be serious, if you can make me laugh."

"What?"

"You heard me, Ollie. Make me laugh and I'll stop screwing around..." He grinned. "...for a while, anyway."

Oliver scoured his memory and smiled. "Okay, when I was a teenager, every Friday night my high school buddies and I hung out. Rob had a Portuguese grandmother who lived with him. Given that we were all underage, we'd wait until Rob's parents took off for their bowling league before we'd ask Vavo to go to the store with us. 'Okay,' she'd say, and off we'd go—to the liquor store. Each guy would pony up whatever he had and give Rob the money, who then handed it over to his grandmother."

Robert was already smiling.

"Dressed in her black dress, black shawl and pink house slippers," Oliver continued, "she'd hover like a seagull near the front counter, while we entered the store pretending to buy salt and vinegar potato chips and Slim Jims. As though we didn't know her, we'd volunteer to carry her beer to the counter—and then out to her car.

"Occasionally, she'd scream out, 'Is that it, boys? You no want something else?'"

His dad tried to conceal his laughter.

"We'd scurry off in opposite directions, pretending that we didn't know her," Oliver went on. "The clerk behind the counter always shook his head, disgusted but not caring enough to make a thing out of it."

Oliver nodded. "This went on for several years, until the oldest of us could finally buy booze for our degenerate crew. Truthfully, I could never tell whether Vavo knew that buying alcohol for minors was wrong. She spoke broken English, and very little of it. In her culture, drinking beer or wine was natural—regardless of age. Few Portuguese kids at school ever abused alcohol because they could have it any time they wanted. It was the rest of us delinquents who were being deprived the fruit of the vine. As a young punk, anything that was forbidden was coveted."

The old man nodded that he understood.

"Vavo was the sweetest, kindest little old lady you could ever meet. During our adolescence, she was the perfect babysitter. And if we got really lucky on those crazy Friday nights, she'd let one of us drive her car home; no driver's permit, no license—no problem. To a 16-year-old, Vavo was the definition of cool."

His father laughed, grabbing his side in pain. "Now that's funny," he said. "How did I not know that story until now?"

"Because you were drinking even heavier than I was back then."

The old man's smile vanished.

"I'm just being honest," Oliver said, playfully.

His dad nodded. "Enough with the honesty for a while, okay? I've got enough guilt to last me the rest of my life."

"Guilt?"

"Sure." His dad stared at him. "You don't carry around any guilt as a father?"

"Are you kidding me?" Oliver said. "You have no idea how many sleepless nights I've had because of the things I should have done and didn't." His Adam's apple rose and fell several times before he could speak. "And just as much guilt for the things I did and probably shouldn't have."

"How so?" the old man asked.

"I tried everything to teach Jonah to swim, but nothing worked. The fear was mind-numbing for the poor kid. Although it tortured me—killed a piece of me inside, actually—I finally threw the screaming kid into the pool, just like you'd done to me."

His dad laughed. "Attaboy."

"Even though I broke Jonah's fear with tough love, I still felt awful about the whole experience," he explained, "much longer than I probably should have."

The sickly man dismissed the foolish talk with a flick of his wrist.

"It was the same thing getting him to ride a roller coaster. Although I felt like throwing up, I forced Jonah to ride the coaster—unsure whether I was being a good father or a terrible one in the process."

"And you've had guilt over that?" his father asked, baffled.

"I have."

"But you helped him."

"True, but the way I helped him has always haunted me."

"It never did for me," his dad admitted.

"Yeah, but I have a heart," Oliver teased. "That's the big difference between us."

They both laughed.

Oliver gave it some more thought, realizing that his son was slow in learning most everything. It took years—too many of them—to take Jonah's training wheels off when learning to ride a bicycle. Oliver couldn't tell if it was from fear or laziness. *I figure it was a combination of the two.* He'd always been happy to offer his children—especially his son—a safety net. *Unfortunately, Jonah confused it for a hammock.* Panic welled up inside him, threatening to stop his heart. *And now he's going to be a father, and there's no way on God's green earth that I've prepared him for that.*

"What is it?" the old man asked. "I can see the chipmunks running a hundred miles an hour behind those brown eyes of yours."

"I have some big news to share, Dad," Oliver reluctantly announced. *The man's dying,* he figured, *there's no reason to keep anything from him at this point.*

"And you waited until now to tell me?" He smirked. "Kind of harsh to hold out on me at this stage in the game, don't you think?"

"Guess who's going to be a great-grandfather?" he asked his father, unsure of the old-timer's reaction.

He shrugged. "I give up."

"You are." Oliver smiled.

"Layla?" his dad asked, struggling to sit up.

Oliver shook his head. "Jonah."

"You've gotta be shitting me?" his father said, in shock.

"I shit you not."

The old-timer sat with this new information for a while. "Makes perfect sense in the bigger picture, I suppose," he said, nodding, "the torch being passed, and all."

"Are you kidding me?" Oliver squealed.

"What?"

"This is the last reaction I expected from you."

"What are you gonna do, Ollie?" he said. "It's life."

"What?" he repeated, in shock.

"I'm sure Jonah and his girl didn't plan it this way, but it's the hand they've been dealt." He shrugged. "We just play the cards the best way we know how."

Still flabbergasted, Oliver was about to respond when his father laughed aloud. "I'm telling you, Ollie, you're going to love being a Grandpa," he said, his eyes misting over, "and you're going to be great at the job."

"I hope so, Dad," he mumbled, still struggling to reconcile his father's reaction.

"Are you kidding me? I've never met a man better suited for the job in my life." The old man smiled. "Besides, it's nearly impossible to mess it up." He chuckled. "Look at how screwed up I am, and the kids still love me."

"That's true," Oliver teased.

His dad reached for his hand. "Welcome to the greatest club in the world, son. I can't tell you how happy I am for you." He nodded. "And I'm grateful that I was here to see it."

"It might be nice if you could hang around long enough to meet the baby," Oliver suggested, hopefully.

"In this world or the next," his dad said, smiling. "It's God's plan, not mine."

Ain't that the truth, he thought, his mind racing out of control.

The old-timer kept smiling. "Trust me, if you were the one laying here, you'd see this baby for exactly what it is—a beautiful gift from God."

Oliver's eyes watered so much that he couldn't contain the tears.

◇◇◇

After returning home from the hospital, Oliver found Ginny waiting for him in the living room.

"I'd like to go to church this Sunday," she said, "okay?"

He didn't need to even think about it. "Okay," he agreed. "My dad can use the prayers."

She nodded. "Amongst other people in this family."

He matched her nod, thinking, *We definitely need some backup.*

"And there's something else I need," she added.

"What's that?"

"You."

"What?"

"I need my husband to make love to me tonight," she explained.

Oliver's instant excitement was peppered with fears of his intermittent performance issues.

Seeing this, Ginny grabbed his hand. "Let's go," she said, "there's never been a thing we can't fix together."

◇◇◇

The priceless stained glass windows filtered in colors of warmth and joy. The concave ceiling stretched forty feet to an exquisite portrait of plump cherubs battling demonic figures. Statues carved from marble kept vigil over centuries of tradition. A giant wooden crucifix hung above the altar and Oliver genuflected before taking his seat in the narrow pew. After speaking silently to the Lord, he skimmed through the weekly handout and scanned the crowd. *It's like years ago*, he thought, *when Saint Thomas More was standing room only*. Today, most communicants were elderly folks, those nearing the gates of heaven. Appropriately enough, they sat up front, while the younger families claimed the rear of the church.

On bended knee, Oliver prayed hard before mass began. *Father, forgive me for not coming to church more regularly and for only talking to you when I need something but, as you know, my dad is in pretty bad shape and needs all the help he can get right now. And Layla is all by herself overseas. Please shroud them in your angels and watch over them.* He looked sideways at his praying wife. *Our entire family needs your help,* he added. *In Jesus' name. Amen.*

With the help of an antique organ, the first notes of a small choir rang out, calling the congregation to its feet. On the first note, families surrendered their children to a teacher who waited in the rear. Kids were considered an interruption. Yet, not so long ago, both young and old alike—entire families—worshipped together. Somewhere along the way, the little unpredictable people were deemed nuisances and rounded up prior to mass. *It's sad,* Oliver thought. Worshipping alongside children always made him feel closer to God. *It seems the Lord would be more apt to listen to a tiny voice.*

The procession started at the rear of the church, with an altar boy guiding the way. A crucifix, fixed atop a long wooden pole, bobbed along, while the second boy steadied the oversized Holy Bible. Dressed in white and green, the priest nodded into aisle after aisle as he made his way toward the front. Oliver snickered. *Everything the Catholic Church does is ceremonial,* he thought, *even the priest's entrance.*

Father Bousquet commenced the Sunday mass and went through his perfected routine. Although it had been a long time since he'd attended, Oliver could have recited every word. People rose, stood and knelt without being directed. It was always the same: safe, predictable, and controlled.

After both readings and the Gospel, wicker baskets were passed from one person to the next to collect donations. Upon blessing the offerings, the enthusiastic priest asked that everyone offer each other a sign of peace. This was always Oliver's favorite. After shaking several hands, saying, "Peace be with you," he turned to his awaiting wife.

She leaned in and kissed his cheek. "Peace be with *us*," she whispered.

The simple message sent shivers down his spine. He kissed her back. "Amen to that," he whispered.

After receiving the Holy Eucharist, Oliver returned to the pew and silently spoke to God again. *Please Lord, bless my dad. Bless my children and my wife. Forgive us of our sins, and help us to do our best with the gifts you have given us. In Jesus' name. Amen.*

Kneeling beside him in the hard pew, Ginny finished her prayers in a whisper—loud enough for Oliver to hear her. "Please God," she whispered, "please help us to build a bridge that'll close the distance between us and unite us once again. We cannot do it alone. We've tried. Amen."

He stared at her in disbelief. *Her message wasn't only for God*, he realized, *and I'm clearly not the only one who wants a healthier marriage.*

◊◊◊

Doing anything he could to find a single moment of peace—a brief escape from reality—Oliver was reading a copy of *Ashes* in his recliner when he reached the story's wedding scene.

The white stretch limo pulled up, a dramatic pause preceding the gray-haired chauffeur opening the rear door. With a gloved hand, he politely helped the new Mrs. Mario Arruda out. Immediately, Miranda and Mario were met by a wave of applause. Yet, all eyes were glued on the bride. Some of those eyes watered. Others gazed dreamily from wishing themselves the same happiness.

Tom's niece was rapture, the perfect picture of beauty. Her makeup had been professionally applied; her permed hair, two hundred dollars prettier than the day before. Yet, it was the gown that stole the breath of the well-dressed mob that milled about. Miranda wore pure white, the lace and frills falling to a train that stretched ten feet behind her. She could not look more beautiful, Tom thought.

As he watched his full-grown niece from a distance, equal amounts of joy and guilt fought for his attention. At least you're here now, he told himself.

As Miranda's mom—Jason's ex-wife, Janice—fluffed her gown, the rest of the wedding party arrived. Betrayed by playful giggles, they'd already toasted the new couple more than once. The bridesmaids and Maid of Honor were dressed in pink chiffon. Like the bride, each wore tiny white flowers in her hair. Mario's best man and ushers strutted in black tuxedos with tails. The hats and canes added a touch of formal elegance. For the wedding of such a young couple, it's quite chic, Tom thought.

Although it was rainy season, the forecast promised a calm day. One could only hope. As the sun set on the water's flat horizon, the large wedding party gathered at the rustic gazebo to take pictures. Everyone beamed, especially Miranda. She constantly grabbed for Mario and stole every kiss she could.

Different poses and combinations of people were stiffly ordered by the photographer—all done only to be placed in an album and thrown on some closet shelf to collect years of dust, Tom thought, feeling sorry for himself. Still, in the unseasonably warm breeze, the wedding party took turns smiling. Miranda and Mario made sure that even years from now, they'd have concrete proof that on at least one day of their lives they'd experienced perfection. By the end of the shoot, a full moon broke through to shimmer on the bay's rippling water. Smiling, Tom started for the bathroom...

Yawning, Oliver began to analyze his own marriage.

For a long while, it had been a real struggle to remember when he and Ginny had once been so in love. *There was a time when I thought we'd found heaven on earth,* he pondered, shaking his head. *So how did we end up in hell?*

Feeling a pit in his stomach, Oliver sat for a few moments in silence when a different thought struck him. *What if we never had to live like this? What if my old man's right, and Ginny and I can go back to where we started?* His father's words rang loudly in his mind, *"For better or for worse; in sickness and in health, remember? I know I still remember my vows, and your mother's been gone for quite a while now."*

For far too long, the idea of rediscovering each other seemed laughable. *But we weren't always like this,* he repeated in his head. *I must keep trying. We both do. That stupid vacation cannot be our last shot. I won't allow it. She's my wife and we've put too much in.* Catapulting himself from his chair, he went searching the house for his and Ginny's wedding video. *I still love Ginny,* he thought, surprising himself with the unfamiliar thought. *I really do.*

It took a while, but he finally found the VHS tape and headed into Jonah's dungeon where an old VCR waited to provide evidence of their love.

Luna Bella Harbor hosted only the most prestigious and important functions. One step inside removed all questions as to why. The foyer welcomed visitors with a floor of white marble and plush green plants. It was gorgeous, with high-vaulted ceilings, antique moldings, and a wall of enormous windows that faced the ocean. Waves crashed off jagged rocks and continually sprayed the glass with a sea mist. One could almost taste the salt. Crystal chandeliers lit mahogany and brass-accented bars that sat beside fireside alcoves. A winding staircase led to the ballroom upstairs. Just past the coat check, an arrow pointed to some sinfully indulgent bathrooms. Inside, doting attendants offered cologne and fluffy towels. Amidst the luxurious sophistication, kids with untucked shirts and runny noses ran around and did what all-normal kids do: they explored and screamed in delight at each new discovery. The adolescents simply scanned the room in search of their prey. Weddings always moved stagnant hearts and inspired romance, even in the boys who were shy.

There were flowers everywhere. Most of them were out-of-season lilies that needed to be flown in. It was clear that Ginny's dad spared no expense in sending off his precious little girl. The best caterer in the Western Hemisphere—Fazzina's Cucina—had been hired to prepare a virtual cornucopia of delights. From cheese and fruit arrangements to the detailed ice sculpture of two smooching angels, the main course promised filet mignon, glazed baby carrots, and some type of potatoes no one could pronounce. For dessert, Ginny's childhood favorite completed the menu—fresh carrot cake with whipped cream cheese icing.

It was open bar, with as much beer and wine as anyone could consume. No one drank the hard stuff in those days anyway. Ginny's dad wanted a live band, claiming he would have gladly paid the extra two thousand, but Ginny, if only for the sake of her friends who loved to dance, insisted on a DJ. One never knew what to expect from a band. Oliver agreed. In fact, he'd agreed to everything. It was Ginny's big day and anything she wanted, she got. Weddings were different for girls. While grooms-in-waiting played baseball and chased frogs, their future wives were already preparing.

Bottles of expensive wine sat atop each table, while teenage waiters saving for college poured half-glasses in preparation for the toast. Favors had also been put near each place setting, evidence that months of careful thought had gone into every detail.

Three linen-covered tables were set up across the dance floor from the DJ The first held a giant wishing well, constructed to collect the cards. It filled quickly. The table in the middle held a three-tier cake, with a running fountain in the middle and a young couple on top. The tiny plastic lovers actually appeared to be looking down into the reflections the fountain created. The final table was used to gather presents. Neatly wrapped gifts covered in white and silver overflowed onto each other.

When Father Ballard, the priest who announced Oliver and Ginny as man and wife, arrived, a runaway cork from a bottle of champagne ricocheted squarely off his head. After brushing off his own sleeve, Ginny's father apologized for spilling the bubbly contents all over the good reverend and then began laughing hysterically. Thankfully, his pious victim joined him. Clearly, nothing could ruin this proud day. It was the best, as if his entire life had been spent preparing to give away his little girl's hand. It was almost a life's accomplishment that could not be put into words.

Oliver watched in awe as he and his young bride took to the parquet floor for their first dance as man and wife. Moving in closer to the TV, he studied her face; her smile was genuine and contagious. *She was really happy then*, he remembered, *and so was I*. He paused the video tape—to where she was staring into his loving eyes. In that big, crowded room, it was only them—Oliver and Ginny—in that moment in time. They were together, as one. He rewound the tape several times to relive the moment, filling his heart with equal amounts of hope and love as he did. *We need to get back to that*, he told himself. *But is it possible? What would I tell Jonah, if he were in the same situation?*

The words immediately came to him. *Marriage requires work. I don't care who you are.*

And then he heard his own father's voice in his head. *Baby steps, Ollie. All champion runners start off with baby steps.*

He paused the tape again to a perfect frame of he and Ginny gazing into each other's eyes. *Somewhere deep down, the spark that started it all is still there*, he thought, *a smoldering fire. I just know it!* He nodded a few times, his eyes filling with tears. *I just need to blow harder on it and give it the oxygen it needs to jump back to life.*

What I wouldn't do to see Ginny smile again, Oliver thought, *really smile*. It suddenly hit him. *I need to ask her out on a date*, he decided. *She'll think I'm messing with her at first, but she'll come around.*

Without hesitation, he called her cell phone.

After three rings, she picked up. "Hello."

"Hi, it's me."

"Oh, hey," she said, her voice flat, "what's up? Is it your dad?"

"No, no," he said, "I wanted to give you a call to ask you if you wanted to go out on a date with me."

"I'm at the market, Oliver," she replied, her voice sounding suspicious, "and the place is packed."

He paused to feel the sting. "This is important," he said, lowering his tone.

She was quiet on the other end.

He cleared his throat. "Sorry Ginny, I'll let you go."

"W...wait," she said. "I'm sorry. It's just so chaotic here right now. I was trying to find a quiet corner to talk."

He waited hopefully in the silence.

"I'd love to go on a date with you, Oliver," she whispered.

"Good," he said, "then I'll plan a nice night for us. It's been too long."

"I agree," she said, "it has." This was followed by a click and then silence.

I have a date, Oliver thought, feeling more excited about his marriage than he had for years. He thought about the shit-eating grin his father was guaranteed to wear when he heard the news. He chuckled. *Thanks Dad.*

Slowly returning to reality, Oliver checked his cell phone for the time. *It's 3:46 p.m. here which means it's 9:46 p.m. in Montenegro.* Shrugging, he called his dearly-missed daughter, being forced to leave yet another message. "Layla, I have bad news." He cleared his throat. "Your grandfather's health is declining, and we need to make arrangements for you to communicate with him...maybe we can set up a Facetime session?" *Before it's too late,* he thought, keeping that part to himself.

CHAPTER 11

A full moon passed when Layla's beautiful face appeared on the bright laptop screen. She had a great smile, with two rows of pearl white teeth—thanks to years of her dad's overtime and some significant dental reengineering.

"There's my angel," Robert said, smiling through a coughing fit, "I knew you'd find a way to come see me."

Oliver adjusted the laptop on his father's lap. "Just don't touch anything and you'll be fine, Dad," he said, before popping his head in front of the screen. "Hi, babe," he told Layla, "I'm going to step out of the room so you and Grandpa can have some privacy, okay?"

"Okay, Dad. Thanks."

"Love you."

"Love you too, Dad," she said.

Keeping his word, Oliver quickly left the room.

Robert palmed the thin computer on his lap and made a funny face. "I thought he'd never leave us."

Layla laughed for a moment, before her eyes turned sad. "Oh, Grandpa," she whimpered, sounding two decades younger.

"I knew you'd visit me," he repeated, studying her porcelain face. "How's Monte Carlo?"

"It's Montenegro."

"I knew that. I was just teasing."

"Sure, you were." She had her father's chocolate eyes and her mother's perfect bone structure.

"Well, they haven't zapped any of that sass out of you. That's good."

"Never," she said.

"Good girl." He took in some much-needed oxygen. "So, you're happy there?"

"I am. I think I've found my purpose, Grandpa. I always knew that I wanted to be a teacher. Now I realize that I *need* to be a teacher."

"It's your calling then." He smiled, or at least tried. "What a blessing to discover that early in your life," he whispered. "I'm so happy for you... and proud."

She took a few rapid breaths.

"Layla Earle," he said, "you have no idea how glad I am to hear all of this before I head home."

Layla began crying, her body visibly stiffening.

"Don't you dare feel bad for me, sweetheart. I slept indoors most of my life," he whispered, grinning. "I was lucky like that."

"Even now, you've got jokes, Gramps," she whimpered, shaking her head.

"Now more than ever," he confessed, before diving back into her eyes. His grin faded away. "Will you come home to teach, or stay abroad?"

"I don't know if I can be happy living there anymore," she confessed.

"Really? And why's that?"

"The people. I'd like to live where the people are different."

"You mean the people in your family, right?" he said, calling it out.

She half-shrugged.

Robert's smile returned. "I remember a story that a wise friend once told me. Do you have time to hear it?"

"Of course," she said, leaning in closer to the screen.

He cleared his throat. "An old man was sitting with his grandson on the front porch of a gas station. A car pulled up, stuffed with luggage and boxes. 'Hey buddy, how are the people in this town,' the driver asked, 'friendly or not? We're thinking about moving.'

"'What are the people like in the town you live in now?' the old man asked.

"'Terrible,' the man said. 'We can't stand any of them, which is why we're moving,' the driver explained.

"'I believe you'll find that the folks in this town are pretty much the same.'

"'Sorry to hear that,' the man said, driving off.

"Two weeks later, the old man and his grandson were sitting on that same porch when a different car pulled up. The driver got out and asked, 'Excuse me, sir, but can I ask...what are the people like in this town? Are they warm to newcomers? We're thinking about moving.'

"'What are the people like in the town you live in now?' the old man asked, while his grandson looked on.

"'They're the most wonderful folks in the world,' the driver said, 'In fact, we hate to leave, but—'

"'No need to worry, my friend,' the old man interrupted, 'the folks in this town are just as wonderful.'

"'Great, thanks! I appreciate the insight,' the man said, driving off.

"The little boy turned to his grandfather. 'I don't understand, Grandpa. You told that man a few weeks back that our townsfolk were terrible people and then you told this man that they're wonderful.'

"'Boy,' the old-timer said, 'It's folks' attitudes that decide how happy they are, and what they think of those around them. People carry their judgements with them—good or bad.'" Robert smiled. "The one person you can never escape from is yourself, so make sure you keep a good attitude."

Robert brought the laptop closer to his face and smiled. "We can't run from ourselves or our families, Layla. Believe me, I've tried."

"I get it, Gramps."

He studied her face. "Whether you come back or stay, just make sure you're doing it for the right reasons. You'll teach wherever you end up, we both know that. But the people you surround yourself with will help to define your life."

Kissing two of her fingers, Layla placed them to the computer screen. "Thank you," she whispered.

"No, sweetheart, thank you. From the moment you were born, you've been one of the greatest gifts God has ever given me, and I've thanked him on bended knee every day since."

Her eyes leaked faster. "I love you," she whimpered.

"I love you too," he said, "and nothing—not even death—can ever change that."

They stared at each other in wonderful silence for a while when Layla announced, "My dad said he asked my mother out on a date."

"He did?" Robert said, surprised by this.

"He did."

"It's about damn time."

They both laughed.

"The only thing I ever wanted from them is that they try," she said.

Robert kissed his own fingers and placed them to the screen. "It looks like you're finally getting your wish then."

◊◊◊

"All right then, Pete, we'll see you on the other side," Robert said, watching his next guest exit the room.

"Who was that?" his son asked, just arriving.

"Some buffoon I used to work with, Ollie," Robert explained. "I thought he came to pay me the money he owes me, but no such luck. I think he was just trying to confirm that I'm really on my way out."

"Dad, that's..."

Robert pointed toward the door. "Trust me, Pistol Pete Hill leaving this room is what you call addition by subtraction. He's always been an individual playing a team sport." He gave his head one final shake before returning to his son.

"How was your online visit with Layla?" his son asked.

He nodded. "She looks great. I'm proud of that kid."

"Me too," Oliver said. "Listen, I have a couple of announcements." His face looked content for the first time in several long weeks.

"Oh yeah?"

"I've decided that I'm going to fight for my wife," he announced. "Life's too short to let my family just slip away from me."

"Good for you!"

"I just hope it's not too late, Dad."

"At least you'll know, without any questions or regrets." He half-shrugged. "But you won't know if it's too late until you give it the old college try."

"Well, I took the first step and asked Ginny out on a proper date— and she accepted!"

Although he acted surprised, even on his deathbed he couldn't help but to gloat. "I hate to say that I told you so, Ollie, but—"

"But you told me so," his son finished for him.

"So where are you taking the pretty lady?"

"Somewhere quiet where we can talk. It's been a long time."

"Good for you. I'm happy for you." He nodded. "If you can't fight for your own wife, then who can you fight for?"

His son nodded in agreement. "I had some solid coaching." He smiled wide.

"You don't say?" he said, doing all he could not to giggle.

"I think we're finally on the right track."

"You have no idea how grateful I am to hear all of this!"

"And I need to show you this," Oliver said, as excited as the boy he'd once been on Christmas morning. He handed over the morning newspaper.

Robert grabbed it from him and read,

Robert Earle Laughter & Wishes Comedy Night
Benefit for Dylan Vasconcellos

His eyes immediately filled, making it hard to read.

Friends of Dylan Vasconcellos will be hosting the first annual "Robert Earle Laughter & Wishes Comedy Night" at the Liberal Club in Fall River, MA on Thursday, November 17th.

Four hilarious stand-up comics will take the stage to make the audience laugh themselves all the way to their wallets and purses. The doors will open at 6:30 p.m., the show starts at 8:00 p.m., and for a minimum donation of $25.00, we promise a night to remember.

Fall River's own funny man, as well as one of the hottest, up-and-coming comics in the industry, Smokin' Joe Holden, will be hosting the event.

The host of The Wicked Funny Comedy Tour on NESN's Dirty Water TV, Dave Russo is also a winner of the Boston Comedy Festival. Besides headlining at the Tropicana in Las Vegas, he has also appeared on the popular E! Entertainment series, The Entertainer, hosted by Wayne Newton.

Comic Chris Tabb has appeared on BET's Comic View, NESN's Comedy All-Stars, opened nationally around the country for Monique, and is one of the fastest rising stars in Boston comedy.

The show's headliner, The Comedy Diva, Stephanie Peters, has appeared on Denis Leary's annual show, Comics Come

Home. Stephanie won the Marshall's Women in Comedy Festival where she opened for Joy Behar (from ABC's The View). Stephanie's outrageous stories and zany opinions have made her a favorite with audiences.

Door prizes, a silent auction, and a Pick-and-Pull raffle promise restaurant gift certificates, sports memorabilia, and tickets to the best amusements and shows throughout New England. All proceeds from Laughter and Wishes will benefit Dylan Vasconcellos.

If you would like to purchase a ticket(s), please contact Oliver Earle at 508-675-3677.

"Thank you, Ollie," he whimpered, folding the paper and tucking it under his bed sheets to read again later.

"Of course, Dad," he said. "Once my merry band of volunteers and I complete the preparation, ticket sales will be the true test."

Robert never realized that he could feel great—and terrible—all at the same time. "You do realize I won't be there this year?"

"I'll be there for you," Oliver said.

"Thank you, son."

"And every year after that."

Robert began to quietly cry, making Oliver do the same.

Once he composed himself to speak, Robert teased, "A woman comedian, huh?"

"Yup, that's right, Archie Bunker, and she's one of the best in the business." They both laughed.

After a while, Robert said, "I couldn't be any more proud of you than I am." He nodded. "I'm so proud of the man you've become."

Oliver actually choked on the unexpected compliment.

Robert scolded himself for taking so long to put his feelings into words. *It's what I've felt for my boy since his very first breath.*

"Proud of me for what?" Oliver mumbled.

"For everything," he said, trying to get comfortable in his bed. "You're even standing up and fighting for love now."

He smiled. "What about you?" his son asked, scrambling to recover. "You never fell in love again after Mom passed. Why not?"

Robert gave it some thought. "I dated a few times, some nice ladies too. But all it did was make me more sore at your mom for dying on me." He shook his head. "Just the thought of getting to know somebody new all over again was heartbreaking. Holding hands with a stranger. I just didn't have the energy or the interest. The entire thing reminded me of how lucky your mom and I were to have found each other, how happy I'd been all my life—how in love we'd been. I felt too blessed to even consider sharing any of that with someone new. It would have felt like I was betraying all those memories with your mom, and the life she and I had built together."

"What about Peggy?" Oliver asked, fighting off a grin.

"She's been a good friend, nothing else. She visits me in the mornings when you're at work and I appreciate that."

"Oh, I bet you do, Dad," he teased. "Nothing else, huh?"

Robert ignored the comment. "Truth be told, even though I never found someone after your mom, your mom—the most important piece of her, anyway—is still with me." He shifted again, still trying to get more comfortable on the bed. "How could I spend time with another woman and ever expect to experience a fraction of the joy I'd known with your mother? The entire practice of dating just seemed foolish to me. I believe we're blessed with one great love in our lives."

Oliver's eyes hit the floor.

"How arrogant to believe that anyone deserves that same blessing twice?"

Oliver nodded.

"Ollie," Robert called out, calling for his son's full attention, "the best part of me was your mother."

"And you always felt that way?"

He nodded. "The scary part was there was once me. And me became us. And it stayed that way for so long that when *us* no longer existed, I didn't know how to just be me again. I felt lost." He shook his head. "Never alone, but definitely lost."

Oliver exhaled deeply.

"And that's the love I wish for you, son." He smiled. "And I really believe that it isn't too late for you to have that."

"I hope that's true, Dad."

"Until you're laying here," Robert said, raising his voice, "it's never too late to create the life you want to live."

"Listen, we need to go fishing before I die," Robert insisted after they'd eaten the Italian grinders that Oliver had smuggled in, "and it needs to be soon."

Oliver visibly cringed at the truth of it. "Don't say that, Dad."

"It's true, Ollie, and it's fine. I've accepted it." He looked at him, gasping for air. "Do you want to go fishing or not?"

"Of course, I do," Oliver said, his eye misting over, "but I'm not sure they'll let you get out of here. You're really sick, Dad."

"You don't think I know that? It's now or never, kid," he said, "and as far as I know, this isn't a prison. If I want to die by the side of a pond—God forbid—then that's my choice. Besides, they don't have enough people working in this joint to stop me and you." He smiled. "As long as we keep it tight and fight together."

Oliver laughed. "No question," he said. "And of course I want to go fishing. Maybe I can ask the kids too."

"Just you and me for this trip," he said.

Oliver looked at him. "But I thought you hate fishing?"

"I do," he admitted, "but you need to understand why." He shook his head. "And I should have explained it a long time ago." This wasn't about extending a kind and sentimental gesture; this was about him needing to express his love in a way—*that can never be questioned or confused for the rest of Oliver's life.*

Oliver opened his mouth but couldn't manage another word.

"Let's go first light," he said, "and then you can take me back here for my final tune-up."

"Okay, Dad," Oliver mumbled.

"Offshore, though. No boats!"

"Got it, no boats."

"And we'll take Luna with us. I have a few things I need to tell her."

Oliver nodded. "Of course."

A grin burrowed its way into the corners of Robert's mouth. "Good," he said, "and we should probably make it interesting."

"How do you mean?"

"Whoever catches the most fish buys the beer, okay?"

"Beer?" Oliver's voice raised a full octave.

Robert laughed. "Okay, Jell-O then."

They shook hands. "Deal."

The logistics were a nightmare—the stack of documents requiring signatures of indemnification before leaving the hospital; borrowing a proper vehicle for transportation; an oxygen bottle attached to a wheelchair that was never designed for the rough terrain they needed to traverse.

Once they reached the pond and settled in—with Luna wagging her tail by Robert's side—Oliver teased, "It's a good thing you waited to take me fishing again when it was easy."

As Robert laughed, he stared at the water while stroking Luna's neck.

"So your birthday's coming up, Dad," Oliver reminded him, casting bait for the first time in years.

"Another birthday would be a win," he replied.

"That's one way to think about it," Oliver said, taking a break to worm his father's hook.

It's funny how life's come full circle, Robert thought. "From where I sit," he said, tilting his face to the sun, "it's the only way to think about it."

Oliver cast the line for his dad before picking up his own fiberglass rod again.

"None of us are getting out of this alive," Robert confirmed, grinning. Just then, his bobber went under. He jerked it once to set the hook and then extended the bent pole to his son. "This one's all yours, kid."

His eyes misting over, Oliver reeled the fish in, making Robert laugh as he fumbled to take it off the hook.

"Yeah, you love fishing all right," Robert teased.

"Not really," Oliver admitted, "but I've always liked spending time with you."

"I know that," Robert said, feeling his heart nearly burst for this blessed opportunity to explain himself, "and there's something you need to know about that, Ollie."

Oliver let the fish go before rebaiting the hook.

"I went to Vietnam and..."

"I know, Dad," Oliver said, "you don't need to talk about it, if it's gonna upset you."

Robert shook him off. "Nam was a bitch. Too many young guys died—just kids, for God's sake! For those of us who did make it home, there was only one message to tell: Never forget those who sacrificed everything and didn't make it back. Many families lost a son, a father, a brother, or a sister—their lives changed forever." He shook his head. "I'm not just speaking for myself, but the Vietnam vets really got screwed, you know."

"I agree," Oliver said.

"No respect and recognition from the government or the citizens of this country." While his hands began to tremble, his breathing became shallow.

"Dad, you don't have to explain."

Robert soldiered on. "I served on the water, Ollie, and saw some things that no man should ever see."

Oliver's eyes filled with tears for his father's long-suffered pain.

Robert extended both forearms. "G.G. doesn't stand for good guy, son. It stands for Georgey Gouveia, my best friend who died over there." Even now, saying it aloud choked him up.

"Georgey Gouveia?" Oliver repeated.

"My buddy from Nam," he confirmed.

His son's eyes went straight to the *G.G.* branded on his forearm. "G.G.," he said aloud. From the shock in his face, he clearly never knew what those two initials stood for until this very moment. "Oh, my God," he muttered.

"It wasn't that I didn't want to go fishing with you, Ollie," Robert said, "At the time..." He stopped to dab the tears from his face. "At the time, I just couldn't."

Oliver dropped his pole and collapsed to the grass beside his father's chair. He began weeping and couldn't stop, healing from the pains and penalties of his childhood.

"I'm sorry, son," Robert said, squeezing his middle-aged boy's convulsing shoulder. "I'm so sorry."

While the red and white bobber disappeared beneath the water's surface a second time, the healing between them was well underway.

"I wish I'd been a better dad, Ollie," he whimpered. "Even though you and I lived under the same roof, I admit that I took you for granted." He shook his head, still disappointed at himself. "I was too busy and I shouldn't have been, not when it came to you. Although it's no excuse, I was pretty messed up for some years because of my military service. I tried my best."

"Please stop apologizing, Dad," Oliver said, cutting him off. "If I'm being honest, I never really understood you or why you did some of the things you did until I had my own children and became a father, myself."

Robert listened, gratefully.

"I now understand that being a parent is a high-wire act of knowing when to push and when to pull back. It's most important to be there for our kids always—to be present." He peered into his dad's eyes. "You did the best you could. I know that now, and I appreciate it!"

Robert studied his son's face. Again, he saw no resentment or anger. *Thank God!*

"Sometimes a parent's best move is to remain silent," Oliver went on, "while the world teaches the tough lessons we all need to learn. The hardest thing is having to sit back and not save our kids when it would be so easy to do so."

"Amen to that," Robert said.

"Whether we acknowledge it or not, all parents bring their own baggage into the relationship with their children." He stopped. "If I'm being truthful with you, Dad, my fear of disappointing my father—you—was hard-coded in me and has been my baggage." He shrugged. "I never wanted my children to suffer the same, even when they did disappoint me." He nodded. "Especially then."

Robert nodded, struggling to keep his emotions under lock and key. "Well, you can let that shit go," he mumbled.

Oliver looked at him. "Please don't ever apologize to me again, Dad. I wouldn't be who I am if it wasn't for you and everything you taught me."

Robert began to cry again, unashamed. His boy's kind words were healing his soul. *Thank you, son!* He grabbed Oliver's hand and held on for dear life.

As they sat together at the water's edge, holding hands, both wept freely—Robert never imagining such a thing.

They dropped Luna back off at the house, where Robert and his mutt shared an emotional goodbye. "You be a good girl," he told the whimpering dog, "and make sure you listen to Ollie. I'll be waiting for you when you're ready to come home." He kissed the dog.

"Do you want to stop for a bite to eat?" Oliver asked, obviously struggling to maintain his composure.

He shook his head. "I don't think I could keep it down right now, Ollie. My insides are churning pretty good."

They were nearly back to the hospital when Robert announced, "I think righting a wrong may be one of the most noble pursuits we can ever undertake." He nodded. "You don't want to be bringing extra baggage into the next world, Ollie," he added with a firm nod. "Trust me on this one."

"As far as I'm concerned, you'll be travelling luggage-free, Dad."

"That's been the goal," he said, before starting to fight for oxygen. "I'm ready to go, Ollie," he wheezed. "What I want, I can't get here."

"And what's that?" Oliver asked, pressing down hard on the accelerator.

"For the good Lord to smile at me."

Tears streamed down his son's handsome face.

"When it's time for me to go home to my father, it's important that I'm able to look back on this crazy ride and smile," the sickly man explained between gasps of air, "with love in my heart and peace in my mind. I'm grateful, for the good and the bad—all of it." He paused to breathe. "For those who loved me and even those who refused to, I learned from each and every one."

"Save your breath, Dad," Oliver said, "I need to get you back to the hospital and..."

He waved him off. "When I was a young man, I admired brawn. I grew older and began to respect brains. But only when I really matured did I realize that the one true key to a successful, accomplished life is kindness." He stopped to increase his oxygen intake. "If you're nothing else, Ollie, be kind. It's enough...more than enough." He extended his bony hand across the front seat for a shake.

With one hand on the wheel, Oliver accepted it. They shook.

"You'll never be alone, son," he said, "I can guarantee you that."

"And you'll never be forgotten, Dad," Oliver replied. "You have my word."

◊◊◊

Robert's pain medicine was being increased by the day, sending him into la-la land. Although he nodded off throughout the day, he was still sometimes aware of what was going on around him—like being in two worlds at one time. He could hear Oliver talking and focused on his son's distressed voice.

"I feel lost, Dad," the middle-aged man confessed, "and sometimes I feel alone."

You're never alone, son, Robert replied in his mind, *I'm here with you, always have been.*

"As a kid, I never really forgave you and Mom for making me an only child. Maybe that's where I learned to feel alone? You weren't around a lot back then and..." His words drifted off.

Ugh... Robert concentrated harder.

"So I insisted that Ginny and I have at least two kids...to keep each other company." There was a pause. "You once told me that being a good dad is synonymous with being a decent man." He cleared his throat. "You can't imagine how often I wonder whether I've achieved either."

Are you crazy, Ollie? You're a wonderful dad and a great man! Every father has his doubts, son, and none of us are perfect, but you...

"I wonder if you felt the same way when you were my age?"

Of course I did, and every day after that from the moment you were born.

"I suppose it's more important to concentrate on what I can do from here on."

Yes.

"And that's what I'll do.

That's my boy...

Robert was suspended in deep slumber when his mind began to spin out of control. *I'm dying*, he told himself. Both his breathing and heart rate simultaneously quickened. *I'm actually dying.*

He then watched as a parade of friendly faces—those who had long passed away—floated by him. Ma, Ruthie, Georgey, his brother, Bay. The anxiety symptoms began to subside. *I've got some good people waiting on me*, he thought. *There should be nothing to worry about.* As he watched the parade pass him by a second time, he could hear his own childish giggle. *I'm going home*, he realized. *I'm finally going home!*

◊◊◊

After fidgeting with his supper, Robert began fashioning two sailor's knots with the rope Oliver had brought him—one for each of his grandchildren. The sailor knot's design was best known in summer bracelets: kids shrunk them to their wrists in ocean water, wore them all summer long until they were filthy, and then had them cut off, revealing a ring of untanned skin that commemorated a season of good memories made with friends and family. Robert, however, was focused on creating a much more intricate design for his grandchildren's keepsakes—*something that's sure to endure*, he thought.

"Most folks believe that these simple knots were created by sailors during their long voyages as a way of remembering their loved ones," he explained to Oliver, while his blotched veiny hands worked the ropes. "They're a symbol of friendship and love." He stopped for a second to look up. "Something for the kids to remember me by."

"Layla and Jonah don't need something to remember you by, Dad," Oliver said, choking on the words, "but it's definitely something they'll cherish forever." He nodded. "I know I would," he added under his breath.

With a dismissive nod, Robert continued with the tedious work. "It won't be long for me now," he whispered as he worked.

"You don't know that," his son said, still refusing to accept the inevitable.

"I do, Ollie," he said. "Your mom comes to visit me now."

"When?" Oliver asked, his face contorted in disbelief.

"Every night." He nodded. "Every night for the past week."

"Every night?" Oliver repeated, his voice cracking. "Do you see her, Dad? Can you talk to her?"

He shook his head. "I can feel her presence. I'd know Ruthie in a crowded room before I ever set eyes on her."

Twin tears raced down his son's cheeks.

"Your mother was loyal to a fault," he said, yanking Oliver back into the room. He smirked. "I could lie about anything and that woman would swear to it."

Oliver laughed. "Ain't that the truth,"

"Did you know that I used to hide her Christmas gifts in the cleaning closet where she'd never find them?"

Oliver laughed. "You're so bad."

"It's true." His eyes still shined brightly when he thought about her. "Your mother was many wonderful things, but being domesticated wasn't one of them."

"I guess it wasn't one of your top five requirements on the list, huh?" Oliver teased.

Shaking his head, Robert maintained his giant smile. "Not even close."

"If she wasn't my mother, I might ask you what those were."

"I'd never tell anyway. That was between Ruthie and me."

Another miraculous hour passed when Robert cleared his throat. "Make sure you remember to grab my shoebox money when I finally get out of here."

"Shoebox money?" Oliver repeated, confused.

He forced a smile. "The wad of cash hidden in a shoebox on the top shelf of my bedroom closet."

Oliver's forehead creased in surprise.

"Don't forget about it, okay? I want you to get yourself and Ginny some ice cream with that money." He shrugged. "There might even be enough there for you to take her out on that date?"

Oliver grinned. "I don't want your money, Dad."

"It ain't much, believe me."

"How much?" Oliver asked.

"Enough for a few ice cream cones, sprinkles and all."

His son laughed.

Robert looked at him until their eyes locked. "Stop worrying about me, Ollie. I'll be okay," he claimed, reaching for his son's hand again.

"I...I..." Oliver stuttered.

"I'll be fine when the time comes. I can feel it."

Oliver swallowed hard, struggling to speak. "But how will *I* know you're okay, Dad?"

"I'll send you a sign."

"What kind of sign?"

He thought about it for a moment until it struck him like a bolt of lightning. "I'll send you feathers."

"Feathers?"

"Yes, bird feathers, and not the small white ones either." He nodded, his smile growing wider. "I'll send you grey and brown feathers—big ones, okay?" His eyes drifted off, as he was already picturing them.

"Okay, Dad," Oliver managed. "I'll be on the lookout for grey and brown feathers."

"No need, Ollie," he said, "they'll find you, I promise." He could feel his son's heart breaking, piece-by-bloody piece—and it fractured his own heart. He clamped down harder on his boy's hand. "I'll be okay, son," he repeated, "I know it as much as I've ever known anything."

"Okay, Dad. I'll be waiting on those feathers."

With a single nod, Robert closed his eyes. "I'm so tired, Ollie," he admitted, "tell me a story."

"A story?"

"Yeah, a story."

"What are you, five years old again?" his son teased.

He opened one eye. "I can be any age I want to be right now."

"That's true," Oliver said. "If you want to return to being a little boy again, then who am I to—"

"And make it a funny one," Robert added, interrupting. "I'm about done with serious."

"O...okay," Oliver said, thinking about it. "Unfortunately, I have more serious stories to share than funny ones," he admitted. "I'm going to have to fix that."

"Glad to hear it!" he said. "Laughter is good for the soul, Ollie."

"I'm starting to learn that. Oh, I've got one!" he called out.

Robert took a deep breath, relaxing his body. "Lay it on me."

"Ginny and I were at the Christening of a very good friend's grandson. The families have been very close for years."

Robert nodded, his eyes still closed, his mind at peace.

"Anyway, this little guy, Jack—the baby's brother—had to use the bathroom to pee. Considering that he calls me Uncle Oliver, I told his parents that I'd be happy to take him. Given the chaos of the moment, they seemed happy that I volunteered.

"So, we walked to the basement of the church and finally located the small, cramped men's room. I opened the stall door, flipped the lid on the toilet and positioned him in front of me. *If he gets his suit wet, then we're both in trouble*, I figured."

Robert laughed, already enjoying the tale.

"So as I was helping him pull his pants down, I realized he was too short to hit the bowl, so I lifted him from both sides of his waist. We were just in time because he wasn't waiting to start the water works. While he urinated, he squirmed a bit, uncomfortable with being off the ground. 'Don't worry,' I told him, 'Uncle's got you.'

"He looked up at me—still peeing.

"'I got you, Jack,' I confirmed.

"As he finished his business, I asked him to stand near the stall door so that I could pee too. Turning my back to him, I began to take a leak—realizing the window of opportunity was only as long as his level of patience. I figured, *The last thing I need right now is to find out that Jack's a flight risk.* Suddenly, I felt two small hands rest on both sides of my waist."

Robert laughed harder.

"'Don't worry, Uncle,' the little guy said, 'I got you.'

"I started laughing—right up until the moment I pictured someone walking in on us and thinking the absolute worse. *If this door opens*, I thought, *I may have to talk to the cops as well as the priest.*

"'I got you,' Jack repeated, never letting go of me until I finished."

Robert's eyes flew open; he could feel his face turning red from laughing.

"So together, Jack and I bellied up to the sink. I lifted him again, so he could wash his hands. 'Thanks for the help,' I told him.

"He looked at me in the mirror and nodded. 'You're welcome,' he said, his face serious."

Robert laughed right up until saying, "Thank you for that, Ollie. I needed it."

"You're welcome, Dad," Oliver said, "I got you."

Robert closed his eyes again and smiled. *Don't I know it, son.*

Once Oliver left for the night and Robert could be alone—*a rare commodity these days*, he thought—he started in on his final masterpiece. The double-fisherman's knot was also known as the impossible knot because, although it was easy enough to tie, it was nearly impossible to break apart. Used to tie two ends of a rope together, it was actually two knots that slid together. Over time, the knots essentially sealed themselves as one, and the only way to undo them was to cut them out.

Doing his best to sit up straight in the bed, Robert set his two pieces of rope side-by-side. He took the end of the first rope and wound it loosely two times near the end of the second rope. He then took the first rope and pulled it back through the inside of the loops or coils that he'd just created and pulled hard to tighten them—creating the first knot. He then took the short end of the second rope, and pulled a little to give himself more rope to work with. Taking that lengthened second rope, he repeated his earlier steps, only to wind the second rope in the opposite direction than he'd wound the first rope. After he created and tightened the second knot, he pulled on each rope's main ends and the two knots slid together. "And there it is," he whispered, "bound together forever."

Although he'd never remembered feeling more exhausted, he wore a smile on his face. *Forever*, he thought, before nodding off.

CHAPTER 12

Jonah was stepping out of class when he spotted his father approaching on the college quad. "What are you doing here, Dad?" He thought about it. "And how did you get here? Your car..."

"I borrowed your mom's car today," his father explained. "Listen, I needed to talk to you, and what I have to tell you might get lost over texts."

While a small herd of coeds stampeded around them, they both took a seat on an empty bench.

"Do you trust me?" his dad asked, looking him in the eye.

"Of course I do, Dad," Jonah said, enthusiastically, "ever since I was a kid, you've had my back." His mind flashed back to one of countless examples.

He was young, maybe twelve, when his dad walked into his bedroom and caught him pleasuring himself to a flickering computer screen. *Oh shit.* Red-faced, he immediately covered up, while his father quickly left the room.

A half hour later, someone knocked long and hard on his bedroom door before entering; it was his dad again.

Jonah couldn't even meet his eyes.

"I just wanted to apologize," his father said, closing the door behind him. "I should've knocked before."

"I wasn't doing anything, Dad," the preadolescent fibbed.

His father took a seat on the edge of his twin bed. "No need to be embarrassed, Jonah," he said, ignoring the lie. "What you were doing is normal and very natural, especially for a young man your age."

Jonah reluctantly looked up at him.

"We all do it," his dad confirmed.

"*We* do?"

The man nodded. "We do, son." He grinned. "But remember, we're not chimpanzees. We don't do it in the middle of the mall or other public places."

Jonah fought off a smile.

"We do it in privacy, discreetly," his father added with a nod, "and without shame, okay?"

He returned the nod.

"Okay," his father confirmed, before leaving the room. "If you ever need to talk about sex, I'm here—no embarrassment or judgment."

"Good," his dad said, awaiting his return to the present. "Then trust me now." He leaned in until they were face-to-face. "You are not small, Jonah," his dad whispered, like he knew this message was exactly what Jonah needed to hear. "You're a giant, son."

"I know that," Jonah said, gratefully.

"Oh yeah, how?"

"Because you made sure of it."

"Just remember that," his dad said, before standing up and walking away.

What? Jonah thought, *You came all the way down here just to tell me that?* He watched as the kind man's silhouette grew smaller and smaller in the distance. *Thanks Dad!*

◊◊◊

Marissa DeSousa was first generation American. Both of her parents had emigrated from the Azores, so to say that her father was old school Portuguese was about as accurate a description as there was. Jonah lost his breath when they pulled up to the house. "Are you sure they have no idea you're pregnant?" he asked his anxious girlfriend.

"I think my mother has her suspicions that something's going on, but she doesn't know."

"And your father?"

"Not a clue."

"Great," he said. As he stepped out of the car, his legs turned to jelly.

As if they were heading toward the electric chair, they took the long walk up the colorful flagstone path to the kitchen door.

Marissa's mother was standing at the stove, cooking something that smelled extra spicy.

"Mom," Marissa said, her voice quivering, "Jonah and I need to talk to you and dad about something."

"Your daddy just got home from work," she said. "He's very tired."

"I know Ma, but this is important. We—"

"Louis," she screamed, "come here please!"

Jonah had met the giant a half dozen times, hoping that each time would get easier. It never did. He was a man of few words and an uneasy stare.

A terrifying thought flashed through Jonah's mind. *If Mr. DeSousa went on a rampage, the only thing that could probably stop him is his wife.*

The bear of a man stomped into the room. He was wearing worn jeans, a green button down shirt, and steel-toed work boots—the entire outfit covered in layers of dirt that matched his massive paws.

That shirt has to be a 3X, Jonah thought, trying to slow his breathing.

"What is it?" he asked, glancing suspiciously at Jonah. "Time to eat?"

"Can we all sit down at the table?" Marissa suggested.

The man's eyes immediately found Jonah's, snatching away a lung full of air from him. "What's this?" he asked, already annoyed.

As if someone had kicked his legs out from under him, Jonah collapsed into the first available seat at the table.

"Mommy, Daddy," Marissa began, reaching for Jonah's sweaty hand. "We have something we need to tell you." She began to cry.

"What is it, sweetheart?" her mother asked, hurrying to embrace her daughter.

"I am... I'm..."

"Please don't say you're pregnant," her mother mumbled.

Jonah watched as her father's eyes darted from one person at the table to the next, clearly confused about what was going on.

"I am," Marissa confessed, crying harder.

"What?" the confused man asked. "What's going on?"

Weeping alongside her daughter, the woman told her husband, "Marissa's going to have a baby."

Jonah took a deep breath to be able to speak. "It's not how we planned it, Mr. and Mrs. DeSousa," he blurted, "but we're going to do this together." Struggling to be strong, he nodded. "We're going to have a family."

While his nostrils flared, the man's dark eyes constricted to furious slits. He lifted his giant fist into the air, slamming it on the table—making everyone jump.

Jonah's heart skipped three beats. Instantly, his forehead glistened with sweat, his hands began to tremble, and his breathing became so shallow that he felt dizzy.

The Portuguese bear stood and pointed to the door. "You get the hell out of my house right now," he hissed through gritted teeth, "or I'll be spending the rest of my life in prison."

"But Daddy," Marissa screamed, "it's not..."

For a split second, his eyes found his daughter's before filling with equal amounts of disappointment and disgust.

"Now!" he screamed, returning his attention to Jonah.

Jonah didn't know how he managed it, but he was able to backpedal toward the door. "Marissa," he called out.

Mr. DeSousa threw his chair across the floor, taking an aggressive step toward him.

Jonah found the door handle behind him, his hand slipping on the knob. He finally opened it and, on his way out, he caught Marissa's eyes. "I love you," he yelled—watching as the furious man was coming for him.

Jonah was halfway home before he was able to breathe again. The truth hurt him. *Marissa's parents will never want me to see her again.* He began to cry, and this made him feel even more ashamed. *It's my baby too,* he told himself. *In time, they'll come to accept it and will realize that I'm not going anywhere.* He shook his head. *Her parents may not like it, and they may never like me, but Marissa and the baby are my family. I'm not going anywhere,* he repeated in his head.

As soon as Jonah pulled into his driveway, he texted Marissa. *I hope you're okay? I'm so sorry. Can you meet me? I'll do whatever you need me to do. Love you!* He had no idea what to say or do.

More than an hour went by, each minute filling him with more dread. His cell phone finally beeped. It was a text message from Marissa. *I'm okay, but my parents are so hurt. My father is furious and my mother is brokenhearted. I was supposed to be the first person in our family to get a college degree and make something of myself. I know I can still do that. But they don't.*

There's no way I can meet you right now, Jonah. I'll be in touch over the next couple of days. I love you too, and I'm sorry you had to go through that. I tried to warn you. My father is a very proud man and, in his culture, we've dishonored his name. I hope you can understand that. This is going to take some time. I'll call you soon. Love you!

Jonah reread the text message three times before he began to cry again. *I need to make this right*, he thought, *for Marissa and the baby.* He nodded with conviction. *I need to be a man for my family, as well as Marissa's parents.*

◊◊◊

Jonah picked up his father from work again.

"Sorry for the trouble," his dad said, as he threw several snack wrappers onto the passenger side floor so he could take a seat.

"It's all good," Jonah told him. "Any update from Keith Tripp?" He quickly found his father's eyes. "Not that giving you rides is a problem."

"I spoke to him yesterday. He said he had to order some part that wasn't in stock. The car should be ready in a week."

They both looked at each other and smiled.

"It's all good, Dad," Jonah repeated. "So how was work?" he asked, trying to keep the spotlight off himself.

"Well..." His father stopped. "To be honest with you, it sucked."

"Then why not try to find a new job?" he asked. "With all your experience and—"

"It's not so easy at my age," his dad interrupted, "especially given the money I make."

"That much, huh?" Jonah said, his eyebrows dancing up and down in jest.

"Enough to put you and your sister through college."

Both eyebrows landed flat.

"Don't worry about me," he said. "I'm fine."

"But you're not happy," Jonah innocently reminded him.

"That's true, at least not at work." He grinned. "But I never expected to find my happiness at work anyway. It's just the place that funds it."

Jonah nodded. *I get it*, he thought, *but I'm hoping to find both.*

"So have you and Marissa told her parents yet?" his dad asked, as they headed for home.

And it begins, Jonah thought, nodding. "We did."

"And how did they take it?"

"They freaked out worse than you and Mom."

His father nodded. "Well, it's hard to blame them, right?"

Jonah thought about it. "I understand the shock, Dad, I do...but everyone needs to understand that this is a done deal."

They drove another mile before his father cleared his throat. "Drop me off at the hospital. I'll have Mom come pick me up later."

"Okay," Jonah said, steering a right onto New Boston Road.

The very moment Jonah stepped into the house, his mother ambushed him.

"Let's go, Jonah. We have to hurry," his mom said, grabbing her pocketbook and heading for the front door.

"Wha...what's going on?"

"We need to grab some apples before the orchard closes," she said, smiling mischievously.

"Are you kidding me?"

"No, I'm not kidding," his mother said, "I need to make my famous apple crisp. It's your father's favorite and we both know that he can use a win right now."

Jonah hesitated.

"Let's just go," his mom said, "there are food trucks there."

Turning on his heels, Jonah started out of the house again.

"When we get home, maybe we can make candy apples like we used to?" she suggested.

Jonah shook his head. "Sorry Mom, but there are limits."

She laughed. "Are there?"

◊◊◊

It was late night when Jonah stepped into his mother and father's bedroom. "Can we talk? I've made some decisions," he announced.

"Some more decisions?" his father quipped.

"I've decided that I'm going to find a full-time job so that I can take care of Marissa and the baby."

"But your education?" his mother said in protest, sitting up in bed.

"I'll take night classes, I promise. I finally understand which direction I should be heading in, so I have no intentions of giving up." He nodded. "But I need to put Marissa and the baby first."

His father looked at him long after it had become uncomfortable. "Jonah, you may be digging yourself out of this hole for a very long time, do you realize that?"

"That might be true, Dad," he said, "but I also need to be the man that you raised me to be." He could feel his eyes swelling with emotion. "I love Marissa. I know the timing isn't perfect for us to start a family, but that's exactly what we've done. I'm going to take care of my family," he confirmed, taking in a deep breath, "and I'm going to ask Marissa to marry me."

"But Jonah..." his mom began.

"She's the one, Mom. I know that, and I want to spend the rest of my life with her. While I work, she can go to school and become a lawyer. Once she starts working in her field, I'll go back to school full-time and finish my degree." He looked directly at his father. "I'll work two or three jobs if I have to. And I don't care how long it takes me to get my family past this difficult start. It's exactly what I'm going to do."

His father remained silent.

"I have to be a man about this, Dad. I have to take care of my family."

While his mom continued to shake her head, a wry smile crept into his father's face. "I understand," his dad said, causing his wife's head to snap up at him. He met her eyes. "Jonah wasn't raised to be a coward, Ginny." He looked back at Jonah. "I understand, son," he repeated, "and you have our full support."

"Thank you," Jonah said, taking the first breath of relief since hearing that he was going to be a dad.

"We need to go visit your grandfather tomorrow," his dad said. "He wants to talk to you."

Oh boy, Jonah thought, *tomorrow might be another painful one.*

◊◊◊

"I didn't go to Six Flags like you and Layla," his dad told him, as they stepped out of the hospital elevator, "I went to Three Flags, a playground near the local housing project." As the elevator doors closed behind them, Jonah and his father took a right and headed for the old man's room. "What I was trying to explain is that none of us are angels—no matter who it is—your grandfather included."

"I don't care if Grandpa was a drunk when he was younger," he said, "it doesn't change the way I feel about him."

"I never said he was a drunk," his dad corrected him. "I said that he abused alcohol."

"Semantics," he fired back.

"All I'm saying is that, in his time, your saintly grandfather spent quite a bit of time at daddy day care."

"Daddy day care?"

"The local pub."

Jonah grinned. "That just makes me love him even more."

His dad looked at him.

"It's true, Dad. Grandpa's a lot of things, but the one thing he's not is self-righteous." He nodded. "He's flawed, you know? A sinner like the rest of us. In my opinion, that makes him even more lovable."

His father nodded at the logic. "I've never thought of it that way, but I think I agree with you."

"Of course you do, Dad," Jonah teased.

Just then, they noticed that Peggy was just leaving the old man's hospital room. They slowed to greet her in the hallway.

"Wow," the older lady said, looking up at Jonah, "someone got tall."

He smiled, expecting to hear his father follow up with an additional compliment.

"Well," his dad said, "if you stand in manure long enough..." He shrugged.

The woman laughed.

What the hell? Jonah thought. Since his grandfather's illness, he could see some real changes in his dad—*and I'm not sure I like it.*

His father was still laughing when they stepped into the old man's room.

After greeting his grandfather with a kiss, Jonah grabbed the seat in the corner.

His grandpa turned to his dad. "Ollie, do you mind stepping out for a few minutes to give me and Jonah some time alone?"

Oh shit, Jonah thought, his backside puckering.

"Glad to," his dad said, smiling, "I'll go grab a coffee and come back in a bit."

True to form, his grandfather got right into it. "You need to be a good man before you can be a good father, Jonah," he said, peering into his eyes. "They're not mutually exclusive, you know."

"Whoa..." Given all he'd professed—and experienced—over the past few days, Jonah was really taken aback.

The old man's forehead folded in surprise. "Whoa, what?"

"I just didn't expect that from you."

His grandfather leapt into his eyes. "I've never lied to you, boy. Did you expect that I'd start now?"

With his mouth hung open, Jonah wiped his hands on his pant legs, trying to burn off the adrenaline firing through his bloodstream.

"There's the easy way to approach life and then there's the right way, Jonah," the old man continued, "and they're usually not the same thing."

Jonah nodded. "I know that, Grandpa."

"You do?"

"I do." He smiled. "Dad hasn't updated you on recent events, has he?"

The old-timer stared at him. "And what are those?"

"I have every intention of doing the right thing for my girlfriend and our baby," he explained.

"Good, because whether you're ready or not, it's time for you to take your seat at the adult table, Jonah. It's time for you to make your place in the world." The old man inhaled deeply. "This is the life that belongs to only you, so claim it. Own it." He nodded. "Whether you like it or not, that baby is more important than you are now. Sorry, but that's life. It's the cycle."

"I know, Grandpa," he said, showing both patience and respect to the family's dying patriarch.

"Good," the old man repeated, "because I don't have many of these talks left in me."

Unexpectedly, Jonah began crying, and couldn't stop; it was a combination of the grief he already felt for losing his mentor, along with all the worrisome weight he'd been carrying around with him.

He felt a hand grip his shoulder and squeeze. He looked up to find his dad standing beside him—without a coffee in hand. *Where did he come from?*

"It's okay for a man to cry," his father told him. "There's no shame in it. The heart that allows you to stand up and defend yourself or the people you love is the same heart that causes you to cry. No embarrassment, no shame." He tightened his grasp on Jonah's shoulder. "Never forget that."

Jonah reached for his father's hand.

"Welcome to fatherhood, son," his dad whispered.

Continuing to cry, Jonah smiled—his heart full.

"Jonah, before any of us have children, we have no idea how deep a parent's love is," his dad said, "which I believe is just a tiny glimpse of how much God loves us."

Outwardly, Jonah remained quiet. Inside, he was overwhelmed with so many colliding emotions.

"Though I don't believe we could ever comprehend the depth of God's love—not in this lifetime, anyway."

"Amen to that," his grandfather added.

"But just wait and see how much your life will change," his father vowed.

"That much, huh?"

His father nodded. "If you're even a decent dad, your entire life will be all about your child. You'll get lost in fatherhood, Jonah, even losing much of yourself in the process. But believe me when I tell you, the payoff is more awesome than anything you've experienced in your life."

Wiping his eyes, Jonah smiled.

"You won't even remember what your life was like without that baby in it," his grandfather said, "and trust me, you'll be glad you don't."

That's a lot to unpack, Jonah thought, *it really is.*

"For the rest of your life," his dad added.

The bedridden patriarch chuckled, drawing everyone's attention. "And each stage of fatherhood is more challenging than the one before it."

His dad chuckled in agreement.

"As far as I'm concerned, there are five stages to being a dad," his grandfather said.

"I'd agree with that," his father was quick to confirm. "Stage one, protector and provider. Chaser of under-the-bed monsters and valiant changer of dirty diapers. Assistance in walking, talking and kissing boo boos away."

All three men laughed—Jonah through his tears. He listened closely, while his grandfather and father alternated explaining the stages of fatherhood. *I'm gonna need to know this.*

"Very good," his grandfather said. "Stage two is probably teacher of right and wrong; of facing and overcoming fears."

"Yes," his dad added, "and we can probably add kitchen table tutor and after-work sports coach."

His grandfather nodded. "Stage three starts to get a little hairy." He thought about it for a moment. "Moral compass and Guardian of Secrets."

"Along with wingman in misunderstanding the opposite sex and facilitator of *The Talk*," his dad said.

All three of them laughed again.

"Ugh, the dreaded talk," Jonah commented.

"Just think," his grandfather said, "you have years to look forward to being on the other end of that one."

Jonah smiled at the thought of it.

"Stage four includes walking ATM, designated driver, and then anxious driving instructor." His dad chuckled. "You can probably throw in the enforcer of respect and soundboard for all teenage drama." He shrugged. "The bigger the kid, the bigger the problems, you know?"

His grandfather nodded in agreement. "And stage five, the last and most difficult of all the stages, is strictly release." The old man looked directly at Jonah's dad and confirmed, "Our job as dads is to raise our children, not keep them."

His father's eyes glossed over from emotion.

"Most of the things we learn, we learn through trial and error," his grandfather explained, "by just doing it." He looked at his own son. "And then we blame our fathers later on for not showing us."

Jonah's dad offered him a comical shrug. "He's got a good point, doesn't he?"

"He does," Jonah admitted.

"Like your dad would put up Christmas lights and turn to you and say, 'Come here, son, and let me show you how to untangle these beautiful frigging lights,'" the old man added, shaking his head.

His dad laughed.

"We learn how to do things by screwing them up, practicing a few times, and then getting them right—with a whole lot of cussing in between."

"Practicing fatherhood is no different," his dad said, his face turning serious.

"Amen to that," his grandfather concluded.

◊◊◊

After a couple of hours spent with the two best men he knew, Jonah realized, *Life's been so easy for me because I've depended on my parents for everything. But those days are over!*

The two things he never thanked his father for was teaching him how to swim and for his love of roller coasters—*two of the great loves in my life*. It had obviously cost his father some serious angst, but he could have never conquered the fears by himself. He realized that throughout his childhood, he'd been protected by layers of proverbial bubble wrap—thanks to his father. *Those days are long gone.*

Reality struck him like a long-overdue haymaker. *I'm going to be Dad now. And I can handle this*, he thought, picturing his expected child. *I'm a giant*, he told himself, smiling, *and it has to be true because my dad said so.* It was finally starting to sink in. *I can only raise a strong person, if I am one.*

In that instant, he realized that being a father was the true connection to the world he'd always secretly wanted. *I'm going to be the best Dad I can be*, he vowed to himself, *and I'm going to be there for my child until my dying breath—just like Grandpa is for Dad.*

Jonah stepped out of the room to call Marissa. "Hi, babe, it's me."

"Oh, hi."

"How are you feeling?"

"Pregnant," she said.

He chuckled, feeling excited for the first time after hearing that very word. "Is there any way you can meet me somewhere right now?"

"The Comfort Zone, fifteen minutes," she whispered, and hung up.

Marissa was already sitting at one of the wrought iron tables when Jonah pulled up. He took a minute to look at her from the car window. *She's so beautiful*, he thought. *I really do love her.*

When Jonah hurriedly approached her, she leapt to her feet and into his arms. Butterflies still swarmed in his gut when he was with her. "Oh my God, I've missed you so much!"

"I've missed you too," she said, squeezing him tight.

"Do your parents know you're here?" he asked, backing away just enough to see her face.

"My mom does."

"And she's okay with it?"

"She's still very upset, but I think she realizes that you and I are together and that it's not going to change." She shook her head. "Unfortunately, my father's a different story."

"Did you tell them everything we talked about...that I'm looking for a job and that you'll keep going to school once the baby is born?"

"I did, but they're not really hearing any of that right now." Her eyes looked so sad. "All they know is that their teenage daughter is pregnant, and they didn't even think she was having sex. It's going to take some time, Jonah. I hope you realize that."

He nodded. "Marissa, I swear I'm going to do everything I can to prove myself to them. I'm going to..."

"Relax," she said, "we'll both prove ourselves to them." Her smile returned. "And we have years to do it. But for now, we need to take it slow, okay?"

"But I want to be with you. I need to—"

"You are with me," she interrupted. "We're together and that's never going to change. For now, though, we both need to finish out the semester. Hopefully, by then, you'll have found a decent job and..." She paused. "Have your parents accepted the fact that you're going to be a dad?" she asked.

"My parents are upset about how this went down, but believe me when I tell you—they'll support us anyway they can."

"My parents will too, once they get over the shock," she said.

"I know that." He went to one knee. "Marissa, I want to spend the rest of my life with you. Without you...without our baby...I'm nothing. It doesn't matter what college major I take or what job I have, as long as I have you and the baby in my life then I have everything." He was overcome with emotion. "If I can come home to the both of you, then I'm the luckiest man in the world."

A giant smile planted itself into the corners of her beautiful mouth. By now, other people were staring.

Jonah didn't care. "I love you so much," he said, "and I swear I'll love you for the rest of my life. You have my word." He reached up and placed his hand on her abdomen. "Our baby has my word," he promised.

She pulled him to his feet. Snatching his hand into both of hers, she kissed it. "I love you too. I always have. You and I are going to be married. We're going to have this beautiful baby and maybe even own a house someday. But it's not going to be easy for us, not any of it."

"I know that," he admitted.

"But before you ask me to marry you, I need you to ask my father's permission first." She looked around the outdoor patio. "And I love this place, but please pick somewhere a little more romantic, okay?"

Wha...what? Jonah was shocked, and a little bit terrified. *Your father's permission?*

"If my dad gives you his blessing, and I have no doubt that he will because he knows how much I love you and how much you make me happy, then you'll have earned his forgiveness as well as his respect. And respect means everything to him."

The path to redemption, Jonah realized. "Okay," he said, "then that's exactly what I'll do."

"In the meantime, he'll start to see what kind of man you are...what kind of man I'm in love with."

They kissed.

"I love you so much," he said, "and you have no idea how much I've missed you."

"I've missed you too," she confirmed. "Now that my mom has somewhat accepted our situation, it should become easier for us."

"I hope so," he said, "because being separated from you has been the worst thing I've ever had to deal with."

"Me too," she said, kissing him again.

They hugged for a long time, long after the other patrons stopped staring and went about their business again.

Marissa's my everything, Jonah realized, kissing her softly. *We're family.*

◊◊◊

Days later, instead of enjoying a long tournament of video games together, Quinn invited Jonah to a college frat party. For the first time since he'd started partying, Jonah declined the offer—shocking them both.

"You must be kidding me?" Quinn said.

"Sorry bro," Jonah said, feeling bad about abandoning his friend, "but I really need to start getting my shit together, and a frat party's not gonna help."

Quinn snickered. "Great, thanks for ghosting me."

"I'm not trying to ghost you, Quinn. I just—"

Either in shock or anger—or perhaps both—Quinn hung up.

Sorry, bro, Jonah thought.

As the guilty feelings lingered, Jonah confided in his father about the situation. "It really sucks, Dad. Quinn and I have been like brothers since preschool, but I don't want him around the baby if he's not gonna grow up."

His father grinned. "Ahhh, the sacrifices of fatherhood." He nodded. "Get used to it. There will be plenty more similar situations for you to deal with."

"But Quinn's not a friend I want to lose," he explained, feeling awful about it.

"Then you should do whatever you can to work it out. But..." He paused.

"But?"

"You guys are in different places now," his dad explained. "There are lifelong friends, Jonah, and there are seasonal friends. When you go to college, those are your friends for that season of your life. But if you're lucky, blessed, you'll have one or two friends that'll stay with you for the whole ride." He shrugged. "You and Quinn may part ways for a bit—until he matures—but he'll be back. You guys are lifelong friends. I have no doubt about that." He smiled. "You guys have too much history to just throw it all away."

"I hope so," he said, though he was doubtful. *Quinn and I will drift further apart now.* Although he hoped it wasn't true, it felt like the beginning of the end for them. *Two different paths,* he figured. *Fatherhood versus Fraternity Life.*

"Things have a way of working themselves out," his dad added. "Trust me."

We'll see, Jonah thought, before smiling so wide that he thought his face might break in half.

His father studied him. "What is it?" he asked.

"I'm going to do it, Dad," Jonah announced, wearing the same mischievous grin he wore as a little boy.

"Going to do what?"

"I'm going to propose to Marissa, once I can get her father's blessing."

Instantly, his father's face lit up. The joyful look only lasted a moment. "Son, if you're only marrying Marissa because—"

"I love her, Dad," he quickly vowed.

"I'm glad to hear that you'll be asking her father first. It's the right thing to do." He nodded. "Grandpa's going to love hearing this, Jonah. He'll be very proud." He placed his hand on his son's shoulder and gave it a squeeze. "I know I am."

"Thanks, Dad." Jonah said, feeling overwhelmed with emotion. "We're having a baby!" he said, overcome with joy. "Any advice?"

His father opened his mouth to answer, but nothing came out for a few long moments. "Jonah," he finally said, "the greatest thing about being a dad for me was watching you and Layla grow up." He nodded. "The hardest part about being a dad for me was watching you and Layla grow up." As his dad's eyes filled, they seemed to choke off his throat. "You'll understood soon enough."

They hugged.

"So what are you hoping for, a boy or a girl?"

Jonah nodded. "You know what, I don't really care, as long as the baby's healthy—ten fingers and ten toes, you know?"

"I do," his dad said. "That's my boy," he added, his chest swelling with even more pride. Throwing his arm around his shoulders, he said, "Now let's go upstairs, so you can tell both your mother and me about your future plans. I'm not a great liar, but I'll do my best to pretend that I don't already know."

"What do think Mom will say?"

"My guess—she'll probably insist that we get started on the wedding plans right away, so you guys will be ready when you finally get Mr. DeSousa's blessing." He laughed. "She's going to be happy for you, son. We both will."

◊◊◊

The following morning, Jonah's cell phone buzzed. He looked at the caller ID. *I have no idea who this is.* Fighting off his initial impulse to screen the call, curiosity got the best of him. "Hello?"

"Jonah Earle?" a deep voice asked.

"Speaking."

"This is Georgey Austin, the managing editor at Electronic Gaming Monthly."

Jonah's body instinctively stiffened. "Hello, Mr. Austin."

"Do you have a minute?" the man asked.

"Absolutely!"

"Listen, our entire team has reviewed your product review on *Into the Breach*. It's really some fantastic work."

"Really?" Jonah asked, wishing he hadn't sounded so unsure of himself.

"Yes, really, and we'd like to publish the piece in next month's edition."

The news took Jonah's breath away; for a moment, he couldn't breathe.

"What do you think of that?" Mr. Austin asked, breaking the silence.

"I think it's amazing," Jonah managed. "Thank you...thank you so much."

There was a chuckle. "And I'd like you to send me a few more reviews, Jonah," the baritone voice added. "If the work is as good as your first review, then we'll talk about you writing for us on a monthly basis as one of our resident reviewers. We can talk about salary and benefits at that time."

Jonah still struggled to breathe.

"How does that sound?" the editor asked.

"It sounds like a dream come true," Jonah answered, honestly.

The chuckle became a laugh. "Perfect."

"I'll get those pieces to you right away," Jonah blurted.

"I appreciate that, but please don't sacrifice quality for expediency. Remember, this may be the final audition before you get the role."

Jonah's entire body buzzed with adrenaline. "I won't rush the work," he said, "I promise."

"Good," Mr. Austin said, "we'll talk soon then." He hung up.

"Yes!" Jonah screamed. "Yes!" *This could be my dream come true*, he repeated in his head. *I need to get writing.*

He immediately called Marissa. "Guess what!" he said.

"What?"

"Do you remember when I told you that I sent off a product review for a new video game?"

"Yeah?"

"They finally got back to me. The editor of Electronic Gaming Monthly; it's an American video game magazine that offers video game news, product reviews and—"

"What did they say, Jonah?" she asked, chomping at the bit.

"He said that he'd like to publish the piece," Jonah replied, overwhelmed with joy to share the remarkable news. "He also asked me to send him a few more. If the work is as good as my first piece, then I may be able to write reviews full-time for them!"

"Are you serious? Full time?"

"Can you imagine, Marissa? I might actually be able to make a decent living playing video games and writing about them." A lump formed in his throat. "I think this might be my big break!"

"Oh Jonah, I'm so proud of you."

"Thank you," he said, his voice squeaking from emotion.

"So what do your parents think about you playing video games for a living?" she asked, playfully.

"I haven't told them yet. I just found out and called you first." He chuckled. "I'm guessing they'll both go into shock."

She laughed. "I'm so proud of you," she repeated.

"Thank you for believing in me," he said.

"I love you," she said.

"And I love you more," he said, filled with more hope than he'd ever known.

◊◊◊

Jonah visited his grandfather, this time of his own accord. "How are you feeling, Gramps?" he asked.

"Exactly the way I look," he answered, "like an empty hourglass."

Jonah cringed.

The old man patted the side of his bed. "Come sit with me."

Jonah took a seat beside the dying patriarch. "We're making good progress on the fundraiser, Gramps. A lot of the donations for the raffles and auction have already come in. We just need to put the baskets together."

"Thank you." His grandfather locked onto his eyes. "What you're about to do, Jonah, will make all the difference in the world for someone, for Dylan, and this will have a ripple effect that you'll probably never see...or completely understand."

That's all I've ever dreamed of, he realized, *doing something big that will make a real difference.*

The old man grabbed his hand so there was no chance for escape. "Can you just imagine—you're gonna be a daddy, Jonah!" He squeezed his hand.

Jonah thought about it for a moment, realizing, *This might be the last time I can gain any wisdom from this man.* "What should I know, Grandpa?"

"Know?"

"About being a good dad. What do I need to know?"

"Just be there and make sure your child knows that you're there. I didn't always get it right, but when I did it was because I showed up."

"And?"

The feeble man smiled. "That's pretty much it." He grinned. "The rest you'll either get right, or you won't. You'll make your mistakes and that's okay. There's no owner's manual to follow." He paused for a long while. "Love is always a given, right? But respect must be earned between a child and his or her father. Remember that."

"I will, Gramps."

"I know you will." He studied his face. "Don't worry so much about it; you're gonna make a fine father."

God, I hope so, he thought, nodding.

"Oh, and one last thing."

"What's that?"

"Please remember that you have my father's last name, Jonah. You have my grandfather's last name, and his father before him. We come from a long line of Earles. Personally, I've always felt a great responsibility that goes with that."

Jonah remained silent; he was attentive and still.

"We only have three things in this world," the old-timer said.

Leaning in closer to the ailing man, Jonah awaited the payoff.

"Our name, our word, and our deeds," he listed. "I've been very careful not to dishonor our family name—their name—and I'd really appreciate it if you remembered to take the same care with it."

Having the name Earle always seemed ironic to Jonah, given that his family was the furthest thing from royalty. He nodded.

"I need to hear it from you."

"I will," Jonah said. "I'll always respect my family name and teach my children to do the same."

"Good," the old man said, grinning. "I could never ask for anything more from you." He patted Jonah's hand.

"I'll make you proud of me, Gramps," Jonah whispered. "I promise."

The sage grinned. "I'd rather you make yourself proud. In the end, that's what really matters." He nodded. "Once you have that, everyone else will follow suit."

As Jonah bid his farewell and started out of the hospital room, the struggling man called out, "You're an Earle, Jonah, and you carry the weight of that name. Are we clear?"

"Yes, sir, we're clear!"

"That's my boy," he said, closing his eyes.

CHAPTER 13

O n his drive to the hospital, Oliver thought, *Between the old man's failing health and Jonah's shocking news, Ginny and I still haven't been able to go out on our date.* He smiled. *She's been great about it, though. I'm even getting lucky again.* Thinking about the previous night, he couldn't wipe the smile from his face.

They'd begun making love—real love—again. Both gave selflessly, taking their time in extended foreplay. From slow and gentle to a passionate sprint toward the finish line, they lay side-by-side, covered in a film of sweat.

"God, I've missed that," he said, panting.

"Me too," Ginny said, nuzzling closer to him—where they both fell asleep, naked and at peace.

Oliver's attention returned to the windshield. *I still can't believe it,* he thought. *My erectile dysfunction may have actually brought us closer together.* Ginny's compassion and understanding was exactly what he'd needed; she'd removed all pressure, allowing them to be truly intimate once again.

As he pulled into the hospital's busy parking lot, he pictured his dad sitting by the pond. *At least now I know why he'd only taken me fishing that one time, and why it took him all those years to get back to the water's edge.* He swallowed hard. *It also makes perfect sense why—for most of my life—he thought everything was a joke.*

He parked the car when his thoughts turned to his children. *It wasn't until I reunited with my son—really reconnected—at my father's deathbed that I've come to discover the path I was always supposed to be on,* he realized. *And it's the same damn thing that I've needed from my father my entire life—to just be Dad.* Once again, he vowed to dedicate his life to making his children's lives better. *From now on, I'm going to teach Layla and Jonah instead of doing everything for them.* It seemed odd that he'd only recently learned this.

Stepping out of the car with a warm bucket of chicken tucked under his arm, he realized, *I haven't seen Dr. Borden-Brown for a few weeks now, and at a time that I probably need therapy most.* He snickered. *At least sitting with my dad is saving me the co-pay.*

Even though the smell was much more likely to give him away, Oliver checked to see if the coast was clear before sneaking the half-crushed bucket of southern fried chicken into his father's hospital room. *How could I not?* he thought, after the master manipulator had said, "Even death row inmates get to pick their final meal, Ollie."

"Did you make it past Nurse Cratchet?" his dad joked.

"I think so, but we'd better be fast about it."

"Promise me one thing, son," the old man said, his face set like granite.

"Name it."

"If anyone comes through that door and tries to confiscate this chicken," he said, before biting into the crispy chicken leg and rolling his eyes, "that you height luck hell...cup'em a hay for me."

Although his last words were terribly mangled by the shredded chicken in his mouth, Oliver still understood every word. "Sure Dad, I'll fight like hell to keep them away from you."

His father nodded his gratitude, tearing into bite-after-bite. "Oh, wow," the old man said, talking with his mouth full, "that's better than good." He moaned with each bite.

Now there's a groan I could get used to, Oliver thought, comparing the same sound to poor man's pain. Watching his dad fade away more and more each day was the kind of experience that would either bend a man's knee or strengthen his spine. Oliver wasn't quite sure what it was doing to him. *What I do know is that Jonah's baby is going to take my father's place in this world.* He'd never had such a strong gut feeling in his life.

The nurse's ominous shadow suddenly passed by the room. Oliver jumped to his feet, making a beeline to the door to buy his father more time if needed. "False alarm," he announced, cautiously reclaiming his hard plastic seat.

"Attaboy," the hippie patient pushed past the gorging, his eyes still wide with food lust. "Now this is how they should be feeding me here."

"I'm not sure that's a great idea," Oliver started. "You'd be—"

"It's not like it's going to kill me any quicker," the old man interrupted.

Oliver opened his mouth to speak again.

"Colonel Harland Sanders," his dad said, grabbing another extra crispy leg, "a brilliant military strategist." As he took another big bite, his eyes rolled to the back of his head in delight. "And he also knew how to make some mean fried chicken."

"Just hurry," Oliver said, keeping watch for any nurses.

"Yeah, sure," his dad said, talking and chewing at the same time. "God forbid we get into trouble in this shithole."

Oliver laughed.

"What could they possibly to do to us?" He grinned, the grease glistening around his mouth like the rings of Saturn.

"Me? They couldn't really do anything to me, Dad, but you..." He grinned.

His father stopped eating.

"Let's see, there's enemas and catheters," he began, counting on his fingers, "and a sponge bath from that male nurse that keeps winking at you."

"Male nurse? I ain't seen no male nurse winking at me!"

Oliver started laughing. "That's one thing I could always count on," he teased.

"Oh yeah, and what's that?"

"Your prejudices."

The old-timer considered the comment before letting it go with another T-Rex attack on the chicken bucket.

Oliver kept on laughing.

"Well, won't you look at this," his dad said in between chews, "my son's finally yanked the stick out of his ass and found his sense of humor." He winked at him. "Maybe sitting here every day with me has been good for you, after all?"

He nodded. "I have no doubt about that. But you're wrong about the sense of humor. I've had one of those for years."

"Is that right?" his father asked before gnawing more flesh from the bone.

He nodded again. "I got married, didn't I?"

The old man laughed twice before he began choking on his contraband dinner.

Oliver hurried to sit him up and lean him forward. Within seconds, the old man cleared his own airway. "That was a lot of noise," Oliver whispered. "I'm thinking that somebody may want that sponge bath after all."

His father threw the chicken bone into the bucket, pushing it away. "I'll stink first," he mumbled.

Oliver grinned. *Mission already accomplished, Pepe Le Pew.*

Oliver had just returned from the cafeteria for a quick bite to eat when his father announced, "All my gaskets and seals are worn beyond repair," he said, acknowledging how his body was now breaking down.

"Nice, Dad," he said.

"In one way, that's a good thing," the old man said, "believe me."

"And how's that?"

"It means that I got every mile out of this trip I've been blessed to take."

Oliver thought about it and nodded.

His father started laughing.

"What is it?" he asked.

"When we were young, your mother and I spent a long weekend camping out on a nude beach. We didn't have a care in the world back then. We were only interested in living freely with each other."

"Ugh...no more details please."

The old man chuckled again. "Whatever you do, Ollie," he said, "when it's time for you to turn yours in, make sure there isn't a single drop left in the tank."

Oliver remained silent.

"Understand?"

"I do," he said, sounding like he'd gargled on the two words.

"Get everything you can out of this life, Ollie."

Oliver nodded again; he was sure to spend countless hours contemplating this lesson. "Didn't Dr. Godin suggest a treatment to strengthen your heart?"

"He did," his father said, "but that's like rearranging deck chairs on the Titanic." He shrugged. "A little too late, right?"

He shook his head.

They sat quietly, side-by-side, when his dad said, "I told you that your mom visits me, right?"

He nodded. "You did, Dad." He looked over at the empty plastic chair in the corner.

"Well, she's been staying with me most of the night now."

"Really?" Oliver said, trying to buy his brain time to reconcile his dad's new reality. He studied his father's face. *He's not joking*, he realized. *He thinks she's been here.* He considered it. *Maybe it's the start of dementia? Or the pain meds making him hallucinate?*

Coughing, the old man gestured toward the chair in the corner. "She sits right there."

"Mom?" Oliver repeated. That one word filled him with an equal amount of love and sorrowful longing. He searched his mind for his beloved mother. Although he was young when she passed from cancer, he could still picture her: she was a tiny human with a giant personality—the bricks and mortar of their small family. Oliver's memories of her were now more like a set of feelings than actual photos in his mind.

He vaguely remembered how she'd left and, as he went back, his moist eyes stared into space. *A black dress hanging in dry cleaner's plastic; my dad's angry outbursts and awful sobs; a table covered in casserole dishes. I was too young back then to realize the permanence of my mom's premature death and that it would become the perfect excuse for my father to start swimming in a beer bottle.*

He continued to search his memory for her. *Even though she loved her sweets, she'd lost so much weight that it felt like I was hugging a coat hanger,* he thought. "Ma, you're nothing but bones," he'd told her.

"I finally beat anorexia," she joked. "Just wait until you get older, Oliver." *She shook her head. "We'll see how fit you look."*

When she passed away from the cruel bout with cancer, the family dynamics instantly changed.

He looked at the empty chair. *Love and miss you, Ma*, he told her in his mind. *Please look after the old man for me.*

"At least I'll get to see ole Georgey Gouveia again," his father said, ending Oliver's quick jaunt down memory lane. "He's owed me a pack of Lucky Strikes for years now."

I'm not sure smoking's allowed where you're heading. Oliver thought, catching himself. *At least I hope not.*

"Looks like I'll finally be able to collect from the deadbeat," his dad joked.

"Do you want to talk about it?" Oliver asked.

"Talk about what?"

"Your service in Vietnam."

He shook his head. "I can't go back there any further than I did at that pond, Ollie," he whispered. "I won't go back there. Not even now."

"Okay, Dad," Oliver said, quickly changing the subject. "How about those Red Sox?"

His father looked at him and grinned. "Nice recovery."

"I learned from the best."

"I appreciate that."

Georgey Gouveia, Oliver thought, *what I wouldn't give to know more about you.* While his dad slept, he took note of the old faded tattoos on the man's forearms.. Once bulging from Popeye-sized arms, they were now shrunken and distorted: A little devil holding a pitchfork branded into his right forearm; an angel's wings with initials—*GG*—on his left forearm. As a boy, when he'd asked what it stood for, the old man simply grinned. "*Good guy.*"

Oliver was sure that the contrast of the dueling ink was as telling about his father's life as anything. *The stories behind the ink are probably something to hear,* he thought. *Unfortunately, he's never shared them.*

He became fixated on the dying man lying in the hospital bed before him. *I remember when he slept on his side facing the bedroom door with the pillow stuffed between his arm and his head, his giant hand outstretched and his pinkie finger resting on the edge of the headboard. He snored like a bear, the greatest signal that the coast was clear for me to go raise hell, and maybe even get away with it.*

Back then, Dad wore his hair slicked back, DA-style, a pack of non-filtered Pall Malls rolled up in the right sleeve of his yellowed t-shirt. Oliver either minded his old man, or felt his leather belt across his backside.

When he was growing up, his father sometimes crashed out in a worn leather recliner. During those times, when he asked his dad's permission to go somewhere, the old man's nonchalant shrug was a clear sign that it was okay to go. *There were more than a few occasions when Dad's indifference was a true blessing.*

When it was cold out, Mom drank tea while Dad still drank beer. On many Saturdays, the old man was escorted from the 'Vets Club' with a drunken man propped under each arm. *Sometimes they'd place him behind the wheel. Other times, one of them would drive him home and leave him snoring on our doorstep.* He shook his head. *I always wondered if he'd died.*

Steering toward the positive, Oliver pictured one of the family's many barbecues. It was dusk and the family was all there—his dad laughing the loudest. While the transistor radio squawked out a play-by-play of the Boston Red Sox, he and his friends played chase in the yard—surrounded by all the people he loved. He remembered catching the first firefly of the season and then casting wishes on the first star of the night. At the time, he never realized that he was standing in a place and time that he'd forever consider a glimpse of heaven.

And then there was that one fishing experience, he thought. He'd tried not to go there, but his mind had already begun to slide down the slippery slope.

Oliver did his chores and lots of them, sometimes at the expense of playing with friends, or back muscles that burned from his shoulder blades straight down to his sweaty butt crack.

If I want a few bucks in my pocket, though, I have no choice, he realized. *My father's never gonna give me a nickel that I don't earn.*

He could still feel the bass in the big man's voice. "You may not believe this now, Ollie, but someday you're gonna thank me."

"How'd I do, Dad?" he asked, looking for approval on one of his completed chores.

"Not bad, son." The old man nodded. "A solid work ethic and a strong back is all you'll ever need in this world, son. Trust me." He leaned in toward him to drive his next point home. "Ollie, being dependent on someone else is like being put into a cage. You can never control your own destiny." He smiled. "Now go back to work, you lazy bum."

Oliver did—until his aching shoulders felt like he'd backed into a hornet's nest.

The memory of fishing with his dad was still so vivid in his mind. It was just past dawn, warm for an early morning. They walked through a long, flowered field before reaching a wood line, a blue body of water shimmering just behind it. *The pond.*

He felt bad for the worms. And then he felt bad for the unlucky fish that convulsed from the end of the bloody hook. Even still, it was time spent alone with his father, and he would have suffered much worst to be with him. "Maybe we can try fishing from a boat sometime?" he suggested.

His dad glared at him. "Get that idea out of your head, Ollie. I'll never step on another boat as long as I live."

But why? Oliver wondered, knowing better than to ask.

When the day had begun, Oliver hoped fishing would become a regularly shared activity with his dad. As the years unfolded, he realized that the poor worms and slimy fish would never pose another problem for him. He and his father never fished again. *The old man was too busy working, or helping other people.* He just assumed that his dad would rather spend his time elsewhere—*and with anyone but me.*

He looked at his dad, lying still on his deathbed. *At least I know the truth now,* he thought. *He made sure of that.*

◊◊◊

"I owe you an apology," his dad mumbled, emerging from his sleep.

"For what?" Oliver said, pouring the old man a fresh cup of water, "I thought we agreed, no more apologies."

"The list is longer than I care to admit," his dad said, completely ignoring the comment. "When I heard you talking to Jonah about how it was okay to cry, I was impressed—and I gained even more respect for you."

Oliver was stunned into silence. Although he never replied—for fear of his words breaking into pieces—he could feel his face burn red. He'd never heard such high praise from his father. *And he's being genuine.*

"I guess I never had the strength to be able to do it myself," the old man admitted, "to feel that comfortable in my own skin, even though I honestly believed at the time that I didn't care what others thought." He rested his sapphire eyes on him. "I'm sorry, Ollie. I should've been stronger for you than that."

"It's okay, Dad, really. And please, enough with the apologies."

"It's actually not okay. Back then, I figured there was no room for anything that felt like weakness—not for the roles I played as provider and protector." He shook his head in shame. "Crying felt like weakness. But I see now that I was wrong. It was weak of me to think otherwise." He tried to shake off the old transgression. "Thankfully, you righted that wrong with your own son, so the chain of ignorance is broken." His head shifted to a nod. "I'm grateful."

◊◊◊

Flipping through the channels with the cable remote, Oliver stopped at the show, *Gunsmoke.*

"I used to really love this show," his dad said.

"I remember," Oliver said, placing the remote back by his father's side.

"I should have been a cowboy," the old man commented, hypnotized by the gunslingers on the wall-mounted TV.

"I thought you were?"

They both laughed. "Close, I guess."

"Looking back now, what would you have been if you could have picked any job?"

His father never missed a single beat. Turning his head to face Oliver, he said, "Your dad."

"Come on, I'm serious."

"And so am I. Name one job in the world, Ollie, that's more important than being somebody's father?"

Oliver didn't need to think long about it either. "None that I can think of."

"Exactly!" He nodded, proudly. "Cowboy, astronaut, button maker—none of it would have meant a whole lot to me if I couldn't have shared what I learned with you and your children." He returned to the old Western TV show flickering above.

Bored from all the dust kicked up by the horses, Oliver commented, "I think I was born in the wrong time."

"Oh yeah, and how's that?" The old man's eyes never left his program.

"I don't know. Even when I was a kid, I had a sense that I didn't belong...that I'd missed my time, you know?"

His dad half-shrugged. "That's probably normal. My guess is that most folks have felt that way at some point in their lives." He turned to look at his son again. "Maybe it's just easier to look back and believe that the past was kinder, simpler—even easier." He grinned. "But it wasn't."

"Oh really? And how do you know that, old wise one?"

The grin widened. "Even I know life's what we make it." He nodded. "It's all in our attitudes, son. This show could be the greatest thing I've ever seen, but it might suck for you."

"I'm not sure that's an attitude thing, Dad."

"You know what I mean." He coughed. "The example might have missed the mark, but you get the point."

Oliver nodded. "I still say I was born at the wrong time."

His father abandoned the TV show to offer his undivided attention.

"I love Frank Sinatra and Dean Martin," Oliver explained, "and they were both before my time."

"Actually, I think their work is timeless." The old man smiled. "The summer wind..." he sang, poorly, "came blowing in...from across the—"

"Please stop," Oliver interrupted. "I think you cured me. I'll never listen to Sinatra again."

"Come fly with me..." his dad belted out, before stopping himself. "Old blue eyes was the definition of class," he said, "the original smooth operator."

Oliver laughed.

"It's no wonder you thought you should've been born earlier."

"Maybe," Oliver surrendered.

"Can I go back to my show now?"

"Absolutely, but you're done torturing me with it. For all we know, it's a *Gunsmoke* marathon."

"Oh, let's hope so."

He looks so tired tonight, Oliver thought. *I should probably cut this visit short and let him get some rest.* "I'm gonna go, Dad," he announced, standing. "You need to get some sleep to keep your strength up."

"Strength," the old man repeated, starting to chuckle but ending with a coughing fit.

"I'll be back in the morning," he said, approaching his father and kissing him on the forehead like it was something they'd done for years—only it wasn't.

Oliver quickly turned and headed for the door.

"I'll be here...I think."

Oliver shook his head. "Love you, Dad."

"And I love you, Oliver," the old man said, loud enough for the cafeteria staff five floors down to hear him.

His eyes filling, he walked out. *He hasn't called me Oliver in years,* he thought, *and he's never told me he loved me so strongly.* He wiped his eyes. *We must be getting close to the end.*

CHAPTER 14

Even though he was growing weaker and frailer, sleep was not coming so easy for Robert anymore—his mind filled with thoughts that needed to be released before he could finally rest.

He stared out the hospital window, his eyes imbued with tears of wonder and gratitude. The sun was rising ever so slowly; it was as beautiful as the first sunrise he'd ever witnessed. It looked like someone was unwrapping a present and taking their sweet time about it. Each moment was filled with the anticipation of the next glimpse, the next miraculous peek. *I'm gonna miss it*, he thought.

He considered the seasons that he'd no longer enjoy. *Fall has always been my favorite.* Once the heat subsided, the air turned cooler and more comfortable. In New England, the colorful foliage was a show that never got old—reds, oranges, and yellows bursting on the trees, painting the perfect Norman Rockwell background. Most foods and drinks included pumpkin or cinnamon flavors—*which I also love.* The distinct smell of burned hardwoods from bonfires. People donned in old comfy sweaters, or hooded sweatshirts advertising one East Coast college or another. The cargo shorts and T-shirts gladly traded in for worn jeans and red flannel shirts. He always had his copper flask at the ready, filled with something to keep his insides warm.

And winter, he thought, grinning. Every New England winter proved to be a season of endurance. From frosted windows, the world resembled the inside of a holiday snow globe. But out in the elements, the cold was biting, stinging. It was an act of self-preservation to dress in layers, covering every inch of skin—most days, it was the only insurance against frostbite. The days grew short and dark. In turn, the heating bills grew heavy. There was snow, mountains and mountains of snow. Unless you enjoyed snowmobiling or skiing, it was a major nuisance: from scraping frozen windows and shoveling driveways to slipping and sliding your way to work with the rest of the morning drones. Christmas was the only real payoff, a Currier and Ives oasis located right smack in the middle of an endless desert of ice and snow.

I'm gonna miss it all.

Robert spent the next few hours reminiscing. *Before the memories are lost forever,* he figured.

Back in the day, we lived up on Pinewood Avenue, just off of Copperhead Road, and we stayed alive in the winter by feeding a wood stove. The rest of the year we survived on whatever we hunted or caught in the Westport River.

His first job was setting bowling pins at Lincoln Park. *I'd never recommend the work to anyone, though. With all the drunks and punks that made their way through there, it was a pretty dangerous gig.*

And then I grew up and hit the lottery. I married Ruth and she gave me Ollie. His eyes filled. *Even though our marriage had its fair share of ups and downs, we were happy back then...until she passed away on me.*

As a young widower, he eventually settled into his routine, living a second life with one new soulmate after the next, each one of them a four-legged mutt that he took the time and patience to train.

I did my thing, he thought, *and I let other people do theirs.* He was a real Swamp Yankee, drinking most of his beer in the back of Trippy's Garage, deep in the woods.

I did it my way, he realized, smiling wide, *no excuses, no apologies.*

Just as soon as Old Faithful—Oliver—stepped into the room, Nurse Sue entered. She was the earthy type, with a little extra crunch. "Time to make the bladder gladder, Mr. Earle," Sue said.

He looked at his son. "They try to kill you off quicker here with bad humor," he muttered under his breath—only it was hardly under his breath.

Sue looked at Oliver. "How did you deal with him all these years?" she asked, kiddingly.

"In small doses," Oliver replied.

"And now it's an overdose," Robert said, laughing hard at his own joke. He looked at his son. "I've still got it, kid."

"What's that," Oliver asked, "scurvy?"

Robert nodded. "Finally!" he yelled out.

"What?"

"It's taken all this time, but I've finally rubbed off on you."

Oliver looked at Sue, who smirked. "You might want to take a long shower when you get home," she said.

They all laughed.

"We're almost ready to pull the trigger on the fundraiser, Dad," Oliver reported, "and I'm so grateful to Ginny and Jonah for helping me pull it together."

"No more grateful than I am, son," he said, "to all of you." He shook his head. "If only I could've frozen time," he added, sighing heavily, "but that's not how it works, does it? We get what we get and, except for a brief stretch overseas, I've been luckier than most. I know at least that much."

"That's good, Dad," Oliver said, his eyes already watering.

"What I wanted from this world, needed from it, Ollie," he said, nearly frantic to impart every last piece of knowledge he could, "could never come from anyone in it. What I wanted for my life had to come from God. Once I realized that, I did all I could to fill the bank with good deeds."

Oliver nodded that he understood.

Robert lost his breath, panicking to find it again.

"Dad, you don't need to talk right now," his son told him, "We can—"

"But I do," he wheezed, cutting him off. "Just let me finish, okay?" As Oliver nodded, he grabbed his son's hand and squeezed down hard. "Don't be the fool I was, son. Love like there's no tomorrow, Ollie, because..." He paused to breathe. "Because for all we know, there isn't. There's only today, only now." He shook his head, taking in more oxygen. "And shower most of that love on your family."

"I will, Dad," Oliver promised, placing his free hand on top of his father's.

"Please do." He was now really struggling to breathe. "I want to speak with my grandchildren," he managed, "I have a few final things..." He gasped for air.

"Okay Dad, I'll arrange it."

With a single nod, Robert passed out from exhaustion.

◊◊◊

That afternoon, Jonah sat at his grandfather's bedside, holding a laptop so that Layla could join them.

"How are you feeling, Grandpa?" she asked.

"Better now," he said, his voice weak. "I'm glad you're both here. I need you to know…" He paused to breathe.

"Oh, Grandpa," Layla cried.

"Have you ever looked at a picture or a painting, and thought, *I really miss that place?*"

They nodded.

"Well, that's how I feel about dying." Both of his eyebrows rose. "It's a deja vu kind of thing, a longing."

"You're not mad that it's…" Layla stopped.

"Even if I wanted to, I couldn't get angry anymore," he admitted. "I've traveled way beyond that foolishness." He grinned. "All I feel now is gratitude."

"Dad said that the hospital priest was in to see you?" Jonah said.

He nodded. "He was. But I'm not worried about religion either. If you believe God is unconditional love, then how can you fear the afterlife?"

"You can't," Jonah said.

"Listen guys, I want you both to know that life is all about the little things, the moments," he said, "and it's in those moments that your real journey takes place. When you look back—like I've been able to these past few weeks—it's so clear how our attitudes dictate the type of lives we live." He nodded. "It's all about the little things."

Both Layla and Jonah nodded again in sync.

"Concentrate on those little things and get as many of them right as you can, okay?"

"We will."

"Good." He grinned. "And go easy on yourselves when it comes to shame or guilt. There's no road map for this trip. Each of us can only do the best we can. Sometimes, we fall short." He coughed. "That's just life." He hacked again. "And that goes for your parents too."

They both nodded.

"It's not about the results, but the effort," Layla said, giving him a break to breathe.

"I couldn't have said it better myself, sweetheart." He took a few breaths; each one was more difficult than the one before it. Tears were shed all around.

Robert was struggling for air when he looked sideways to see his son standing in his doorway.

Jonah looked up too. "Hi, Dad," he said.

"Hi, Daddy," Layla called out from the screen.

"Hi, beautiful," Oliver called back. Looking at Jonah, he pointed toward the bed. "How's Grumpy doing today?"

"Not great," he mouthed, presuming his grandfather couldn't see him.

"Now there's an understatement, if I ever barely heard one," Robert said.

Oliver went to his bedside. "Ginny said she'll be in later to see you." He nodded. "Looking forward to it."

"She said you guys had talked about something which she hasn't done yet, and she wants to explain why." He shrugged. "Whatever that means."

Grinning, Robert nodded again. "Thanks for letting me know."

Oliver gestured toward his children. "I'm the one who should be thanking you...for having my back."

Robert shrugged. "Just making my amends for lost time, is all."

"Debt paid in full," Oliver commented.

Robert smiled. *Not quite yet.*

As they sat together—talking and laughing—minutes felt like seconds; the hours like minutes.

"Grandpa, tell us one of your famous stories about Dad," Layla asked a half world away.

"Only if it's a funny one," he replied, thinking, *I wish I had the time to share them all.*

"Of course, it'll be a funny one," Oliver said. "What else would it be?"

Robert searched his memory. It didn't take long. "It was the start of shark season when I purchased one of those seal suits for your late grandmother," he joked.

Oliver, Layla, and Jonah laughed.

"Anyway, we were at the beach and your dad was eating a sandwich—an Italian grinder, if I remember correctly?" Robert said, happy to share another tale with his grandkids.

Oliver nodded in confirmation. "From Marcucci's."

"Oh, those are the best," Jonah said.

"My favorite," Layla agreed.

Robert nodded in agreement. "Anyway, your dad's hanging that sub out in the wind when a seagull swooped in and dive-bombed him, snatching it right out of his little hand."

Looking over at her father, Layla laughed hard. "Oh, he must have freaked out."

"You have no idea!"

"Did he scream like a girl?" Jonah asked.

Oliver shook his head.

"Oh, he screamed all right, though I'm not sure I'd insult any girl given what came out of his mouth that day."

"Yeah okay, Dad," Oliver stammered, "very funny."

"Thanks, Grandpa," Layla said, giggling.

Although Robert and the kids laughed hysterically at his expense, Oliver seemed to enjoy it—even if he was being torn to shreds. "Those sea chickens are dirty thieves," he said, joining in on the fun.

The laughter continued; it was the perfect medicine for each of their souls. They were creating another memory that would be cherished for all time—or at least whatever time remained—and they all knew it.

◊◊◊

Once the kids left for the night, Robert approached his dinner like an untrained monkey.

"Go easy, Sloppy Joe," Oliver teased him. "You look like an over-grown baby chewing on a teething cookie."

He smiled, thinking, *It's about damn time I could get him to mess with me!* "How are Luna and Sophie getting along?"

"Surprisingly well."

"No bullshit?"

"No bullshit."

For whatever reason, Robert suddenly thought about all the dogs he'd owned, all that had passed before him. *Buttons was the first in a long line of many,* he recalled, *and the only thing that mutt ever gave me was an early understanding of loss when he'd gotten struck by a car.* Although he remembered being intrigued by the dog's newfound freedom, the grief was consuming.

"Take care of Luna for me," he told his emotional son, "it won't be long before she joins me." The statement was telling, given that he'd never been the most overtly spiritual man.

"I will, Dad."

"I appreciate that, and so will she." He grinned. "She's a pain in the backside, but she's worth it."

"She's not the only one," Oliver said, making him grin.

"That's true enough." He took a few deep breaths. "Things are better between you and Ginny, huh?"

A smile overtook his son's tired face. "Much better," he reported. "We're watching our favorite shows together again, and she's started making a pot of coffee for me in the morning before I head off to work." He chuckled. "We're tackling the laundry together now, washing the dishes side-by-side—and what's even better is that we talk through it all." He nodded. "Things are much better," he repeated, his eyes a thousand miles away.

"That's good to hear," Robert said. "It's all about the little things."

Oliver's eyes went wide, as he returned from his daydream. "I just remembered, we're out of peppermint tea. I need to stop at the market and grab some on the way home."

"Peppermint tea?" Robert said, his face twisting in disgust. "You like peppermint tea?"

Oliver smiled. "Not at all," he said, "but my wife loves it."

"Good man," Robert muttered. "The little things."

◊◊◊

Oliver arrived earlier than usual the next day.

Even he can sense that the time is near, Robert thought. "Are you okay?" he asked his son right away.

Oliver nodded. "I am, Dad, thanks." Choked up, he struggled to compose himself. "I just wish that you had more..." He stopped.

"Ollie," Robert said, grabbing his son's hand, "I did the best I could, I really did. And that's all you can ask of yourself. Stop worrying about me. I'm finally going home." He managed a smile. "Do you know how long it's been since I kissed my mother's cheek, or walked alongside my father—or played ball with my brother?"

Ollie couldn't hold back the tears.

"I'm ready. I've been ready for some time now." He grinned through the pain. "Oh, to taste my Mama's blueberry pie again." He looked at his son. "I'm sorry to say it, but you've never tasted pie like hers in your life."

They both laughed—Oliver, through his sniffles.

"To run in an open hay field with my brother and the old Pinewood Avenue gang, maybe even climb a willow tree..." He stopped, choked on the emotion of going home again. "To slow dance with your mother again, and give Georgey Gouveia a long overdue hug..."

Oliver nodded, believing more than he ever had.

Robert could picture all of it; he knew in both his mind and heart that these scenes would be unfolding soon—*very soon*. After a few deep breaths, he said, "Anyone can master the double fisherman's knot, Ollie. As you may recall, although it's pretty easy to tie, it's nearly impossible to break apart."

His son nodded, confirming that he remembered.

With trembling hands, he handed his son the keepsake. "You and I are a knot that can never be untangled or untied, Ollie—don't you ever forget that."

A deluge of tears sprung free from his boy's eyes.

"While I'm off on my new adventure," he said, "know that I'm still with you, always thinking of you, and that ain't ever going to change."

Oliver stared at the knotted rope. "Tha...thank you, Dad," he stuttered.

"No, son," he muttered, "thank you."

"I'll watch for the feathers," his son wept.

"They'll find you," he promised, "don't you worry about that."

CHAPTER 15

Ever vigilant at his father's bedside, Oliver was so tired he could feel the blood vessels pulsating in his eyes. Looking down at his Impossible Knot, he thought, *Dad's given me a gift I can never repay—at least not to him.*

The old man snored.

"Jonah's on the right path now, Dad," he whispered to his sleeping father. "He's finally landed a full-time job...in the video gaming industry, of all things." He chuckled at the irony of it. "He's going to be fine. We're all..." Emotion stopped him from speaking another word.

Feeling overwhelmed with gratitude, he thought about their recent talks and decided, *We're all just trying to make the most of the time we're given.* He looked at his peaceful father. *Even Dad was just trying to get through each day the best way he knew how.* It made him smile.

◊◊◊

As the old man grew weaker, he was diagnosed with double pneumonia again. "Your lungs are filling with fluid again, Mr. Earle," the spectacled doctor advised, "and they need to be drained."

With the wide eyes of a young boy, he asked, "Ollie, how long do you figure that needle is?" He was clearly terrified about the procedure.

"No bigger than the one they put in your arm to get blood, Dad," he told him. It felt strange that the table was now turned, and that he was the one providing comfort—even courage—to his father.

With gritted teeth, his father leaned forward in the bed and closed his eyes tight. After being numbed with a local anesthesia, they inserted the long spike into his back and sucked out nearly a quart of fluid that didn't look much different from Mountain Dew, only a bit murkier.

◊◊◊

The following afternoon, Dr. Pin—a vascular surgeon—addressed Oliver the moment he stepped into his dad's room. "I just explained to your father that his legs are filled with clots, causing incredibly poor circulation. Even more concerning is the possibility that one or more of those clots might travel to his heart or lungs."

"But how did..."

"It could be caused from old blood being pumped down from his malfunctioning heart."

You've got to be kidding me, Oliver thought, feeling the next domino tumble toward the end of his father's life. A different, more hopeful thought hit him. *Would they really be doing this surgery if Dad's that close to death?*

"We've cleared an operating room for this afternoon and—"

"This afternoon?"

"Your dad is very sick and we need to perform emergency surgery." He lowered his voice. "We'll try our best to avoid amputation."

The old man's blue peepers flew open. "I'll be a son-of-a-bitch," he groaned.

Oliver's knees buckled, threatening to take him to the floor. He glanced over at his frightened father.

"Looks like I finally hit Powerball," his dad added, maintaining his signature sarcasm.

Oh, my God...

Confident they were at the end, Oliver knew he should be calling everyone to come pay their respects and say their final goodbyes. Although rare for him, he chose to be selfish, needing the time—the last precious moments—for himself. Pondering the man's final seconds on earth, every moment, every breath would be remembered and cherished for all eternity.

Oddly enough, he thought about all of the negative experiences he and his father had shared along their rocky road. He recalled looking forward to this very moment, when he could call the man on his random acts of neglect. *I hated him for a long time,* he thought, *even despised him, sometimes wishing that he'd get struck by a bus.* But those old childhood wounds and festering resentments had long healed, covered over by years of scar tissue. He felt very differently now. Being a dad, himself, he now understood. *No matter how twisted Dad could be, he was only doing his best.*

"I love you, son," the old man said, breaking the trance. "You know that, right?" His words were dripping with emotion.

Oliver nodded. "I do."

"And I can't tell you how proud I am of you."

His father's words packed a wallop that he never expected. He never realized how much he needed to hear them.

"You're the man I wished I could have been, Ollie, and you have no idea the satisfaction I feel in that."

"Dad, you don't have to—" he interrupted, squeezing his skeletal hand.

"Let me finish, Oliver. It's important you know this." He squeezed his hand back; it was weak, but understood. "Because you turned out to be the man you are, my life has been a great success. Thank you for that."

Tears raced down both of Oliver's cheeks. He tried to speak but his sobs and convulsions would not allow it. It didn't matter. For him and his father, the truth was often found between the pauses in the conversation rather than just in the words spoken.

"You don't need to say a word," the old man confirmed. "I just need you to know that." He handed Oliver a sealed envelope. "This is for you to read when I'm gone."

"I'll see you when you get out of surgery, Dad."

"Sure, Ollie," his struggling father said, shooting him a wink, "I'll see you on the other side of this."

◊◊◊

Oliver and Ginny looked up at the same time to find Layla's small silhouette standing in the doorway. Letting go of each other's hand, they stood together.

"Mom," Layla cried, hurrying into Ginny's extended arms.

Oliver joined them in the embrace.

"I came as soon as I could," she whimpered.

Oliver nodded. "We know, babe."

"How is he?" Layla asked.

"He's in surgery," Oliver reported.

Layla wept.

"We need to pray," Ginny said. "Your grandfather needs prayers right now."

The one-hour surgery took nearly five. Oliver, Ginny, Peggy, and the kids were all huddled together in the CCU waiting room when Dr. Pin entered. After removing his light blue cap, he explained, "The surgery went as well as could be expected. We finished the first leg, but need for him to get stronger before we can work on the second leg."

Oh, that's not good, Oliver thought. "And when will that be?"

The medicine man shrugged. "That's up to him and how quickly he heals."

"But do you think—"

"Your dad is a very sick man, Mr. Earle," the man announced, interrupting. "You should know that he suffered two cardiac arrests during surgery. Fortunately, we were able to bring him back both times."

"No!" Jonah blurted.

For a moment, the world felt like it had stopped spinning. Oliver searched the doctor's eyes, thinking, *This man is obviously having difficulty being kind and honest at the same time.*

"We've made him comfortable, but at this point he needs prayers more than anything."

Layla was the first to cry, sounding like she once did as a little girl.

"Where is he now?" Oliver asked, trying to be the strong one.

"He's being transported to the Intensive Care Unit and..."

Oliver's knees went weak again.

Ginny collapsed into the waiting room chair and wept.

"We've intubated him and he'll remain sedated with pain meds while his body fights to heal." He shook his head. "I'm so sorry I don't have better news for you."

"Thank you," Oliver told the man. "We appreciate all of your time and effort." It sounded business-like, although it wasn't intended that way.

The surgeon nodded. "Of course," he said. "Are there any questions I can answer?"

"Can we do something for you?" Oliver asked. The man's forehead was creasing in confusion when he added, "Maybe get you an ice cream, or something? You've obviously had a long day." *It's exactly what Dad would have said,* he realized.

Everyone laughed; the stupid comment was enough to break the terrible tension.

No more fear, Dad, Oliver told his father in his head, knowing this was a blessing. *No more pain.* And then another wave of reality struck. *Will I ever talk to him again?* The unanswered question made him lose his breath.

◊◊◊

Hand-in-hand, Oliver and Ginny stepped into the ICU room. His father looked like a beastly cyborg, making Oliver catch his breath again. "Oh Dad..."

For a man who'd never taken so much as an aspirin, a horrific tree of IV meds were being pumped into both of his shriveled arms. A blue vented tube was jammed down his throat, the hissing machine a stark reminder that he could no longer breathe—or complain—on his own.

Nothing's more difficult than to say goodbye without being able to use the word, he thought.

"I'm here, Oliver," Ginny said, wrapping her arms around his waist. "You don't have to be alone anymore."

"I know that," he said, starting to sob. "When I was a kid, it was just him and me, so when he got sick..."

"I know," she said. "I understand." She rested her head on his chest. "But I'm here now, and I'm not going anywhere."

Thank God, he thought, before looking at his dying father. *You've done this, haven't you?*

Out in the corridor, Oliver threw his arms around both his children. After two long embraces, he grabbed his daughter's hand and led her and Jonah into the room, where their mom greeted them.

"Oh God," Layla gasped, hurrying to his side where she began to weep.

Oliver looked at Jonah, who was struggling to be strong. "Remember, there's no shame in crying," he told his boy. "Lord knows I've done plenty of it over the past few days." He hugged his son again. "You love him and this hurts like hell, so don't hold it in."

With a single nod, dual teardrops raced down Jonah's crimson cheeks.

For a while, Oliver became hypnotized by the subtle rise and fall of his father's chest.

Breaking his cruel trance of grief, Layla said, "Thank you, Grandpa, for all you've done for us." She paused to choke back her pain. A dramatic attack of grief ended the explanation. She couldn't speak anymore.

Oliver wrapped his arm around her shoulders and squeezed her tight, trying all he could to offer her strength.

In the same broken whisper, she looked up at her father and concluded, "Grandpa's right. Life's too short."

"We just need to remember that, sweetheart," he said, the tears breaking free once more.

Ginny stood to join them in a group hug.

The nurse entered the room. "It's a miracle that he's still holding on."

For a second, the family grinned proudly at each other. *Of course, he is,* Oliver thought. *He'll go when he's ready to go and not a second earlier.* "How long?" he managed at a stutter.

She shrugged. "That's up to your father. It's his will alone that's allowed him to stay with you this long."

A new wave of sobs swept over the family.

"Oh, Grandpa," Layla whispered.

Besides the unrelenting grief, Oliver realized that the entire room was immersed in light—bringing their family closer together. *You are so loved, Dad, I hope you can feel that.* He held onto his father's large hand as tightly as he did when he was a small boy, knowing that there was little time left with the man who'd fed and clothed him, rocked him to sleep, played catch and Santa, disciplined him, taught by example, encouraged dreams—*but most of all, loved me.*

All of the machines and monitors in the world could never measure the strength of Dad's spirit, he thought, before leaning in to the man's ear to selflessly say goodbye. "There's no need to fight any longer, Dad. You've given us the time we needed to say goodbye." He took a deep breath. "We don't want you to suffer any longer."

Everyone lay their trembling hands upon the old man, each taking his or her turn saying goodbye.

His father's latest gift was not lost on him. *His death has brought our family back together. Our shared grief is creating common ground again—enough for the healing to truly begin.*

As more tears streamed down each of their faces, Robert Earle declined—but still fought to hang on.

◊◊◊

It was three o'clock in the morning when Oliver's cell phone rang. Startled from his restless sleep, he looked at the caller ID. *It's the hospital*, he thought, his heart plummeting straight into his feet.

"Mr. Earle, my name is Brandon. I'm one of the nurses over here at the ICU."

"Hi Brandon," Oliver said, feeling a giant wave of nausea roll over him.

"Your father's very ill."

"I know," Oliver said, trying not to dry heave.

There was a long, terrible pause. "There is no DNR order on file. Is that correct?"

"It is, but..." He paused to take a deep breath. "But my dad didn't want to suffer...or prolong the inevitable." Oliver never imagined having to offer such devastating information.

"Your father's struggling," the nurse explained, with more compassion in his voice than Oliver had ever mustered. "You might want to get in here, and contact anyone who needs to say goodbye."

Oliver began crying. "Okay," he whimpered, "I'll be right there."

When the call ended, Oliver turned to find Ginny crawling across the bed toward him for a hug.

"My dad's..." He stopped.

"I know, babe," she whispered, starting to cry. "Do you want me to go with you?"

"No," he said, "I need to do this myself."

"You don't have to be alone, Oliver," she reminded him.

"I know that," he said, hugging her tighter. "I'm not." He kissed her. "Thank you."

"For what?"

"For being here for me."

"You're my husband, Oliver. I'll always be here for you."

Given the situation, it seemed peculiar, but he could feel a giant weight slip off his shoulders. "I love you too," he said, quickly kissing her again.

"And I love you."

Skipping the usual shower, Oliver hurried to get dressed, talking to himself the entire time. *I should be ready for this, but I'm not,* he thought, his tears washing his face. *I'm not ready at all.* He stifled a gasp. *He's my dad, and I'm about to lose him. Oh, dear God...*

◊◊◊

Oliver arrived at the ICU in record time. He wept at his dad's deathbed—holding the man's giant hand, his other resting on his father's forehead. As the cycle turned from sorrow and anger to gratitude, he whispered, "Thank you for everything, Dad."

The old man's blood pressure plummeted with each shallow breath.

"Go home, Dad...in peace," he told him, "we both know there are good people waiting for you." He sobbed so violently that he struggled to breathe. "You've done your job well, Dad," he wept. "The family's good. I can take it from here." The very idea struck panic in his heart.

His dad's breaths were coming slower now, the rise and fall of his chest nearly non-existent.

Oliver's knees wobbled, while his eyes burned with grief.

"You were always so much fun," he told his father, "so full of life." He smiled through the tears. "I remember the day you took me to Fenway Park to see the Red Sox play. I walked into the men's room and you stepped in right behind me. As we stood side-by-side at that long nasty trough, you yelled out, 'Is there a Frank in here? I'm supposed to meet a Frank Furter here.' While the line of men froze, you looked at me and smiled. 'Maybe he's in one of stalls?' you hollered. The place went dead silent. I finished my business, washed my hands, and then hightailed it out of there. We were back on the busy concourse when I told you, 'Dad, you can't do that!' You only laughed. 'Oh, but you can, Ollie,' you said. 'You just have to be prepared for the possibility that some big guy named Frank Furter might come looking for you.'" Finishing the story, he began to laugh.

At that very moment, the beep of the heart monitor turned to one flat tone. As though he'd taken his cue, his father finally called it quits and ascended home.

I was crying one minute, but as soon as I laughed, Dad went home to be with his parents and my Mom again, he thought, sobbing. *He must have figured that if I can still laugh, then his work is done.*

As the color drained from his father's face, he leaned in and kissed his cheek. *Have a safe trip home, Dad, and please tell Mom I miss her.* He felt the slightest breeze brush past him, making him sob even harder. *Goodbye Dad.*

He held his father's calloused hand long after it had turned cold, mourning so deeply that he felt like he might have his own heart attack. He could barely think, never mind speak. The only clear words he could offer his dying father was "Thank you, Dad." Through the unrelenting grief, he also realized, *This has been a true blessing.* It was a divine gift for him to be there and share this experience with his father, and it was not lost on him.

Door-to-door, the man lived 73 years, he realized, *dying on the exact day he'd been born.* "Happy Birthday, Dad," he whispered, before kissing his forehead for the last time and leaving the room.

On the way out of the ICU, he wanted to tell the poor folks across the hall, "I hope you guys have better luck than we did." He knew his father would have gotten a kick out of it. *Probably not the best idea,* he decided.

Stepping out of the hospital, Oliver's mind felt like it was floating; he began to recall memories with his father as vivid as the days they'd shared them, and silently thanked him for each one. He felt a pang of joy, even peace. The next moment, his thoughts returned to reality and his entire body screamed out in agony.

Dad's been dying for weeks, but that doesn't seem to make it any easier, he thought. *It's going to take me a long time to accept it.* Parts of his father—the parts deep inside that mattered—had already left before he was wheeled into the ICU. Oliver's soul ached. In his heart, he was already mourning the moments they'd missed together, as well as those they'd never be able to share again.

After some tearful phone calls, he drove drunk on sorrow to a local diner where he sat in a booth alone. Nothing else mattered in these moments—work, success, failure, even the other relationships in his life. Everything he'd worked so hard for all his life—fought to hold onto—he finally realized it was all fleeting. *It's all temporary,* he thought, *and we're only caretakers for a short time.*

As numbness took hold, all he could feel was apathy. *I just don't care about anything right now.* It was an attitude he hadn't known in decades.

As he sipped hot coffee, he remembered, *Dad's letter!* Plunging his hand into his coat pocket, he discovered that it was still there—sealed. He quickly opened it and read:

Dear Ollie,

I could apologize again for everything I did wrong, which was plenty, but then I look at the man you've become, the man you are, and I find it impossible to apologize for that. I figure I must have had something to do with it. And even if I only had a small hand in helping to form who you are, it's given me enough pride for a lifetime.

You are a better dad than I could have ever dreamed of being, a better man. I think maybe that's the real goal of any man, that his children will become more educated, more accomplished, even more kind... More evolved, I guess.

Oliver, live each day to its fullest. They all count. Whether you're young or old, there's joy and hope in every moment— if only you're willing to look for it. If you love something or someone, fight for it. The way I see it now, love is the only good reason to fight for anything. It's gonna go quick, Ollie, so don't waste another day.

I'm proud of you, son, and I love you. Nothing will ever change that. Know that I'll be standing in your corner—always.

Oliver gasped.

When your work is done, I'll see you on the other side. In the meantime, enjoy the feathers.

Love, Dad

◊◊◊

Two grief-stricken days passed when Oliver returned to his father's apartment to go through the old man's things. It didn't take long before he discovered an old shoe box of memorabilia from his father's war service.

Right up until the end, his dad talked very little about his service in Vietnam. Oliver wanted to know more—*besides the old salt's love of knot-tying.* The only thing he'd ever gotten out of his dad about the war was, "When a man sees his friends die, he doesn't talk about it—end of story." *I think he felt guilty that he was the lucky one—that he made it back, not everyone did.*

Oliver unfolded a yellowed newspaper article and read: *The USS Ingersoll began training for a WestPac deployment. She sailed for the Far East on June 9, 1965 and on July 5ᵗʰ, she began coastal surveillance patrols. In late July, she joined the naval gunfire support group off the coast of Quang Ngai. On October 10, 1965, she was assigned to plane guard duty in the South China Sea. Within the war zone, she participated in Operation Sea Dragon, anti-shipping and interdiction operations, and plane guard duty for USS Kitty Hawk (CVA-63). On December 5ᵗʰ, a North Vietnamese coastal battery fired on the destroyer, whose counterfire silenced the enemy guns. Ingersoll continued to operate in the war zone and other enemy waters until returning home in the spring of 1967.*

For service during Vietnam era, the USS Ingersoll and her eligible personnel earned the Europe bar for the previously awarded Navy Occupation Medal, the China Service Medal, the National Defense Medal, the Vietnam Service Medal, the RVN Gallantry Cross and the RVN Campaign Medal.

After his own country spit on him, Robert Earle had obviously decided to deep-six the whole experience—slamming the haunted door behind him, locking it and throwing away the key.

Oliver finally came to understand why his father had spent years trying to drink away the painful memories of Vietnam. He thought back on his childhood. *The old man always drank beer. In fact, with the exception of a single cup of coffee in the morning, he only drank beer. He called it his "medicine."*

Oliver also discovered that there was $4,000 in that shoebox his dad told him about. *That's a lot of ice cream, Dad,* he thought, realizing that his father had prepared to pay for his own funeral service. *Even though he's gone, he still refuses to be a burden.* His eyes swelled with tears, until they broke free and plunged down his cheeks.

Dad was a giver, not a taker, Oliver confirmed. *He was a worker who never once gamed the system, dying with just enough money to bury himself.* He grinned. *But his greatest gift was my last name, Earle.* With that surname, Oliver was reminded that he was here to serve others—*family first, and then everybody else.* The good, the bad—it all made him who he was, just like his father before him. *Dad wasn't perfect, but he did his best,* he decided, eternally grateful for being the man his father raised him to be. *My last name is Earle,* he thought, *and everything I say and do from this moment on will be to honor that name.*

◊◊◊

Immediate family—to include Peggy—gathered at Oliver and Ginny's house to celebrate Robert Earle's life. They went through his things—yellowed photos, record albums, dated documents—each item revealing as much about who he was than any words could.

"Look at this," Ginny announced, with both Luna and Sophie laying quietly at her feet, "he saved two silver dollars for his grandchildren."

With an emotional nod, Layla and Jonah each accepted their keepsakes.

"I can't help but to picture all the dogs that Grandpa loved fighting to get to him first in heaven."

"And from this day forward," Jonah announced, "there will be a can of Miller High Life kept in the refrigerator, off-limits to everyone except Grandpa."

Smiling, Oliver nodded.

Ginny grabbed his arm. "You know that as soon as Dad opened his eyes in heaven, he said, 'I'll be a son-of-a-bitch.'"

"No doubt," Oliver said, but he couldn't manage much more. He felt like he'd been reduced to a four-year-old again. Losing his dad was wreaking havoc on his inner child, making him feel panicked. *I feel so lost right now,* he thought, *even orphaned.* It seemed so odd, given that he was middle-aged.

As the family sat in mourning, an incredible amount of love and support was showered upon them. There were deliveries of fruit and bagel baskets and casserole dishes.

One thing's for sure, Oliver thought, *we're not alone.* Knowing this brought a sense of peace.

Even his old college mentor, Professor McKee, reached out to him—via email—with some words of comfort. *When we become the foundation, only then can we appreciate our foundations,* he wrote. *Pain passes as memories fill some of the void. I know you have some wonderful memories, experiences, and wisdom to pass on. Hang in there, Oliver—grieve, share, then stand tall and carry on. The privilege and responsibility are now in good hands—yours.*

He smiled. *It's no wonder I always loved that man.*

Even more valuable during this painful time was the fact that their family was together.

"How's Marissa been feeling?" Ginny asked Jonah.

"She's home resting now," he reported, looking worried. "She hasn't been feeling well at all."

"Morning sickness is the worst, believe me. Just make sure you're there for her, Jonah, and give her whatever she wants." She smiled.

"Of course, Ma," Jonah said, "although the only thing she wants lately is a bucket."

Her smile erased, Ginny shook her head. "The worst," she repeated.

A few more days passed when Oliver found an audio message of his father's voice on his cell phone. He stepped out into the yard to listen to it. *Ollie, it's me. I'm not sure why we have these damn phones, if no one ever picks up?* There was a pause. *Well, call me when you get this. Love you.* There was a second pause. *Oh, it's Dad by the way.*

The man's baritone voice reverberated in Oliver's soul. *I miss you so much already,* he thought, looking skyward. After saving the message and then listening to it a half dozen more times, he wept shamelessly.

Oliver felt nothing but gratitude for all he'd experienced—the incredible joys, as well as the paralyzing fears. He thought about his parents—realizing that he'd gotten his heart and his faith from his mother. But he received his backbone, or work ethic, from his father. *And the old man's backbone was forged from steel.*

Stepping back into the house, he grabbed Layla and Jonah, "What do you guys think about going fishing with me?"

They exchanged a surprised look before nodding.

Parked in front of Terminal C at Logan Airport in Boston, Oliver removed Layla's luggage from the trunk while she and her mother hugged.

"I don't want to go," Layla confessed, breaking one hug to lock onto another.

"But you have to," Oliver said, squeezing her tight, "it's your future."

"We don't want you to leave either," Ginny said, "but it's where you need to be right now, sweetheart."

Oliver peered into his daughter's dark mocha eyes. "Your grandfather's really proud of you. He told me so."

"I'll be back," she said, reaching for her carry-on bag.

"Good," they said, wrapping their arms around each other's waists.

"No, I mean it," Layla said. "I'll be back."

◊◊◊

"You've canceled our sessions for nearly a month," Dr. Borden Brown said, "that's not like you."

He tried not to shrug, but couldn't help himself. "My apologies, I've had a lot going on lately." His sponge was completely wrung out; he needed to take a break, allowing it to absorb more. *Besides*, he thought, *I've had enough therapy over the past few weeks to last me a lifetime.*

"Even more reason for us to meet, wouldn't you say?"

"My dad passed away," he abruptly announced.

"Oh, I'm so sorry."

"I was with him. It was peaceful." He nodded. "It was a blessing all around."

She took her first note.

"And as a result of the incredible loss, it's brought our family much closer together."

The woman's pen continued to fly.

"Layla just returned to Montenegro."

"That's a good thing, right?"

"It is," he agreed. "And Ginny and I have decided to give our marriage a fighting chance." He smiled. "Just as I figured, there's more than enough love bubbling beneath the resentment and bitterness."

The doctor couldn't write fast enough in her notebook.

"How are things in the bedroom?" she asked, without batting an eye.

"My doctor prescribed Cialis." He shrugged. "It's the best insurance policy I've ever purchased. I pop a half tab a couple hours before the big event and then it's game on."

In spite of her usual decorum, she laughed at the description.

He smiled wider. "Oh, and if that wasn't enough, Jonah and Marissa are going to make me a grandfather soon."

"That's wonderful. Are you ready to be a grandfather?"

"It's a few months off, but yes...I am," he said, "more than I've ever been ready for anything in my life. A wise man recently told me that it's the best job ever."

She laughed, before searching his face. "Are we going to continue on with our sessions?"

He nodded. "Oh, absolutely, my job still sucks."

She jotted down another note; this time she was able to fight off the smile.

"Although I'm getting better with that too," he reported, suddenly feeling a blanket of peace being draped over him. *This job is what I do*, he thought. *It's not who I am.* He nodded to himself. *I'm a husband and a father. That's who I am.* He smiled. *And those jobs are so much more important than where I make my money.*

"How so?" she asked.

"I just need to keep reminding myself that I'm taking care of my family, and that's the only job that matters." He shrugged. "The rest means so much less."

"Good for you," she said. "Well, it certainly appears that you've made some significant progress since we last met."

"That's what I am," he said, jokingly, "a work in progress."

"Aren't we all?"

Oliver was late to work—again—when he decided to steer his car into the coffee shop's long drive-through line. *I feel like buying someone breakfast*, he decided.

◊◊◊

The Aviary was the newest, up-and-coming restaurant in the area. According to their website: *Inspired by the open architecture of St. Barth's and named for the birds who visited the site while it was built, The Aviary provides*

a sense of escape minutes from Providence. Dine seated on the lush patio, in-
side by the fire, or underneath the sculptural birdcages suspended above the bar.
Whatever your vantage point, your meal will be remarkable.

Oliver clicked on *Reservations*, thinking, *It seems like the perfect place*
to fall deeper in love.

To Ginny's delight, they were seated outside at a small round table, situated between two standing heat lamps; a hurricane lamp between them
and a crescent moon hanging above.

"It's so beautiful here," she whispered, "even for November."

"It sure is," he said, staring at her illuminated face.

Her eyes thanked him.

"For an appetizer," he told the waitress, "I'll have the deviled eggs.
And give me the Bolognese for my entrée."

"Deviled eggs?" Ginny turned her nose up at him. "You're so weird,"
she said, making the waitress laugh.

"And you love it," he said.

"I really do," she said, before placing her order. "The bacon wrapped
dates for me and—"

"And I'm the weird one?" he commented.

The waitress looked up from her pad. "You guys are a fun couple,
aren't you?"

He looked at his wife. "I've always liked to think so."

Ginny smiled. "And please give me the flattop steak, cooked medium, with fingerling potatoes, and a side of baked macaroni and cheese."

"That comes separate in a small cast iron skillet."

"Perfect."

While Ginny sipped on her blueberry lemonade and Oliver drank
a few Sam Adams Oktoberfest, they talked and laughed and immersed
themselves in each other's company.

At one point, she reached her hand across the table. He grabbed it
and held on. *This does feel like a first date*, he thought, loving it. *What an*
amazing night! The waitress was doting and the food was incredible—*but*
neither compares to the company.

Ginny reached into her purse, retrieved a light blue envelope, placed
it on the table and slid it over to him—wearing a smile the entire time.
"This is for you," she whispered, "for us."

"What is this?" he asked, opening it.

"What does it look like?"

Aruba? he read, looking up at her.

"One full week, just the two of us," she explained, winking, "so we can get it right this time."

Oh, my God, he thought, *this is awesome.*

"I've been waiting a long time to give this to you," Ginny explained, "but between Jonah's big surprise and your dad's declining health..." She shrugged. "The time never seemed appropriate." He smiled wider. "Your dad knew about it, and he was happy we were giving our vacation a second chance."

Oliver grinned at his wife's play on words. "This is so amazing, Ginny," he said, getting up to kiss her. "Thank you."

"I can't wait to go," she said, "but we just need to make sure that whatever week we pick, it's nowhere near Marissa's due date."

Oliver nodded in agreement. "Speaking of that, are you ready to be a grandma?" he asked.

"Oh, I'm ready," she said. "You?"

"I can't wait."

"Although I'd rather not think about that for the next few hours," she said.

"And why's that?"

"Because I need some alone time with my husband." She was nearly purring.

An instant rush of adrenaline shot through Oliver's body, causing him to quickly raise his hand. "Check please!" he called out at a volume much louder than appropriate.

"No dessert?" the waitress asked, as she hurried over.

"It's waiting for us at home," Oliver said.

Ginny stifled a laugh behind her cloth napkin.

As they walked along the illuminated path to the parking lot, Oliver spotted a large brown feather lying before them. "Oh, my God!"

"What is it?" Ginny asked.

"It's my father," he explained, picking up the feather.

"Your father?"

He stopped to face his wife. "My old man told me he'd send me a sign to let me know that he's okay." His eyes filled. "He promised he'd send large brown and gray feathers, so I'd know he made it home safely."

Her eyes immediately misted over. "Of course he did," she said, "he was the second most thoughtful man I've ever known."

Oliver smiled at the implied compliment, thinking, *Thank you, Dad. I know you're always with me. I can feel you. But please do me a favor, don't follow us home tonight.* He nearly squealed at the thought of it. *It looks like we'll need some privacy.*

Ginny looked at him, trying to read his thoughts.

"I love you too," he told her.

"I love you," she replied, grabbing his arm and picking up the pace.

CHAPTER 16

Jonah looked skyward. *Gramps, I'm going to ask Mr. DeSousa for his permission to take Marissa's hand in marriage today,* he told his grandfather in his head. *I'd appreciate it if you could help me stand tall when I talk to him.* He shook his head. *It's not going to be easy.*

Not an hour later, Jonah was taking in some deep, cleansing breaths. "Thank you, Mr. DeSousa, for allowing me back into your home." He cleared the emotional debris from his throat. "Before I ask what I've come here to ask you, I'd like to explain a few things."

Nodding, the giant man took a seat at his kitchen table.

Jonah remained standing. "Sir, I love your daughter more than my own soul, and these are not just words. It's how I've felt since the moment I met her. Marissa's everything to me. I know we're young and that...that the..." He could hear his heart drumming hard in his ears and stopped for a moment—an eternity. "And that Marissa's pregnancy wasn't planned." He peered hard into the Portuguese man's dark eyes. "But it wasn't a mistake, Mr. DeSousa." He got choked up, having to pause again. It was enough time to see the large man's eyes also mist over. "Please forgive me for disrespecting you and your family. That was never my intention." He nodded. "But that said, I cannot—and will not—apologize for this baby...for my child, your grandchild." He nodded several more times, affording him the time to take in more oxygen. "Mr. DeSousa, sir, may I please have your permission to ask for your daughter's hand in marriage?"

The intimidating man stared at him.

At least he hasn't lunged for my throat yet, Jonah thought. "I want Marissa to be my wife, and it's important that we have your blessing," he added. "And if that takes more time for you to give that, then I—"

"You love her?" Mr. DeSousa asked, cutting him off.

"More than my own soul," Jonah repeated.

"Would you have asked her to marry you, if she didn't get pregnant?"

Jonah tried not to smile. "Truthfully, I've thought a lot about that, and there's no doubt that I would have. It might've been further down the line, but I've always known in my heart that Marissa would be my wife. I love her. I love our baby. I'd do anything to—"

"You have my blessing," the man said.

Jonah could hear Marissa squealing in delight from the other room.

Mr. DeSousa stood, towering over Jonah. This time, there were no aggressive moves or attempted assaults. Instead, he extended his giant hand.

Jonah grabbed it and gave it a shake, realizing that his own hand—in the grasp of his future father-in-law's—looked like it belonged to a small child.

Mr. DeSousa smiled. "Maria," he called out to his wife, who was clearly eavesdropping with Marissa behind the kitchen door, "grab the Cachaca. We need to drink on it."

Once both aged shot glasses were filled to the rim with the Portuguese moonshine, Mr. DeSousa raised his glass, gesturing that Jonah do the same. "Welcome to the family, Jonah," the patriarch said, and downed his shot.

Jonah placed the glass to his lips, hoping, *Please don't let me spit up this flavored kerosene.* He drank the shot and, although he coughed twice, he was able to keep it down.

Mr. DeSousa laughed. "You'll get used to it," he said, slapping Jonah on the back before filling the glasses to the top again.

Wiping his mouth with the back of his hand, Jonah returned the smile. "I'm looking forward to it," he said, steeling himself for another vicious assault on his stomach. He grabbed the shot glass again. *I think Mr. DeSousa and Grandpa would have gotten along well.* He looked toward the ceiling. *Thanks for the strength, Gramps.*

◊◊◊

November 17th finally arrived. Before setting up the hall, Oliver, Ginny, Jonah, Marissa, and Peggy went out for a late lunch at Lina's Place, each of them ordering their meal before sharing the current details of their lives.

"So, are you ready for this baby?" Oliver asked Marissa.

Nodding, she opened her mouth to speak.

"If it were up to me," Jonah blurted, smiling, "we'd be at the hospital right now."

"How are you feeling?" Ginny asked Marissa.

"Like I'm really pregnant."

Everyone laughed.

How wonderful, Oliver thought, his excitement making his hair stand on end.

"Except for the morning sickness, I don't mind it at all."

"It'll get better," Ginny said, placing her hand on Marissa's arm, "and it'll be worth every second of suffering that these boys will never understand." She grinned.

While Peggy laughed, Oliver and Jonah's eyes found the table, remaining there for an extended moment.

Once the coast was clear, Oliver began to hand out assignments. "Jonah and Marissa, can you please pick up the balloons from the supermarket and the pastries from the high school's culinary arts program? Then meet me, Mom, and Peggy at the hall."

As they walked out of the restaurant, Oliver watched as Jonah threw his arm around Marissa. "Do you think we're ready for this tonight?"

"God, I hope so," she sighed.

Me too, Oliver thought, trying to shrug off the pressure that pushed down on him.

Oliver, Ginny, and Peggy headed out to Fall River. When they got to the hall, they discovered that the place was completely desolate. They had to arrange all the tables and chairs, so it would fit like a perfect puzzle. As the kids joined them, everyone accepted their role. The boys set up the tables and chairs, while the girls laid out tablecloths, placing raffle items and snacks on the tables. Once the silent auction table was finalized, the banners and balloons were put out.

No sooner had the family finished their work and changed their clothes when a noisy crowd stampeded into the hall. Although there was no need to turn away anyone at the door, it was a sold out show—with 250 people filling the seats, each one eagerly waiting to laugh.

With his father on his mind—and in his heart—Oliver grabbed the microphone. Standing beside his family, he happily made the night's first announcement. "From the bottom of our hearts, and in my father's good name, I want to thank each and every one of you for offering your support tonight. Without people like you, these wonderful causes would never be supported."

Jonah and Marissa applauded the audience. The crowd happily returned it to them.

"So, please have a great time tonight," Oliver added. "Allow yourself to be generous and know that for some kid who's faced unspeakable obstacles, you've just made all the difference in the world."

The hall echoed with more applause, with Ginny clapping the loudest.

Jonah grabbed the microphone next. "So without further ado, let's get on with the show," he announced. "If you don't laugh tonight, you might want to consider checking your medication."

Smokin' Joe Holden took the stage and, from the first word out of his mouth, people were rolling in the aisles. With the help of a busy cash bar, Oliver felt a few pounds slip off his shoulders.

The comedy was sensational, with the crowd roaring for two straight hours.

Even when the jokes ended, the night did not. People had really gotten into the pick-and-pull raffle, putting all the tickets they bought into the cups of the prizes they wanted to win. The more coveted prizes included a weekend get-away for two on Cape Cod, several rounds of golf, and three private vineyard tours.

Jonah called out the numbers drawn, while Ginny, Marissa and Peggy distributed the baskets to the twenty-five lucky winners.

Without feeling a hint of anxiety, Oliver took the stage one last time and announced, "It's with incredible gratitude that our grand total tonight is $11,123—more than enough for Dylan's chair ramp." His eyes filled. "We thank you. My dad thanks you!"

Ginny wrapped her arm around her husband's waist, leaned into the microphone and said, "Our entire family wants to thank you all for coming out tonight and supporting this incredible cause. There have been many local businesses that have stepped up and pledged their support. Among them are Hutchins & Sons Enterprises, Andrew Souza Mason Contractor, Rodrigues Home Maintenance, Express Printing, and the North Attleboro Patrolman's Union."

Everyone applauded.

"We also need to acknowledge the folks who volunteered their time and effort," Oliver added, "and made the *First Annual Robert Earle Laughter & Wishes Comedy Benefit* a reality. Lastly, we'd like to thank Joe Holden and his cast of comedians. I need to warn him that *Laughter & Wishes II* is only a year away!"

With a final round of applause, the hall emptied out.

It was late when Oliver texted Layla. *We did it, babe,* he wrote. *We surpassed our goal!*

He then went to his knees and told his dad, *We raised over eleven thousand dollars for your buddy, Dylan, Dad!* "Thank you for this gift," he whispered. "I now see why you went out of your way to help someone new every year." A single tear tumbled down his cheek. "Your life made a real difference. I hope you know that." He looked toward the ceiling. "And I hope you know how much I love and miss you, although I know in my heart that you're still with me—always."

◊◊◊

"You have your grandfather's heart," Jonah's dad told him.

Actually, I have your heart, Dad, Jonah told the man in his head. *I just need to carry on what you've taught me while I was watching you from the back seat of your car.*

Although his dad was absolutely crushed over losing his own father, he was still right there for him.

Showing even more signs of maturity, Jonah decided to turn the table and make it about someone other than himself—for the first time. "I'm fine, Dad. Enough about me." He placed his hand on his father's arm. "I know you're in a lot of pain right now, and I need you to know that I'm here for you."

His father became emotional, betraying a mix of joy and grief. "You have no idea how much I needed to hear that, son."

◊◊◊

Days turned into weeks, while the world returned to normal—or as normal as it could be without Robert Earle in it.

"I'm on my way, Marissa. I'll be there as soon as I can!" Jonah promised, smiling. "I love you," he added before throwing his cell phone onto the passenger's seat.

He was still pressing down on the accelerator when he saw the blue lights flashing in his rearview mirror, the siren growing louder behind him. *Not now*, he thought, feeling panicked. *Please, not now!*

He immediately pulled over to the side of the road and rolled down his window. Rifling through the car's glovebox, he found his vehicle registration just as the cop's dark shadow blocked out the sun.

"License and registration," the baritone voice demanded.

Jonah handed both out the window.

"Do you know why I've pulled you—"

"I was speeding," Jonah confessed, cutting him off, "because my girl-friend's in labor and I'm trying to get to the hospital, so I can be there when our baby's born."

"Stay in the car," the cop said—without congratulations or that mythical offer of police escort.

This cop's obviously more concerned with making his quota than help-ing me out, he thought, waiting for what seemed an eternity. Every second that passed, his mind raced faster: *Please don't let Marissa have the baby without me there! She'd never forgive me. I'd never forgive myself. I want to be able to tell my child that I was there to witness that first breath.* He looked out the window. *Why is this guy taking so long? I need to be there with Marissa!*

The dark shadow finally returned to his window, handing back his credentials along with a hundred dollar fine for speeding. "Slow down," he said. "Next time, I won't go so easy on you."

"Yeah, thanks for that," Jonah said, before rolling his window back up and hoping that their warm exchange had concluded. *I have a baby to meet, you jackass,* he thought, stomping on the gas pedal.

◊◊◊

When Jonah finally entered the birthing room, dressed in blue scrubs and a mask, he hurried over to Marissa's side. "Sorry," he said, "I'll explain later." He nodded at her mom, who returned the gesture. He then grabbed his girlfriend's hand. "How close are we?"

A middle-aged nurse positioned herself between Marissa's legs. "Okay, you're at ten centimeters," she announced; "you need to start pushing."

Jonah was so excited, it felt like there were fish jumping in his veins. He quickly scanned the room for a doctor.

"What about the doctor?" Mrs. DeSousa asked.

"We're fine," the nurse said, "I've delivered more babies in this hospital than all the doctors combined." She looked at Marissa. "Now start pushing."

As Marissa began to bear down, tiny red capillaries began bursting in her face each time she pushed.

Jonah felt his grandfather's presence enter the room. *It's him. He's here!* Goosebumps turned his entire body to sandpaper.

It took a few minutes before the baby's head crowned, dark hair matted with his mother's mucous. "The baby's almost here, Marissa!" Jonah called out. "Just a few more pushes. Come on, babe. You can do it!"

With a final warrior grunt, Marissa pushed their baby boy out into the world.

Oh, my God, Jonah thought, immediately starting to cry alongside his boy. "He's beautiful, Marissa," he whimpered.

With ten fingers and ten toes, the baby looked like a pink honey ham without the netting—screeching out in rage.

Jonah felt buzzed on unconditional love.

After the baby was cleaned up and placed on his Mama's chest, Mrs. DeSousa asked, "Have you two decided on his name?"

Marissa gestured for Jonah to announce it. "His name is Robert Oliver Earle," he said, proudly, before whispering directly to his new son. "Your last name is Earle, Bobby, and that means something." He paused to wipe his eyes. "And your Daddy's gonna be there for you until his final breath. You have my word on that."

Jonah switched his attention to the exhausted boy's mother. "Thank you, Marissa," he said, kissing her. "That was the bravest thing I've ever seen anyone do." He shook his head. "I didn't think I could love you any more than I do."

She kissed him back. "I love you more, Jonah," she whispered, exhausted, "and I love our little family."

That afternoon, while they stared at Bobby, the baby opened his eyes.

"Oh, my God," Jonah said, "he has my grandfather's blue eyes."

Bobby smiled.

And his smile too. He looked up. *Thanks for being with me today, Gramps,* he thought. *Please help me look after our boy here.*

◊◊◊

It was early evening when his mom and dad stormed into the room, his mother already extending her arms to hold the baby.

"Here you go, Grandma," Marissa said, graciously handing him over.

Oliver stood close to his wife's side to get a good look at his grandson. "Bobby," he whimpered, "you just wait until you see how much Grandpa spoils you!" With glistening eyes, he looked to Jonah and Marissa. "Congratulations, you guys. He's perfect."

Jonah threw his arm around his father's shoulder. "Congrats to you too, Grandpa."

"What did you name him?" his father asked.

Jonah's chest swelled with pride. "Robert Oliver Earle."

"You've honored our family, son," his dad whimpered, tears breaking free, "Thank you."

"I finally understand what it means for my son to have our family's last name, to have Grandpa's name," Jonah told him.

His father pulled him in for an even tighter hug. "What can I say," he said, smiling, "a father's love is a father's love, right?"

Jonah nodded. "I get it, Dad," he said, grinning. "I finally get it."

After taking his turn holding the baby, his dad revealed a folded piece of white-lined paper. "I've written a poem for my grandson."

"That's great. Too bad you never wrote one for me," Jonah teased.

The proud man grinned. "I have," he said, "and I'm happy to say that you're finally ready to appreciate it."

For Baby Earle
from Grandpa

If love was a wish from the heavens
and that wish was the best thing on earth:
I would put all the stars in a basket
on the glorious eve of your birth.

If life was a neatly-wrapped present
and that gift was a pleasant surprise:
I would buy all the bows and the boxes,
as quick as the morning dove flies.

If the world was a dream in the making
and that dream was a hope which came true:
I would beg, I would borrow and barter
and offer the whole world to you.

As they prepared to leave the hospital, Jonah's dad pulled him off to the side. "I'll get you that poem I wrote for you," he said, "but for now, I want you to read this." He handed over a sealed envelope. "I love you, Jonah."

"I love you too, Dad, and thank you."

"For what?"

"For everything."

They hugged.

It was late, both Marissa and the baby asleep when Jonah opened the envelope and pulled out the letter. Taking a few deep breaths, he read,

Jonah,

I'm writing this letter for two reasons. The first is to let you know how excited I am for the adventure you're about to embark on. Fatherhood has been the greatest honor of my life. I have no doubt that you'll feel the same. God has blessed you with the most sacred task—to guide and protect another human being.

I can't tell you how much pride I already feel knowing what kind of dad you're going to be. Here's a few things you can expect:

There's no way to prepare for this job. Trust me, you'll have to play it by ear most of the way. But as long as you remember

*that your child's life means more than your own, then you're
in the perfect position to make every decision you need to.
You will worry, more than you've ever worried in your life.
Just know that you're not alone there. All parents suffer. It's
the price we pay for the incredible responsibility we're given.
From your child's birth until your own death, you will know
anxiety well. The good news is that everything will be okay.
You're going to be fine.*

Jonah paused to collect himself. *That seems like a contradiction*, he
thought.

*Raising your baby is something you and Marissa will have
to do on your own. And it would be wrong of me to even try
to help, so I won't. Even still, know that I'm always in your
corner and will be here for you until my dying breath—for
you and your family.*

You're not alone, not ever. Nothing could be more impossible.

Love, Dad

Jonah tiptoed over to the baby's bassinette. "Bobby, it doesn't matter what you do or who you try to become," he whispered, "from this day
forward, you only need to be the person you're meant to be—and that's
you. Regardless of where you end up, I'll always be proud to call you my
son." He leaned further into the portable crib. "Even with all the darkness in this world, you're going to love it here." He kissed him.

In that one moment, Jonah felt overwhelmed with gratitude for all
the people and experiences that had made up the whole of his life.

The baby opened his eyes, looked up from his bassinette and smiled
his grandfather's smile.

The circle is complete, Jonah thought.

◊◊◊

The world had completely thawed and returned to spring when Jonah passed
Erastus M. Brownell's grave—his grandfather's new next-door neighbor—

and kneeled at Robert Earle's gravestone. After offering a prayer, he blessed himself. "Thanks for being there with me, Gramps," he said aloud. "I know you were." He choked back the emotion that tickled the back of his throat. "As bad as I screwed up, everything still worked out okay, just like you said it would." He smiled. "Dad and you were there for me—always there—and that never changed, no matter how stupid I was being." He nodded. *Maybe that's all it takes to be a good dad?* he pondered. *Just be there.* "So that's exactly what I'm going to give my son." His eyes filled.

As he walked away, he thought about the letter his dad had written him. *I need to write a letter to Bobby someday.*

He was nearly out of the cemetery when he spotted a Ziplock bag blowing around in the warm breeze. It landed at his feet. Picking it up, he looked around before reading the letter inside. His hair stood on end. It was addressed to *My Son.*

"Strange," he said aloud and opened it—never realizing that the sealed envelope contained a message of hope from a healing soldier to his unborn son.

Dear Son,

First and most importantly, I love you—more than I could ever explain in a simple letter.

Know that I will always be here for you, my son. No matter the circumstances or the situation, I will be right by your side until my final breath. You have my solemn word.

I must admit that this is not a perfect world that we live in, but it's all we have, so it's important to make the most of it. Attitude is everything. If you can adopt a positive attitude and find hope in each day, then your life will be filled with joy—I promise.

No matter where you live, family and friends are your home. Value education because it's the key to opportunity. And although I never want you to start a fight, I never want you to run from one either. Courage is the only thing that guarantees you can keep your word and stand for your beliefs—and you'd better do both because that's where your character is forged. Also, try to give people the benefit of the doubt. We're all human and we all make mistakes—even you and me. Wearing another's shoes is a good practice.

Make sure you laugh a lot and, although it's good to plan for the future, remember to live in the present. Your life will be a string of moments. Don't waste any of them. Be forgiving of others, as well as of yourself, and strive to have no regrets. As far as we know, we only get one shot at this.

You're responsible for your own life, so please make it a great one. Dream big, and never let anyone tell you that you can't do something. You CAN do anything—ANYTHING!

Be good to yourself. Believe me, it's not as easy as it sounds. Say your prayers, and lean on your faith when things get tough—and unfortunately, things will definitely get rough at times. But remember, it doesn't rain forever. And please be a gentleman. Your life will be the true measure of success for mine. I'm counting on you to be a good man.

Never be selfish. It's a true weakness. Give more than you take, and know that you have my heart.

All My Love, Always,

Dad

Jonah wiped a single tear from his cheek. Instinctively, he wanted to pocket the treasure but knew it would be wrong. Instead, he took a picture of the letter with his cell phone to share the story somewhere down the road with his son. He placed the envelope back into the plastic baggie and lay it back on the ground exactly where he'd found it. *I'm sure others will need to read this as much as I did.*

As he walked away, he couldn't help but smile. *There's no love like a father's love,* he thought. *I just hope I can measure up to the men who have come before me.*

The Greatest Teachers
by Oliver Earle

My children have taught me...

that trust is sealed before the first step,
and real understanding does not require words;
that a baby's breath and angels' wings make the same sound,
and bonds forged on sleepless nights are eternal.

My children have taught me...

that the greatest wonders are found within the smallest moments;
and the grip of a tiny hand slips away much too fast;
that the word "proud" can inspire unimaginable feats,
while the word "disappointed" can scar the soul.

My children have taught me...

that doing something means so much less than being there,
as one day at the park is more valuable than ten visits to the toy store;
that laughter is contagious and can destroy all worries,
and Santa Claus is alive and well—all that's needed is faith.

My children have taught me...

that the most powerful prayers are made up of the simplest words,
humbled, grateful, and spoken from the heart;
and that for most ailments, the best medicine is a kiss
or a hug for someone who wouldn't dream of asking.

My children have taught me...

that friends can be made with no more than a smile,
and real blessings are found amongst family and friends;
that the future promises magic and wonder,
and that dreams must be chased until each one comes true.

Reading the poem over, Oliver discovered that it brought him great melancholy. *It was so long ago.* As he thought about it, his eyes filled. *It was only a moment ago.*

Acknowledgments

First and forever, Jesus Christ—my Lord and Savior. With Him, all things are possible.

Paula, my beautiful wife, for loving me and being the amazing woman she is.

Special thanks go out to my children—Evan, Jacob, Isabella and Carissa—for helping me with the research on this novel. It's taken us years.

Thanks, Dad, for helping me write this book. You were with me in every word.

Mom, Billy, Julie, Caroline, Caleb, Randy, Kathy, Philip, the Baker girls, Darlene, Jeremy, Baker, Aurora, Jen, Jason, Jack, Luke, the DeSousa's, Laura—my beloved family.

Jack Schoonover, Mark Diethelm and Jacob Manchester for their invaluable insights and input.

Lou Aronica, my mentor and friend.

My life has been richly blessed for having known each one of you.

About the Author

Steven Manchester is the author of the soul-awakening novel, *The Menu*, as well as the 80s nostalgia-fest, *Bread Bags & Bullies*. His other works include #1 bestsellers *Twelve Months, The Rockin' Chair, Pressed Pennies* and *Gooseberry Island*; the national bestsellers, *Ashes, The Changing Season* and *Three Shoeboxes*; the multi-award winning novel, *Goodnight Brian*; and the beloved holiday podcast drama, *The Thursday Night Club*. His work has appeared on NBC's *Today Show*, CBS's *The Early Show* and BET's *Nightly News*. Three of Steven's short stories were selected "101 Best" for the *Chicken Soup for the Soul* series. He is a multi-produced playwright as well as the winner of the 2017 Los Angeles Book Festival, 2018 New York Book Festival and 2020 New England Book Festival. When not spending time with his beautiful wife Paula or their children, this Massachusetts author is promoting his works or writing. Visit: www.StevenManchester.com